# My Name is Nobody

## MATTHEW RICHARDSON

PENGUIN BOOKS

PENGUIN BOOKS

UK | USA | Canada | Ireland | Australia
India | New Zealand | South Africa

Penguin Books is part of the Penguin Random House group of companies
whose addresses can be found at global.penguinrandomhouse.com

First published by Michael Joseph 2017
Published in Penguin Books 2018
**004**

Set in 12.02/14.26 pt Garamond MT Std
Typeset in India by Thomson Digital Pvt Ltd, Noida, Delhi
**Printed and bound in Great Britain by Clays Ltd, Elcograf S.p.A.**

A CIP catalogue record for this book is available from the British Library

ISBN: 978-1-405-92479-5

www.greenpenguin.co.uk

To all my family

PENGUIN BOOKS

# My Name is Nobody

Matthew Richardson studied English at Durham University and Merton College, Oxford. After a brief spell as a freelance journalist, he began working as a researcher and speechwriter in Westminster. He has also written speeches for senior figures in the private sector. Matthew is twenty-six, and *My Name is Nobody* is his debut novel.

# Prologue

'I know a secret,' he says. 'A secret that changes everything.'

Solomon Vine pulls out the rickety plastic chair and sits down on the opposite side of the table. The room is stark and empty. Dust clings to the walls.

'That wasn't my question,' Vine says, holding the man's gaze. His voice is without colour, bare of any emotion.

'No. But it is my answer.'

'I don't want your secrets, I want names.'

There is an interruption as the door screeches open. Gabriel Wilde fills the space, offering a slight nod of apology. He pads across the concrete flooring and takes the chair on Vine's left. He slides over a manila folder. Vine doesn't look at it immediately, as if he has already memorized its contents. Instead, it sits there, free of any official marking or classification, anonymous and deniable.

Vine lets a beat of silence fall. He needs to make the suspect hear the full, noiseless force of it. There is no one else here to save him. This isn't official territory, softened by rules and edicts. There are no platoons of lawyers ready to ambush the interrogation. He is theirs, to do with what they will.

'You don't understand,' the man says now. There is a spike of volume in his voice. He leans forwards so his upper-body weight pivots on his elbows. Despite the handcuffs, he fights for dexterity with his hands, prodding his index finger at the table top in rhythm with his voice. 'What I know changes everything. Whatever you think you can do, you are mistaken.'

Vine reaches for the file and brandishes it. He opens the cover and scans the first page.

'Mobile-phone records show recent contact with five British citizens who have travelled to Syria,' he says. 'We have evidence confirming the supply of fake passports and illegal arms. Her Majesty's government has an isolation cell prepared specially for your return home. With the material we have in this folder alone, you will be sent down for life . . . Write down the names of your contacts, and we can talk.'

The man looks up, lips creasing into a smile. It is not a reflex, but a carefully calibrated action, the jaw wounded with amusement.

'There will be no trial, no sentence, no cell,' he says.

'No one will save you, Dr Yousef,' says Vine. 'No one even knows you're here. You have disappeared off the face of the earth. You're lucky you ran into us before the Americans. Though if you would like to be transferred, I'm sure that can be arranged . . .'

He shakes his head. This time the smile thickens into laughter. 'One word from me and they will let me go . . . Trust me, they will call.'

'Who will call?' says Gabriel Wilde, breaking his silence. He gets up from the chair and starts roaming the boxy parameters of the room.

'The people who matter,' says Ahmed Yousef. 'They always do. If they want my secret, they will pay the price. It is the terms of business. Nothing more.'

'A secret that changes everything?' says Wilde. He stops behind Yousef's chair and dips his voice to a whisper. 'It better be a bloody good one. A grass can never be too careful . . .'

'It's the best,' says Yousef. 'They will call. You will see.'

'And if they don't?'

Yousef doesn't answer. He looks to the closed door. As if on cue, there is the flash of the alert light, a throb of red that upsets the blankness of the room. Vine feels the first cramp of unease as he gets up from the table and makes his way to the door.

It is cool outside. There is another sound behind, and Vine turns to see Wilde following him down the long line of grey corridor to the control room. An RMP guard – all fidgety eyes and nervous speed – waits with the phone.

'Who is it?'

'The switch at HQ,' he says, handing over the red receiver. As Vine waits to be connected, the guard turns to Wilde.

'Your wife also called, sir. She needs you back at base. She said it was urgent.'

Wilde doesn't display any twinge of anxiety. Instead, he says to Vine: 'You OK to finish this? I'll be back as soon as I can . . .'

Vine nods, careful not to react at the mention of Rose. The control room is full of monitors, a glassy panorama of concrete floors and airless turnings. He sees Wilde make his way down the hall and in the direction of the car park. A voice emerges through the crackle on the other line.

'Please hold for the Chief . . .'

One burr later, the gravelly tones of Sir Alexander Cecil fill the speaker.

'Is it true?' the voice says.

'I'm sorry?'

'Is it true, Vine? You have Ahmed Yousef in custody?'

'Yes,' he says. 'He's not talking at the moment. But we're getting there. The product he was carrying should be enough to put him away this time.'

There is no response on the end of the line. Vine can feel the weight of it, like a silent throat-clearing. 'I never said this, Vine. Are we clear? This never came from me.'

'I'm sorry?'

'You're to release Ahmed Yousef immediately. I don't care where you drop him, but see that you do so within the next half hour.'

*I know a secret . . . A secret that changes everything . . .*

Vine halts, unable to reply immediately. Sweat begins to gather on his forehead, a tightness pressing on his gut. 'The line's bad. Repeat please.'

'You caught it perfectly well, Vine. Just do it.'

Vine waits for another moment, topping up the composure in his voice. 'What's going on?'

'Nothing's going on,' says Cecil. 'Drop him and continue with whatever you were doing. Don't ask questions. Not this time.'

'Sir, we have direct evidence implicating Ahmed Yousef in the cases of at least five British citizens arriving in Syria. He is a priority-one target on the NSC and CIA Most Wanted lists. We have more than enough material here to prosecute. This makes no sense.'

Cecil's voice frosts over now, the words newly brittle. 'This isn't a discussion, Vine. There are more important things going on here than you can possibly imagine. Carry out this order or I'll damn well get someone else to.'

With that, the line cuts off. Cecil's voice is replaced by a scratchy monotone. Vine hands the receiver back to the RMP guard. He glances at the monitors.

He turns to the guard. 'Is there anyone else in the building?'

'No, sir,' he says. 'Just you, me and the prisoner.'

Vine waits. Once said, the words can't be unsaid. 'Good. I want you to go dark until I say so. If anyone asks, blame it on a power cut.' He notices the scrunch of concern on the man's face. 'Refer any questions to me.'

He looks up at the monitors for a final time to see Gabriel Wilde's car inching out of the driveway – escaping all consequences with immaculate timing. He watches as the guard begins methodically turning the cameras off, each screen blinking fuzzily and then blank.

Then he leaves the building and walks into the blast of heat outside. He unfurls a lighter and a cigarette. The sun bruises his face. He can already feel the pincers moving towards him. Cecil will have engineered things in London to make sure the call was never logged. If it goes wrong, Cecil will be able to plausibly deny he ever gave instructions to let Ahmed Yousef free. But, if Vine doesn't follow through, he will find the full might of the fifth floor against him. The game demands a scapegoat, and he is now theirs.

He keeps on smoking, letting the minutes drift away, trying to will things clearer. Eventually, he douses the final one and turns. As he walks, the words repeat, tumbling over themselves.

*There are more important things going on here than you can possibly imagine . . .*

Curiosity compels him forwards now. The secret looms like a challenge. He treads back through the dour hallways, not yet sure what he will do. But he finds himself suddenly longing to be away from here, tired of patrolling the huts and compounds, starved of oxygen and scenery; tired of the decisions and the choices.

He buzzes back into the secure area and makes his way down the thin final corridor. The interrogation room lies at the end, aglow with a harsher whiteness. Vine wonders again what hold Yousef has on London. What does he know? What grubby deal has he engineered that sees him immune from further questioning? Why would the Chief of the Secret Intelligence Service intervene personally to demand his release?

*I know a secret . . . A secret that changes everything . . .*

Vine reaches the door and pauses for a moment. He feels a new anger begin to work its way up from the pit of his stomach until it fills his throat.

He presses his card against the scanner and hears the door click open. He tries to brush aside any final doubt as he steps into the brighter light. He knows what he will do, what he must do.

It is then that he stops. In front of him is an empty chair, a hollow space where Ahmed Yousef should be. But that isn't it. There is something else wrong. He looks down at the floor and sees the first splashes of colour against the greyness. It seems to ooze and wander according to a logic of its own. Slowly, he traces the source, a lump of shadow behind the table.

Ahmed Yousef is lying on his back, blood haloing around him. It looks like a gunshot wound. Without stopping to calculate the consequences, Vine finds himself pressing the alert button. A keening noise smothers the building.

Soon the steps of the RMP guard sound outside. The door opens with a ponderous click.

He knows they have minutes at best. With the amount of blood loss, they could already be too late. He strains to feel a pulse. But there is just flesh, slippery and raw.

'Call for an urgent medical team,' he shouts. 'We need to evacuate him now.' As the guard turns, Vine says: 'Find out who's been in here and how the hell this could have happened.'

The delay seems to last for ever. He takes out the emergency medical kit and begins doing everything he can to stem the blood loss. But the blood spatters his fingers and up his arms. His clothes become damp and sticky. He tries again to find any signs of consciousness, feels just the fading echo of a pulse.

Minutes later, the guard returns. 'Evac team on their way from base, sir. ETA five minutes.' He starts to walk further into the room then stops and hovers.

'What is it?'

Vine turns. He realizes what he must look like – a butcher, or a surgeon.

'I've found the card that was used to enter the building, sir,' he says. 'Ten minutes ago. With the CCTV down, that's the only identifier we have.'

'And?' Vine says impatiently. 'Who was in here? Who did this?'

The guard doesn't answer at first. He looks nervous, as if unable to summon the words.

'It was you, sir.'

# PART ONE

## November 2016

Solomon Vine took another sip of coffee and pushed his plate away. He signalled for the bill, flashing his debit card. Perhaps he should just make a run for it now. He could be at an airport within an hour, stay over in Paris or Berlin, even deploy some elementary tradecraft if anyone had bothered to notice he was gone. He had often imagined all the lives he could lead – a teacher, labourer, nomad. Anywhere as far away from this as he could get. From England, the establishment, Westminster, Whitehall and, above all, the Secret Intelligence Service.

As he waited for the bill to arrive, he took the postcard from his jacket pocket again. It had landed on his doormat early this morning. He turned it over and read the single line of text on the back, scrawled in biro. It read:

*11 a.m. St James's Park. CN.*

Cosmo Newton, Chair of the Joint Intelligence Committee. Newton still had his number and could have texted. But the card meant he didn't want GCHQ or, worse still, the NSA picking it up. There had been a drip-feed of scandals in the last few months from former Whitehall veterans claiming they'd been bugged by the intelligence fraternity. Since then, most ministers had ditched the phones and gone back to whispered asides in the Members' Dining Room.

Vine paid the bill and then grabbed his coat. He walked slowly, trying to focus on his surroundings. The breeze stabbed at his cheeks. The air smelled of fumes, tangy and raw. He wondered what Newton wanted to tell him. Ever since his suspension, he had been exiled from all meaningful contact. His days were filled with waiting, the rare messages heavy with potential consequences. Perhaps they would grant him one final dignity and send Cosmo Newton to deliver the worst news of all. As Vine walked, he felt his body ache with an old frustration. The illogicality of it all strained at him. He had entertained every possible hypothesis over the previous three months, but still the impossibility of it haunted him like a curse. Ahmed Yousef had been silenced by a ghost. He could hear the interview with Cecil on his return, each moment of hesitation dooming him.

*You ordered the RMP guard to disable all CCTV coverage?*
Correct.

*Only you, Yousef and the RMP guard were in, or near, the building at the time of the incident?*
Correct.

*The RMP guard's movements were accounted for by digital forensics on the computer system of the premises?*
Correct.

*Your card was used to enter the secure area during the time of the attack?*
Correct.

*There are no witnesses to your movements between 1710 and 1730 on the day of the incident?*
Correct.

*Why did you try to kill Ahmed Yousef?*
Vine considered the question again now. He had thought many times about what he would do if left alone with Yousef. The ethics had been juggled, but no answer ever found. Sometimes he wondered if his own memories were deceiving him. In the half-alive moments between sleep and

wakefulness, he saw himself tread the hallway to the interrogation room. He could see the splinter of shock on
Yousef's face as he aimed and fired. He could hear the thump
of sound as his body collided with the stone floor.

Vine tucked those thoughts away. He soon arrived at St
James's Park. Cosmo Newton was seated on a bench straight
ahead, insulated from the weather in an overcoat, hands snug
in brown leather driving gloves, both clasping the handle of
a furled umbrella.

Vine slipped into the gap beside him. There was no formal greeting, not even a flicker of recognition.

'How is exile treating you?' said Newton, after a beat.

'I can't complain.'

'You always were a good liar.'

'I take it this isn't just a social call?'

'Well deduced.'

'So?'

The shadow of a smile crept to the edge of Newton's lips.
'Trust me,' he said, rising from the bench and prodding his
umbrella at the ground. 'This is something you'll want
to hear.'

## 2

'So why do you want to be a spy?' he asks.

Vine pauses, looks again at the strange figure in the tweed jacket, tufty hair, red cords. 'I wasn't aware I did.'

'How do you mean?'

'Professor Donaldson told me this was an interview for the Treasury.'

A gale of laughter, five seconds long at least. Cosmo Newton clenches his pipe between his teeth. 'She did always have a very droll sense of humour. You would prefer the Treasury?'

Vine pushes himself further into his seat. 'Can't say I speak from much experience of either.'

'No, quite.' Newton looks down at the sheet of paper in front of him. From the back, Vine can just about make out Professor Donaldson's sloped handwriting, the trademark red ink. 'Good with numbers, I see.'

'I can muddle my way through, yes.'

'Any languages?'

'I've just about mastered English.'

'But not much foreign experience?'

Vine smiles. 'I don't know how familiar you are with state-run care homes, Mr Newton. But not many have budgets for foreign holidays. Blame the government rather than me on that one.'

Newton looks up, an interested crease on his heavy face. 'You're political, then, are you?'

## 3

'Let me get this straight. You're saying Gabriel Wilde has just . . . *disappeared*?'

Cosmo Newton sighed. 'Left the station in Istanbul at approximately 1915 on the evening of Thursday 3 November. According to the CCTV feed, at least. The first sign of trouble was when he didn't show up for work the next morning. The station alert went out at 0800 and the Ambassador was informed. From witness statements, we think any incident took place roughly between 0100 and around 0200. Forensics found evidence of a struggle. Impossible to judge exactly how many hostiles we could be talking about. From some initial work, we think not more than three. The kitchen was covered in Wilde's blood. But the snatch team were good. We recovered no other DNA matches. It bears all the signs of a professional take-out.'

'Any clues about the identities of the hostiles?'

'No, they were good. Too good.'

Vine coughed lightly and continued to stare ahead. He wrapped his upturned collar tighter around his neck, wincing slightly at the cold. He felt numb at the news, as if the full impact would only hit him hours later. For now, he was content to drift on the guilty thrill of the diversion.

St James's Park was emptying. When they'd first arrived it was dotted with parents pushing buggies, replaced now with a scattering of joggers immune to the chill.

Vine stared up for a minute at the sky. 'What was the follow-up?'

'The Ambassador ordered an immediate search party, unsurprisingly. A team were dispatched to comb the area. Tentative mention was made of trying to use the Cousins and track him by drone, but the relationship has been patchy of late.'

'And the reaction at Vauxhall Cross?'

'Well, there's the rub. That's where the story stops.'

'How do you mean?'

Newton transferred his umbrella between hands, his pace slowing a fraction. 'Cecil won't let so much as a whisper about it penetrate the walls of Whitehall,' he said. 'Wilde was replaced as Head of Station almost instantly, and normal service has been resumed.'

'And the Americans?'

'As far as I know, the drone request was never authorized. They'll have picked up mutterings, of course, but Vauxhall Cross has kept quiet otherwise. Cecil's best plan is to sit pretty and hope Brexit helps sweep it all away.'

'And you? The JIC?'

'We live by rumours alone. Cecil has been consolidating his grip. It isn't worth the while of any staffer to blab. Everyone's too frightened of him. The lessons of the past are there for all to see. I don't need to remind you of that.'

'No . . . so why have you summoned me?'

'I've been shut out,' Newton said. 'Vauxhall Cross has gone into lockdown. Cecil has always seen the JIC as an irrelevance. The Foreign Office doesn't want to know. Whitehall instinctively looks the other way when this sort of scandal breaks. But something's not right. And I need to find out what.'

'Why the fallout?'

Newton grimaced. 'The new Public Accountability Bill, extending the thirty-year rule on public files to all branches of Whitehall.'

Vine laughed. 'Open government.'

'Indeed. If we can read Cabinet minutes, why not what Five, Six and GCHQ got up to? Even so, none of this makes sense. The Public Accountability Bill has been in the works for years. There's something else Cecil's trying to hide. He knows he can't keep Whitehall in the dark about Wilde's situation for ever. Perhaps in the old days, but not now. This is him freelancing, I'm sure of it. Whatever game he's playing, he obviously thinks it is worth the risk.'

'And he thinks he can win.'

Newton stopped. 'The truth is, I want you to do something for me. Something that only you can do.'

'And what might that be?'

Newton sighed, a greyish plume forming. 'Have a good sniff,' he said. 'Inhale the flavours. Swirl it around the glass and see what impression you get. Until the Yousef case is cleared up, you're not going to be back at Vauxhall Cross any time soon. Might help keep you busy.'

'Thanks for the thought.'

Newton looked up at Vine. 'No one else knows Wilde like you did,' he said. 'And I can't trust anyone on the inside. The greatest hope for MI6 in a generation – a man prepared to one day clutch the green pen as Chief – is snatched in the middle of the night, and we're all meant to pretend it never happened.'

Vine pressed his hands deeper into his furred coat pockets. 'So what is my brief?' he said.

'I want you to go and interview the key people. See what was happening at the consulate, within the station. Go through Wilde's history and see if you can find me some answers. There were endless rumours about something he might be working on. He was about to be handpicked as the next Director of Global Operations, then seemed to pack it all in. Everyone thought it was personal problems, but see if it was something more. Go back to the start. Talk to Turnbull at Oxford. His Deputy Head of Station is back in London. Get their thoughts. Here's one name to get you started.' He handed across a card.

Vine took the card and scanned the name. Olivia Cartier MP, Member of Parliament for Kensington.

'One of the last people to see Gabriel Wilde before his disappearance,' said Newton. 'She was at a dinner at the consulate in Istanbul. I've put in a call and she's expecting you.'

Vine stowed it in his coat pocket. He waited for a second before he asked it. Then he gabbled it out, nervous about the consequences. 'The report of the scene. Did anyone see or hear him being taken?'

'The report said two witnesses in the complex heard some movement outside, but there was nothing unusual in that. Wilde was often called in to the consulate at odd hours. He moved out of official accommodation after the separation with Cecil's blessing, claimed it gave him greater cover. No one saw anything or had reason to raise the alarm.'

'And CCTV? Emergency protocol from Wilde?'

Newton swallowed, hesitating slightly. 'What little there was had been down for weeks. You know what it's like out in the field. The on-site team ran all the tests they could, but there was nothing further on the forensics front. He wouldn't have had time to activate any emergency protocol. The snatch teams have been getting better. They'll have shadowed him, found out his routine. It will have been clinical, all mobiles and electronic devices the first thing they destroy. Easier for them, given it wasn't an official embassy residence. It would have been over in a minute.'

Vine removed his hands from his pockets now and folded his arms. 'But we're assuming he was alive when they grabbed him?'

'Probably unconscious, but that's the working assumption. Drugged and bundled into the boot is the best guess. In terms of past experience, there's still some hope that they want to leverage the kidnap for all it's worth, probably a prisoner exchange. If not, use it as a media opportunity. The public execution of an MI6 Head of Station. One hell of a front page.'

'And has there been any communication since?'

Newton shook his head. 'Not that I know of. With every day that passes . . .'

'. . . the worse it gets.'

'Yes. We both know no one comes back from this. Not really.' Newton turned to him. 'I've been sidelined officially. That's why I need you.'

Vine looked around. It was the fear that lurked behind the self-imposed armoury of every MI6 officer, the deadly implications of falling into enemy hands. Despite all that had come between them, he felt sick as he thought of Wilde locked in darkness, the colourful possibilities of the future now fast diminishing, replaced instead by the ghoulish certainty of what lay ahead. They had all undergone hostage training at the Fort, savage interrogation sessions with an SAS team. They had been told how to prepare mentally and physically for torture. But practice was no match for reality.

'. . . and wider implications?' Vine shifted uncomfortably. As he stood here in the park everything that had come between him and Wilde seemed redundant. Instead, he felt the initial kick of friendship return, the irrepressibility of Wilde that he had once so cherished. He realized that he had never had the chance to make it right. Now he probably never would.

Newton's voice quickly regained an operational briskness. 'The consequences are unthinkable,' he said. 'Our most important assets in the Middle East potentially compromised. Our on-going relationship with every Western intelligence agency doomed.' He lowered his voice. 'No matter how long he tries to resist, they all talk eventually. I'm afraid, in some ways, the best we can hope for now is that they killed him quickly.'

Vine felt a shudder at the clinical way he said it, no doubt echoed in the conference rooms of Vauxhall Cross, Cecil and the rest of the fifth floor secretly wishing Wilde away. That was what they were in the end, Vine realized: just so much collateral damage. He was tired of it all. 'And what if I've left this behind? What if I don't want to play this game any more?'

'Because you have no other choice,' said Newton. 'Until your investigation is concluded, you are in limbo.' He fixed Vine another knowing stare. 'And you realize she's back, don't you? Returned to Thames House after the separation.'

Vine found his concentration lost in the swirl of noise around them. He hated the smallness of this world, the claustrophobia of old regrets. Yet something else burned too, the better part of him drawn to the case despite himself.

As he forced his gaze back towards Newton, he wondered whether redemption came in such an unlikely disguise. 'Who's back?' he said.

Newton smiled. 'Rose, of course.'

# 4

Vine looked at the screen again: he was up by a couple of thousand on the day. As the graphs and numbers flickered back at him, he could feel his anxieties recede. It acted as a form of relief. On the markets there was just the formal purity of numbers. He had been an addict ever since Cambridge, long mornings propped up in bed flicking through the pages of the *Financial Times*.

His record spoke for itself. He had played it well just before the dotcom crash, then inched his way into behavioural economics, seeing the madness and shifting his money accordingly in the run-up to the financial crisis. He had taken out any loan available and bet it all against the over-leveraged banking sector. With the property market tanking and the rest of the world haemorrhaging money, he had upgraded from his roomy flat in Pimlico to this place in Wellington Square, Chelsea.

Six months later, he had enough to redecorate the library. It was his temple, a vast rectangular space with polished wooden flooring, a high Regency ceiling frosted with decorative twirls and ornamentation. Each part of the room housed a different collection: general reading on the right, intelligence history on the left, and then the collection up ahead, constantly added to, his newly revived work on Enlightenment mathematics. The rest of the room was bare, a nirvana of nothingness.

He clicked off the screen and turned instead to the secure laptop that Cosmo Newton had biked round following their meeting. He lifted the lid and tapped his way through the multiple layers of security with Newton's own login details. The screen flared into life with a large, searchable JIC database, the Cabinet Office logo filling the top of the screen.

Vine clicked through until he found the folder he needed. He drew up the file containing the brief report from Istanbul Station into Wilde's disappearance. He started reading through it again. The prose was dry and colourless, but the facts were clear. The consulate CCTV feed showed Wilde leaving the premises at 1915 on the evening of Thursday 3 November. The first alert had sounded from the Deputy Head of Station at 0800 on the morning of Friday the 4th. A station team visited Wilde's flat at 0900, before full search protocol was initiated at 1000 on the orders of the Ambassador. A forensic team were helicoptered in and conducted an initial sweep of the flat, before Wilde was officially declared missing.

Vine read through the details for a second time. He clicked on the attachment to the file and made his way through the CCTV photos. He began trying to reconstruct the scenario in his mind. He could see Gabriel Wilde leave, careful as always to notice any watcher stepping into rhythm behind him. The consulate regulations preferred staff to stay within their vehicles as much as possible. But Wilde knew as well as anyone that vehicles were too easy a target for tracking devices and electronic surveillance. He always preferred to risk it on foot, dodging his way through the crowds, a change from muggy days cocooned within the station.

He would make his way back to his flat. Despite himself, he would feel the same nostalgic bite as he contemplated his new arrangements: a single-bed flat, Rose permanently back in the UK, wrestling the electrics to life in the hope of a decent supper. And, always, there was the paranoia of constant suspicion. There were ears everywhere, informants surrounding him. Each movement was logged, listened to and sieved for advantage. It was the new normal of life in the field.

Vine closed the lid of the laptop. He paced back to the large rectangular windows that looked down on the tidy square of lawn below, trying to stop himself thinking of the rest. He had seen enough case reports to last a lifetime. The clinical precision disguised the brutal reality. Shock usually numbed you to begin with. Once you had time to assess the scale of the threat, it was too late. By the amount of blood the forensic team had found, Wilde had marshalled impressive resistance. But it came down to numbers in the end. No one stood a chance against a trained snatch team.

He breathed deeply, the thoughts pounding at him. He closed his eyes and tried to shake them off. Instead, he found himself mulling over the past. Sometimes he wondered if he would ever be able to escape that world of rivalries and jealousies. The cast list was still with him somehow: Wilde, Newton, Cecil, Rose. He felt a familiar nausea dig at him, the same feeling he had experienced in the park. He knew deep down that Newton was right. He would agree to his request. He longed to be back in the action, a chance to walk the halls of Vauxhall Cross one last time with his head held high. But more than that: whatever the consequence of his relationship with Wilde, in that past life he had once been more brother than friend. They had been through too much together. The thought of Wilde being tortured to death would leave him no comfort; he would be restless until he knew why.

The silence held for a second longer, then broke. Vine turned, wondering for a moment if he was imagining it. Then the sound echoed again, puncturing the stillness.

The doorbell was ringing.

# 5

The rules around the identities of members of the Secret Intelligence Service – more commonly known as MI6 – were clear. To the world at large, they were invisible.

The stringent vetting process took a year before you gained STRAP 3 clearance. Once you had survived training at Fort Monckton, you were then inducted into numerous layers of anonymity. There were two principal ways to hide: official cover and a selection of aliases. The official cover was used within the environs of Whitehall, armed with a card proclaiming allegiance to the Foreign and Commonwealth Office. An alias was for outside the manicured streets of SW1. Surnames and backgrounds were slyly altered. The technicians in the basement of Vauxhall Cross produced the props – fake passports, business cards, copycat national insurance numbers. When you bought a property, took out a mortgage or opened a bank account, the trail was obscured behind the scenes, while physical security required constant personal vigilance. Whenever Vine approached Wellington Square, he unconsciously checked his tail. A team from Vauxhall Cross had installed a security camera above his front door and a panic button on the second floor. Paranoia wasn't an add-on. It infected every second of life.

Vine checked on the security feed relayed directly to his computer. On the steps of the house was a man in a red Royal Mail top with a brown package balanced uneasily in his right hand. He zoomed in a fraction and studied the face: an angular jaw, narrow emerald-green eyes and a fuzz of toffee-brown hair greying at the edges. There should be no way that any foreign intelligence service could know about his recent suspension from duty. He regularly had the house swept for bugs, and all personnel information at Vauxhall Cross was fortressed behind the thorniest possible encryption methods. But if they did, they would know that now was the optimum time to strike. The panic button on the second floor would be met by shrugs in the techier rooms of Vauxhall Cross. There would be no immediate search party sent out if he was abducted, no clamour to let teams loose on the streets of London. The paperwork would be quietly edited and the suspension transformed to severance. He would be cast adrift, doomed to wear out his vocal cords pleading for help that would never arrive.

He took one final look at the video feed and then clicked off. Instinct told him to ignore the call, though it would be impossible to pretend the house was uninhabited. The first floor was illuminated, a gash of yellowish light. The windows were too shiny, the front step swept clean of leaves. He was just about to wait it out when the doorbell rang again, the sound even uglier than the last time. The noise held and echoed before finally tapering back to silence.

Eventually, Vine decided that he would answer. There was something about the package that intrigued him. It was always possible – just possible – that this really was nothing more than it appeared to be. But somehow he couldn't quite square that possibility. The logic didn't fit. Very few people outside the Service knew he lived at this address. Spies weren't encouraged to fatten their Rolodexes. If this was from Cosmo Newton, he would have biked it round with a Cabinet Office freelancer as he had with the laptop, stealing down the street and then dropping a message to the burner phone. The very normality of this worried him.

He reached the ground floor and treaded along the hallway, trying to blank out the flurry of cautionary tales that now suggested themselves, tales of operatives scuppered by one moment off their guard. He could still listen to the voice urging him to think again, though he knew his footfall on the stairs would already be enough to give him away to any agent attuned to such nuances.

Vine reached for the latch and drew back the door, faking a casual smile.

The man nodded silently and drew out a PDA. Vine waited for a name to be produced, the moment he could judge whether such a simple everyday exercise was truth or fiction. Technical wizardry meant the innocuous brown package could contain any number of ills: a bug, bomb, or bio-weapon of some kind that would slowly permeate the house and eat through his insides. Often he wished he could edit out such knowledge and hypotheses, but they stuck in his thoughts. He had eaten from the tree of knowledge too long ago.

'Mr Joseph Woods?'

Vine felt his pulse beat harder, palms clammy and throat parched. He locked his features into a neutral expression, trained never to give anything away. But the name echoed through him as he clutched the thin stem of the electronic biro and squiggled letters on to the PDA's surface. Then the package was handed over and, within seconds, Vine saw the man flash him a thin-lipped smile and move back down the steps and away.

He didn't retreat into the safety of the hall but hovered in the doorway for a moment longer, weighing the package in his right palm first and then quickly assessing the shape of it. He glanced down at the label stuck on the front and saw the name Joseph Woods and his address printed in tidy black type. It looked slightly battered at the edges, as if the journey had been a long one. He checked finally for any other obvious signs of trouble – a professionalism in the sealing which suggested it had been manufactured in lab conditions – though saw none.

He closed the door, walked through into the kitchen and placed the package down on the table. He scrutinized it from all angles for one final time and then searched for a pair of scissors. All the while, those three words beat in a constant rhythm: *Mr Joseph Woods*. There were only a handful of people alive who had ever known him under that name. It had been one of his earliest operational assignments, joining up with officers from the CIA to hunt and capture key members of the al-Qaeda leadership in the wake of the attack on the Twin Towers. The details of the operation, including operational aliases, had been limited to the grander incumbents of the fifth floor.

Vine steadied the object with his left hand and then carefully cut into the packaging with the tip of the scissors held in his right. He continued up in a straight line, watching as it split in two. From the recesses of memory, he could hear the stern warnings of the liaison officials from Porton Down, drilling into them the variety of ways hostile actors could embed biological weapons into everyday objects.

Vine reached the end and parted the packaging. It revealed the blank leather cover of a book, larger than a traditional hardback and covered with a light snowing of dust. He checked to make sure it really was dust, before gently inching the book out of the packaging completely and holding it up to the light. It had no jacket or insignia on the front, and no identification marks on the spine or back cover. But the binding looked pricey, and the texture felt smooth and cushiony to the touch.

He placed it back down on the table surface and then slowly opened the leather cover. The paper was thick and aged to a crinkled creamy-brown. He flicked through some empty pages until he saw the first marking, a circle shape with an arrow-like tail. What looked like the pages of a codex stood on the left and right, two crowns above and one underneath. Vine peered closer at the lettering around the frame of the circle and read: UNIVERSITY OF OXFORD. Beneath that symbol stood a further line in italics: *Oldsworth Prize 1999*.

He turned again and found himself looking at a title page. It read: THE ODYSSEY. Then Vine saw the name and felt a rumble of surprise: *The Honourable G. Wilde*. Beneath it was another paragraph, this time handwritten in a flash of blue ink.

Vine took a breath and read the words, his mind fizzing with incomprehension:

*Dear Solomon,*

*In case we don't meet again, I want you to have this. All wisdom lies in this book. Take care of Rose for me.*

*Yours,*
*Gabriel*

# 6

Vine stared at the inscription for several minutes, trying to compute the range of implications. He stood back from the table top and worked to calm his breathing.

The only people alive who knew him by the name of Joseph Woods were the Chief and Director of Global Operations at MI6; the Director of the National Clandestine Service at the CIA; and his partner on those operations, a fellow recruit from Fort Monckton, the Honourable Gabriel Wilde.

Suspicion was so deeply stitched into him that for a moment he wondered whether it was a hoax by one of the others on that list. In the days of the Cold War, the KGB had excelled in mind games as a way to wrong-foot opponents, unpicking an operative's sanity by extrovert displays of power. There was something deeply personal about the book in front of him. It was Gabriel Wilde's own translation of Homer's *Odyssey*, the labour that had secured him the prestigious Oldsworth Prize during his penultimate year at Oxford. The reward was the volume that sat on the table top, Wilde's translation printed in two special editions housed at the Bodleian. Vine had heard Wilde boast of it numerous times. It served as a sign of intellectual vigour for the initiated, far more exclusive than a degree certificate. The jab of unease surfaced again. Was someone with knowledge of Wilde's whereabouts taunting him with their power, able to summon even the most intimate objects?

He looked at the title page, though saw nothing else there apart from three rows of numbers in pencil. He quickly checked them for any obvious mathematical pattern, but they were meaningless; probably library reference codes of some sort.

He scanned back up to the words. *In case we don't meet again, I want you to have this. All wisdom lies in this book. Take care of Rose for me.* The voice sounded like Wilde, though the style was curter than he remembered, as if the youthful cadences had hardened over time to something more concerned with substance than verbal flourish. But what did it mean exactly? Each line seemed to contain its own enigma.

*In case we don't meet again, I want you to have this.*

*All wisdom lies in this book.*

*Take care of Rose for me.*

Vine thought of the details of Wilde's disappearance from the official report. All the evidence pointed to a surprise snatch job: the amount of Wilde's blood that had been found in the flat, and the clinical way the snatch team had avoided leaving any forensic debris to identify themselves. But Vine rolled those six words around: *In case we don't meet again.* They bristled with foreknowledge. Had he known? As Gabriel Wilde hunched over the title page and inscribed these words in the Turkish heat, had he known what was about to happen? Vine looked down at the words again. They seemed to have a newly confessional tone. He turned to the second sentence, a single clause that revelled in its own sense of Delphic mystery: *All wisdom lies in this book.* The confessional tone shifted to the satiric, leading the reader on, before ending with the shiftiest line of all. It seemed so simple, yet was freighted with emotional inconsistencies: *Take care of*

*Rose for me.* The tone of it was off somehow: not just considering their own history, but in the phrasing of it.

He read the sentence out loud, remembering the lessons at the Fort on how to imitate a style. Nowadays it was easy, scanning through correspondence digitally to find out how to mimic the slant of a hand, and then using basic pattern analysis on the syntax to ensure it appeared authentic to anyone who knew Wilde's voice. In a strange way, Vine saw that the very irregularity of the last line authenticated the whole. If someone had been trying to copy Wilde, they would have stuck more slavishly to his normal style. Only Wilde himself would dare use something that jarred so clearly with the pattern.

Vine took up the book again and began leafing through the rest of the pages. He wondered how long it had taken Wilde to complete the translation. There were over 400 pages, each busy with immaculate lines set out in grand, imposing type. Wilde had so often cultivated the air of the dilettante, yet this proved the opposite. The volume was treasured not just for the symbolic value it held, but for the elbow grease that had gone into the composition.

Reaching the end, he flicked through to the start again and lingered over the inscription, trying to silence the emotional feedback and return to first principles. He needed to understand the logic here and find the underlying architecture of the pattern. What was Gabriel Wilde trying to say? What did the inscription mean? Why was it sent? And how did it relate to Wilde's disappearance?

Just as these questions began tumbling around in his subconscious, a noise struck up behind him. A waspy buzz from a burner phone.

Only one person had this number. They were instructed to text day or night with any information.

He picked it up and stared at the message pulsing from the screen.

*I have news. We need to meet.*

# 7

The main entrance of Guy's hospital smelled fiercely of cleaning fluid and coffee. Shuffling bodies queued patiently to dose up on caffeine from the counter on the left. Phones bleeped at the reception desk on the right.

Vine made his way through the lobby, pausing at the bank of lifts. He pressed for the third floor, positioning himself as usual to check he wasn't directly in the sightline of any CCTV cameras. These visits always required a change in appearance. The wingtip brogues and Oxford shirts were replaced by a more informal set-up. Scuffed jackets, jeans tearing at the knee, a Mets baseball cap and a pair of modishly rimmed glasses. It wouldn't fool the latest facial recognition software, but it would be more than enough to stop a bored security contractor from spotting any irregularity.

Getting through the entrance was easy. The real pressure came here. With ongoing budget constraints, the Met could only afford one full-time officer to monitor Yousef. Vine had slowly built up a case file of sorts – name, habits, movements, hobbies. The key weakness was soon obvious: the guard took lunch every day at 1 p.m. on the dot. While he was meant to stay in post at all times – with a nurse ferrying him a takeaway sandwich – he had become lazy, the hospital canteen a welcome relief after hours jammed between the same two corridor walls.

Vine looked at his watch: 1.15 p.m. As the lift doors sighed open, he double-checked the hall was clear. There was no sign of the police guard. Then he began walking in the direction of Ward 9 and through another set of double doors until he was standing outside the right room. Screens crawled with colour on either side. A bed took up the centre of the room, the fragile-looking figure drowned by pillows.

Vine stood watch, as he always did. It was like a vigil. As a British citizen, Ahmed Yousef had been flown straight back to Brize Norton, where he was immediately taken into the custody of the Met. He existed now like a cabinet of secrets, each piece of information still under lock and key.

Every time Vine arrived here, all he heard was that single line taunting him.

*I know a secret . . . A secret that changes everything.*

He could feel the familiar pangs of doubt consume him again. He had tortured himself with every possible logical construction but still couldn't find a proof that worked elegantly enough. Someone, somehow, had set him up that day. He wasn't even meant to have been in Istanbul. He had stepped into something he had yet to understand and had been paying the price for it ever since. He saw Wilde's vehicle inch out of the car park, the feel of the concrete floor under his feet, the blood next to Yousef's body.

Five minutes later, Vine heard steps echoing down the corridor. He turned and smiled as he saw her approach. She classed as the only asset he ran these days, his source on the floor where Yousef continued to hibernate, waiting to flicker back to full consciousness.

Vine put his phone away. He always had to remember to slip into character at this point. He was no longer Solomon Vine but Martin Wright, a freelance journalist willing to lunch anyone who would talk on a background basis.

'Hello, stranger,' he said, as she walked up to him. Becky Reith was twenty-two and had just finished her nursing degree. She now earned £21,000, had a rent of £800 a month and student debts north of £40,000. She didn't say no to free lunches.

'You look in need of some proper food.'

Her face creased with disapproval. 'You know you really shouldn't be up here. If someone caught you . . .'

Vine raised both hands in surrender. *'Mea culpa,'* he said. 'Curiosity got the better of me. I just wanted to get a proper look at our patient. See how he's doing. You said there was news. I thought perhaps . . .'

Becky looked sheepish for a moment. Then she shook her head. 'Not that good, I'm afraid.'

'So,' Vine said. 'The usual?'

The usual was a run-down café on St Thomas Street, cheap yet with its own vinegary cheer. Agent-running was all about avoiding elementary character errors, making sure the asset felt you were on their side. There was no inquiry into her relationships or personal life. He kept it strictly professional, letting her make any moves.

Once inside the cramped shadows of the café, they ordered quickly. Vine listened as Becky continued one of her usual spiels about haughty surgeons, temperamental admin staff, problems with her flatmates. Eventually, Vine steered them back.

'So your text said there had been a development?' he asked, as he took another bite of his burger.

She smiled. 'They think it's nearly over.'

Vine swallowed. 'A chance he might wake up soon, you mean?'

Becky shrugged. She picked up another chip and washed it down with Coke. 'There's always a chance. But they are already making preparations for when he wakes up fully . . . They think it could be any day now.' She began pushing a molehill of coleslaw around her plate. 'You're not going to quote me, are you?'

Vine found himself lost for a moment. The thought was tantalizing. 'What?'

'Your article. I think I'd probably get into trouble. Don't like us lowly nurses speaking out.'

He smiled. 'Don't worry,' he said. 'If I do use anything, I won't attribute it. You're fine.'

They finished their main course, and Vine watched as Becky tucked into a pudding and coffee. Then he walked her back. As they neared the sprawl of the hospital campus, Vine said: 'If he does wake up, I need to know as soon as it happens.'

Becky nodded. 'I'll definitely call.'

Vine watched her shuffle back inside, then looked at his phone. For some reason, the air felt scratchy and irritable on his skin. He needed to get out of here and wash himself clean.

As he reached the entrance to London Bridge station, a calendar reminder pinged on the screen. He looked down at his clothes, realizing he needed to change.

He drew out the card Cosmo Newton had given him in St James's Park and scanned the details. For his next appointment, he would have to pretend to be himself all over again.

## 8

The entrance to Portcullis House was heaving with visitors, the queue snaking out through the revolving doors and round the steps outside. Glazed-eyed policemen supervised the conveyor belt, the muddle of constituents and corporate lobbyists each patiently waiting to turn out their pockets, advertise their innocence.

Vine took off his jacket and placed his wallet and house keys in a grey tray, before walking through the full-body scanner and having a mug shot taken. Once given the nod by the policeman, he followed the line ahead, collected his items and arranged the paper pass with a hazy, colourless image of his face around his neck. He gave his name at reception and then took a seat.

He looked down at the card Newton had given to him: Olivia Cartier MP, Member of Parliament for Kensington. It had no photo, just a portcullis symbol in the right-hand corner. Vine had already done his research: Cheltenham Ladies' College followed by Oxford, a former member of the Intelligence and Security Committee and now Parliamentary Private Secretary to the Defence Secretary. *Who's Who* listed her fifteen-year career in the Foreign Office, serving in Paris, Rome and Washington. Her hobbies included history and travel. She was a typical Wilde courtier: socially fluent, stacks of private money, a good brain and plenty of ambition.

Someone called his name on the tannoy. Olivia Cartier's PA escorted him through the glass doors and then walked him down from Portcullis House to the Palace of Westminster, through the gloom of the colonnade.

Cartier greeted him with a firm handshake. 'How does the terrace sound? Not too cold for you?' she said.

'Not at all,' said Vine.

They began walking down the Medals Corridor. They bought two coffees from the cafeteria, then made their way past one of the uniformed doorkeepers guarding the entrance to the House of Commons terrace.

As they paused momentarily on the steps, scanning the full length to find a spare seat, Vine tried to keep his focus. His mind still spun with the consequences of Gabriel Wilde's disappearance and the inscription in the copy of *The Odyssey*. *In case we don't meet again, I want you to have this. All wisdom lies in this book. Take care of Rose for me.* The better part of him had been stirred by Newton's call and a chance for personal redemption, yet some unspoken part wondered if Wilde had got what he deserved. Vine allowed himself to indulge that sentiment longer than he liked to admit.

He followed Cartier leftwards, away from a gaggle of other MPs and researchers already on to their second pints. She set the tray down and pushed a black coffee towards him.

'So, Newton gave me a ring personally. Said you needed to speak about something. I'm afraid my PA didn't have any papers for me to read on this one?'

Vine settled himself into the hard wood of the chair and looked across at the frothing blue-grey expanse of the Thames to his right. Only one boat was puttering down the middle. Wind-battered tourists clustered uneasily on the deck, trying to avoid the spray.

'Newton told me you knew Gabriel Wilde,' said Vine, voice neutral and eyes trained firmly on Cartier's face, alert enough to catch a reaction.

'Yes. Good old Gabriel,' said Cartier, chuckling to herself. 'I first got to know Wilde when I joined the Intelligence and Security Committee. He was on a brief secondment to Whitehall liaison.'

'That was the first time you met?' asked Vine. 'You didn't cross over at Oxford? Or during your time at the Foreign Office?'

Cartier sipped at her coffee. 'Who knows, probably shared a dining hall at one point. Could say the same for half the people here. But it was the first time we got to know each other properly . . . What's this all for, if you don't mind my asking? Newton was pretty gnomic on the phone. Nothing's happened to him, has it?'

Vine let the question hang for a moment and watched a concerned expression work its way across Cartier's face: forehead depressed, lips pinched, a slight tilt forwards on the chair.

'No,' he said, at last. 'Nothing serious, anyway. Newton wanted me to speak to you because he said you saw him recently.'

Cartier breathed hard and looked upwards, as if trying to summon a calendar in her head. 'Yes. So I did. Sorry, the last few weeks have been a total blur. Problems in the constituency. I was in Istanbul with the Defence Secretary, his PPS for my sins.'

'How did Wilde seem?' Vine asked.

'Fine,' said Cartier, leaning back in her chair. She crossed her legs and steepled her hands. 'Looked pretty tired. We didn't get to speak that much. Got the impression he was under quite a bit of stress, actually. He looked like he hadn't slept for days. I think I told him to take it easy. Have a holiday. If anyone needed it, he did.'

Vine felt a cool gust of wind flick at his cheeks from the river. 'And what about the last year or two? Anything out of the ordinary that you noticed? Did anything change?'

She drew her cheeks in and laughed timidly. 'No. As I said, he often seemed tired, but that's hardly unusual in the field.'

Vine waited for the sentence to trail off before deciding to play his hand, a gentle bluff to see what he could draw out. 'And what if I told you there was speculation that things weren't quite right?'

Cartier looked slightly bemused by the question. 'How do you mean?'

Vine kept his voice steady, as if he had copious evidence to back up what he was about to say. He inched forwards in his chair. Outside the official realms of Vauxhall Cross, he now had only limited resources, relying solely on his own tradecraft to get to the truth. 'A shift in patterns. Not unknown in the field. Too close to the death and destruction. Breaks in routine, getting careless with safety protocols. What the white coats at Vauxhall Cross would call behavioural abnormalities.'

Cartier looked momentarily perturbed. She masked a twinge of unease by taking another swig of coffee. 'Suspicious behaviour, you mean?'

Vine kept his answer firmly neutral. 'It's certainly one possibility.'

'And is this a view shared by the JIC?'

Vine knew he had to be careful. Newton had sent him to find answers, not stir up new trouble. 'I'm afraid I'm not at liberty to say.'

Cartier raised her eyebrows. She sat back and turned towards the river, as if debating whether to reveal something.

At last, she said: 'Well, I'm not entirely sure I should either, then . . .'

Vine felt suddenly alert. He kept his voice level, knowing he couldn't allow anything to break the spell. 'So you did notice something?'

Cartier still looked unsure. She took another gulp of coffee and traced her finger round the rim of the mug. 'This is just shooting the breeze, right,' she said. 'Nothing official. I'm not being recorded? This doesn't go any further?'

Vine shook his head. 'No. This stays between you and me.'

'Good.'

'So?'

Cartier stared to her left, losing herself in the undulating patterns of the river. 'If you want my theory, I got the impression he was working on something. Something big,' she said. 'Whether official or unofficial, I couldn't tell. But when I first knew Gabriel, he was full of life. He could drink everyone else under the table, get twenty minutes sleep and he'd still look fresher than you in the morning. He was absolutely on board with the direction of Western foreign policy. If anything, I'd have marked him down as something of a hawk. Tell me if I'm wrong, but I always got the impression that he was a bit of a neo-con. He could see why Saddam had to be removed. He absolutely accepted the case for the war on terror after 9/11.'

Vine nodded. He felt his pulse begin to quicken. He knew that Wilde, a bullish mask put on in polite company to hide any lingering doubts. 'But recently?'

Cartier turned away from the river. She looked back at Vine. 'I think it was after the coup in Egypt following the Arab Spring. Or at least I always got the impression that was what changed it for him,' she said, her voice less certain, the stagey volume dimmed. 'Then trouble began brewing again in Iraq and the civil war in Syria. He began to see a decade of Western foreign policy in the Middle East had brought nothing but carnage. He was sitting on the sidelines with blood on his hands.'

'He actually used those words?'

Cartier sighed. 'Yes. I think he was looking for a way to make things right. My impression was he had started circumventing official procedure, trying to save it all on his own. Going straight to Cecil and bypassing the MI6 bureaucracy.' Cartier stopped. 'I think there might also have been other problems . . .'

Vine held back, trying not to seem insensitive. 'Personal problems? His marriage?'

'I don't know. But I think he was struggling on numerous fronts.'

'And the final time you saw him? Did he raise any of this then?'

Cartier yawned. She flicked a hand through her hair. The cold had begun to give way to a slight drizzle, the other drinkers and eaters clearing their trays away and moving inside.

'That's the thing,' she said, picking up her coffee mug. 'He said he'd found the answer.' Cartier looked straight at Vine with a bloodshot stare. She seemed uncertain of what she was about to say. 'He said he'd found a way to seek redemption. To wash away the blood on his hands for good.'

# 9

'Cecil wants us to take the next one,' says Vine.

'What's his background?' asks Wilde.

'Lived in Britain for ten years, just back from three months in the arms of the Americans.'

'Enhanced interrogation?'

'No, all-paid trip to Vegas. What the hell do you think?'

'Sorry, silly question.'

'Tech-ops guy, by the sound of it.'

Vine slows the car and opens the window. Both of them flash their security passes for the uniformed figure at the gate and drive through towards the car park.

'Why have Langley let him go?' Wilde asks.

Vine squeezes in between two Land Rovers and then kills the engine. 'They're drowning in cases. Can't send them all to Guantánamo. They can only handle the big fish. Need us to sweat the link men. Number 10 are keen to show our use to the White House.'

'Fair enough.'

They get out of the car. It is dark, dawn barely broken.

Wilde stares at the buildings in front of them. 'These places don't half make you want to top yourself. So depressing.'

Vine locks the car door. He finds himself amused once again at the occasional clarity of Wilde's reactions, the off-duty comments when there is no one in the room left to seduce. It is the instinct of the games field, a sense of fair play. 'And here was me thinking war was supposed to be fun.'

'You know what I mean.'

'Not really.'

'How long do you think it will take?'

'Why? Not another lady waiting for you in London?'

Wilde smiles. 'I've been thinking it's time to settle down.'

'Of course you have.'

'I'm serious.'

Vine laughs. They walk inside, eager for the warmth. There is another flash of passes, and then they are through to a room littered with used coffee cups and takeaway pizza boxes. On the monitor above them is an empty industrial warehouse with a single seat in front of a table, the rest of the screen bare.

A solitary figure, eyes webbed with sleep, gets up and nods. 'You guys taking over?'

'Unfortunately,' says Wilde. 'Where's the coffee machine?'

'Kettle in the corner and jar of Nescafé best you'll get.'

'Anything we should be briefed on?' asks Vine.

The man shakes his head. 'He was in a bad way when we got him. Broken bones, malnourished. We've brought him back to the land of the living. But he's fragile. Still sleeping.'

'Time for a wake-up call then. How many guarding him?'

'Two. But he couldn't run more than ten metres without collapsing. Nothing to worry about on that front.'

The man leaves while Wilde goes in search of the kettle. Vine picks up the secure line and instructs the guards to get the prisoner prepared for interrogation. Twenty minutes later, the phone bleeps.

'He's ready,' says Vine.

Wilde downs the dregs of his second cup of coffee. 'Do you want to play good cop or bad?'

Vine only ever has one answer, the bravado masking the bug of unease in his stomach. 'Bad. So much more fun.'

They pause next to the door, craning up at the monitor to see the prisoner brought in. On the monitor, the door of the warehouse opens, and two RMP guards emerge, both grasping the puny arms of a third man between them. He is dressed in a white t-shirt, baggy tracksuit bottoms and un-laced trainers. He looks thirty, perhaps thirty-five. His hair is shaved short, muscle tone wasted. He seems unsteady on his feet, unable to take the full force of his own weight, face gaunt and shrunken.

Vine forces strength into his voice. 'Showtime.'

'Remind me what this is all for,' Wilde says, finishing a cigarette and stamping it on the ground. 'Him, here . . . *this*.'

Beyond them the base is packing up for the evening, the mosaic of lights gradually dimming. Vine looks out and marvels at how mundane it feels, the normal rhythms and frustrations. Despite its purpose, the scene around them retains a stubbornly normal sheen. Trucks still humming around the base, cramped offices lit with a pale glow, the snatches of half-heard conversation drifting lazily up towards them on the balcony.

'I don't like this any more than you do,' he says, tiredness keeping him from summoning anything more profound.

Wilde turns, almost laughing. 'Are you sure about that?' He sweeps his hand across the view, as if able to topple the lot with the back of his hand. 'Fact of the day. Did I ever tell you my great-grandfather was part of a cavalry charge with Churchill?'

'More than likely.'

'Well, behave yourself and hear it again.'

'If I must.'

'Incredible story. The Battle of Omdurman. On horseback, weapon in hand, staring his enemy in the face. He wrote in his diary that he had looked on death and made his peace with it.'

'A poet as well as a trained killer . . .'

'Wizard with a paintbrush too, as it happens. But that's not the point, Sol.'

'What exactly is the point?'

'I mean what a way to fight a war. Putting everything on the line like that. Charging into the fray with your head held high, praying to God you survived the day.'

'A dead body is dead, no matter how it died. The means don't change the ends.' He looks across at Wilde, the scar of animation on the smooth curves of his face. There has been another terror scare that morning, Whitehall locked down for hours, a chaos of police sirens, helicopters overhead, offices evacuated. Ministers whisked down underground corridors and hugged tight by security details while the rest of the populace tottered about unprotected.

'Surely that's what we're missing in all of this,' says Wilde. 'That sense of nobility. We're viewing this war as if the enemy are atoms, individual units we can manipulate, torture or take out as we choose, and the rest won't be affected.'

Vine stays still. He knows Wilde too well not to recognize the symptoms of his intermittent epiphanies: a captivating brightness to the eyes, voice tinged with a slight husk.

'But they're not,' he continues. 'If we're ever going to win, we need to understand who they are. Their tribes and traditions, loyalties and families. If we think we're just going to impose McDonald's and Burger King from ten thousand feet, then we're doomed.'

'Thus sayeth the archangel Gabriel,' laughs Vine.

'We're not prison guards, Sol, we're spies. Name a Moscow Centre hood that was turned chained to a concrete floor. We need to get him one on one . . . It's the only way. You know it is.'

Vine shakes his head. 'No. Absolutely not. We'd be burned alive. What the hell would the Americans say?'

'Who bloody well cares what the Americans say?' says Wilde, flailing his arms in frustration. 'They butchered the poor bugger and still couldn't get him to talk. It's how we have always done it, the British tradition. Trust me, we'll never get anything out of him if we just keep sitting there.'

Vine looks over at Wilde. Standing closer, he can see a tenseness in the face beneath the smooth veneer.

Wilde stoops to light another cigarette, then tilts his head back and lets loose a cloud of smoke. 'He's not an equation, Sol, he's a human being. We've got to treat him like one.'

Vine glances at his watch. They have endured a whole day with nothing to show for it. The prisoner is barely alive, probably brain-damaged, all secrets evaporated long ago in the chaos of his arrest. He has said nothing, barely even confirmed his name, just shivering in silence. 'How long would you need?'

Wilde smiles and nods in acknowledgement. 'An hour. Tops. Just let us get some air. Let him think I'm a friend, someone he can trust. The fifth floor never needs to know.'

It is four hours exactly after Vine receives the order to stay for a second shift that the phone rings. Wilde has gone to try and sleep, ready for another early-morning start. Vine is still working through case reports on his laptop.

'Yes?' he says.

'Sir, it's Private Henderson from the residence.'

'What is it, Private?'

'We need you here. Now.'

'Of course.' Vine puts the phone back, feels a jab of anxiety at the tone. He closes his laptop, checks his mobile for any missed calls and then asks the RMP guard on duty for the direction to the residence. It is a three-minute walk across the car park and into a separate building.

He flashes his pass and continues up to the first floor. Henderson, a thin man with moist eyes and a round face, is waiting on the stairs.

'What the hell's happened?' asks Vine.

Henderson doesn't answer immediately. He just walks up the stairs and pushes through a door into a narrow hallway. 'This is where we kept him, sir,' he says, pointing at a room on the right. 'One of us in the other room, him in here. Bathroom done up in the middle. We thought he was asleep.'

Already, Vine feels a stab of queasiness. He follows Henderson into the bedroom, a cramped, dusky space made worse by the sight on the bed. The sheets are stained with blood, the sleeper's eyes lidded shut. The wrists are turned upwards. Right by the arm lies a fragment of razor blade.

'Ring the emergency number,' says Vine, his voice edged with panic. He pauses and glances at Henderson. He can feel his heart pounding, trying to will himself to think faster. 'Where's the log book?'

Henderson looks back. 'Sir, I'm not sure . . .'

'Where's the damn log book?' Vine shouts.

'In the other room, sir.'

Vine nods. 'Go downstairs and make the call.' Henderson still dawdles, his body locked with indecision. '*Now.*'

Vine waits until he hears Henderson's feet on the stairs, then walks through to the other room. The log book is on the table, blue biro by the side. He scans the room for cameras, finds none and then opens it to today's date. He runs his finger along the timings and sees the entry.

He stares at the evidence that will condemn them both, his body flooding with anger. Wilde with his rule-breaking, protocol-flouting entitlement. A lifetime charming or buying his way out of trouble.

He can already hear Henderson's voice from the phone downstairs, the call about to end.

After the anger comes the kick of self-preservation. If anyone learns of the outing, both their careers will be over. That much he knows for sure. Such a severe breach of procedure will kick off a major row between Vauxhall Cross and Langley. They will inevitably pay with their careers. He was complicit. He will go down as well.

He hears Henderson coming back up the stairs and looks down again at the evidence that will be used against them.

He considers the other option: shop Wilde, shatter the friendship, his stint as turncoat earning him a slim chance at a desk job on probation at best. But something stops him from doing it. He can see Wilde carted off to prison somewhere as a warning to others, undone by his own residual compassion at the sight of a detainee tortured free of a personality. Whatever else, Vine can't let that happen.

In one quick move, he rips out the page. There is no time to burn it. Ripping it into shreds will leave evidence he can't afford.

Instead, he scrunches it into a ball, forces it into his mouth and chews it down. What doesn't exist can't hurt them. If Henderson or the other guard say anything, he will claim to have seen one of their razors left casually in the bathroom.

As he waits, Wilde's words spin through his mind again. Perhaps he is right, the scene in the bedroom the most humane way this whole enterprise can end.

Just as he swallows the final piece, Henderson's wiry frame is in the doorway.

'They're on their way, sir.'

The London Eye continued its geriatric spin to the right, spectators estranged within the oddly shaped pods, as if afraid of contamination.

Vine tensed his fingers in his coat pockets. He said: 'So you noticed the change about two years ago?'

Fergus Goodwin, Deputy Head of Station in Istanbul, nodded. They continued walking down the Embankment, pushing through the wind. 'Yes. I think it was probably to do with the legal work Rose was doing at the time. He had started to help out with some of her pro bono cases on weekends and that sort of thing. You can spend your entire time barely going beyond the consulate.'

'Anything else?' asked Vine. It fitted with what Olivia Cartier had said about Wilde's louder dissent. 'Did he talk to you about his concerns over Western intervention in the Middle East and the Arab Spring?'

'A bit. Mostly it was about how misunderstood Islamic culture was.' Goodwin dabbed at his nose with a tissue and zipped his jacket further up his chest. His voice was curiously placeless. It had the faintest hint of an American twang, the product of a decade spent in the field. 'He was coming up to forty. I always got the impression he'd had a slightly uneasy relationship with his father. He'd always seemed to me to be the epitome of Englishness, good manners, that sort of public-school charm. But I think he was looking back quite a lot.'

'Was there ever any indication that he had gone beyond just an interest in Islamic culture?' asked Vine, once again trying to find any concrete piece of evidence he could hold on to. 'That he might have considered converting, for instance?'

Goodwin seemed to tense. His mouth pursed, as if snagging on a detail. 'I shouldn't really be talking,' he said.

'This is direct from the JIC,' said Vine. 'I'm just the messenger.'

Goodwin looked across. He was a man on the make with things to lose. Vine envied his situation.

'There was one time when I burst in on him. We needed him urgently for something, I forget exactly what now. He'd left his door open, which was pretty unusual for him, most of the time telling everyone else to be safety conscious.'

'What happened?'

'When I went in, he was clearly preparing for something. He was too good to look surprised, just smiled and thanked me for telling him. I was a bit slow on the uptake, I suppose. But there was a mat . . .'

Vine tried not to let his interest show. He needed to keep coaxing out the information. 'He was praying, you mean?'

Goodwin scrunched up his nose, desperately trying not to commit to an answer. 'Something like that,' he said.

They stopped for a moment to stare out across the water, figures inching along the South Bank opposite just visible through the light spread of mist.

Without another question, Goodwin went on, as if unburdening himself. 'There were also the meetings,' he said, shuffling his feet to try and regain some warmth. 'He started circumventing normal procedure, going out to meet contacts at bizarre hours. Sometimes we wouldn't see him for days. Other times, he refused to share what he was working on. It was as if he was hiding something. I started to get cut out of the process. I was worried he was having a breakdown or . . .'

Vine waited for him to say it. 'Or what?'

'. . . something more damaging. Don't ask me exactly what. But something.'

Vine nodded. As with Olivia Cartier, he couldn't press it too far, with only the tenuous cover of Newton to hide behind. 'And did you do anything about it?'

'I tried the Director first,' he said, looking down at the ground, as if ashamed at grassing on a colleague. 'Then even tried to take it to the Chief himself.'

'To Cecil?'

'Yes.'

Vine couldn't hide his interest any longer. 'What happened?'

Goodwin looked up. His face was riddled with emotion, desperately trying to find the right course of action. 'I got told in no uncertain terms to get back to work. Cecil wasn't interested.' Goodwin shook his head and turned back to the view across the Thames. 'As far as the fifth floor seemed concerned, Gabriel Wilde was untouchable.'

'So what do you have?' asked Newton. He wrestled the cork from the bottle of claret and poured them both a generous glass. They were standing on the balcony of the house in Chester Square owned on his late wife's side.

Vine took a seat on one of the wicker garden chairs, crossed his legs and heard the sound of a bicycle bell cut through the stillness. A cold, butterscotch sun strained at his eyes. He watched Newton fill the seat opposite as he took a first sip of wine.

Vine thought back to the two interviews so far: Olivia Cartier and Fergus Goodwin. He had spent hours trying to match the Gabriel Wilde they described with the version he had known, the middle-aged doubt with the youthful arrogance, religious conversion with libertine morals, anguished principles with realpolitik. It was so difficult to tell truth from fiction, Wilde so adept at transforming one into the other.

'I know that Wilde had begun expressing disdain for US and UK foreign policy, particularly after the Arab Spring and with the start of the civil war in Syria. Olivia Cartier also said Wilde often talked about having blood on his hands, guilt at not being there on the battlefield. Especially the last time they met, just before . . . well, you know. There is also evidence that, while in Istanbul, Wilde began practising as a Muslim.'

'He was a practising Muslim?' Newton's voice was shot through with curiosity. He batted away a stray strand of hair from his brow.

'According to Goodwin.'

'So what do you conclude?'

Vine looked over at Newton, then took another quick spot-check of the balcony. He remembered all the courses they had been forced through during early training, just at the start of digital warfare. He knew how easy it was to get a take on anything if you knew what you were doing. Newton as Chair of the JIC was a top target for the key threat areas. This place could be crawling with bugs, one of the reasons they had chosen to talk outside.

He put his wine glass down on the side-table and folded his arms. 'Something was going on,' said Vine. 'I don't have enough facts yet to know what.'

'But I was right to be suspicious,' said Newton.

'Yes.'

'I'm pleased. Good to know I still have a nose for these things.' Newton remained silent, scratching at an itch on his right leg. 'Dare we indulge in a hypothesis or two?'

Vine smiled. 'You know I always prefer fact over theory.'

'Forgive an old man his whim.'

Vine sat straighter in his chair. He let his thoughts cohere into an outline, the edge of a pattern beginning to emerge. 'There are three possibilities so far,' he said, 'each of varying probability. The first is a random kidnapping. He looked rich, he was a Westerner and he foolishly refused consulate security. Like many before him, Wilde could have been the victim of a local gang. Taken for his money or to demand a ransom from his family. Statistically, the chances of that are reasonable. But the forensic evidence in the flat counts against that. The take-out was too clean, too professional.'

'The second?'

'This was an act of war from an Islamist cell, or a hostile intelligence service working inside Turkey and across the Syrian border. Wilde must have been running some sort of investigation and got too close to the truth. They pounced. They left the blood as a sign of victory. A warning to others.'

Vine looked across at Newton again, trying to interpret his inscrutable expression, the mask-like set of features. It was impossible to tell whether he was convinced.

'And the third hypothesis?' said Newton.

Vine let the conversations swirl through his mind for a final time. He knew how crazy the words sounded. They would be inadmissible to anyone who knew his history with Wilde. Yet the hypothesis couldn't be ignored, underscored by the words that continued to baffle him, the dazzle of blue ink.

*In case we don't meet again, I want you to have this. All wisdom lies in this book. Take care of Rose for me . . .*

'What if Gabriel Wilde was never who he seemed to be? The anger over US foreign policy, the sense of blood on his hands . . .'

*He said he'd found a way to seek redemption . . .*

'What?' said Newton. 'You think he's committed suicide? Run off with intelligence secrets and given them to the *Guardian*?'

Vine had considered all possibilities. But there was always something about Wilde that refused to settle for second-best. The Gabriel Wilde he'd known wouldn't shoot himself in a forest somewhere or down a bottle of pills. He would seek a grand finale.

'What if there's something else going on here?' he said. 'What if he's still out there? If the abduction wasn't quite what it seemed?'

'You mean . . . ?'

'Yes,' said Vine, finally allowing himself the freedom to say the words. 'What if this is all far worse than we think?'

# I2

*2012*

He feels himself tap across the floor of St Martin-in-the-Fields now, glad for dryness after the sour rain outside. He is early, as ever, hugging the routines, the sense of order they instil. He always takes the pew at the back, always at the end closest to the door so he can stare forwards across the serried ranks – the collection of overcoats, mackintoshes, scarves and woollies – all shapes of person crammed obediently into the hard wood of their seats. Others want a closer view of the choir, to inspect the faces of the singers. But he is happy to observe not participate, to watch the world at a distance.

It turns 7.30, and the choir rises, tidily turned out in their spotless black uniforms, the conductor with his exaggerated, jerky enthusiasm and straggly hedge of grey-streaked hair. They are a disorderly bunch appearance-wise, corpulent swell and wand-like thinness. But when they start singing, the strains of Handel's *Messiah* rising slowly through the church, the music seems to smooth out the wrinkles of appearance, the act of performing to straighten their backs, add hauteur to their chins, varnish their workmanlike demeanour.

It is also a relief, a reminder of beauty amid the chaos. Being back in London is a welcome change after too many months of choking on the Beijing smog. London seems like an oasis of calm compared with the noise he has left, the

62

queue-friendly order of the Tube, the patient understanding of street corners. He longed for these moments then, beached in a scrappy flat with the smell and sound of a country's adolescence all around. He longed for the peace of a declining empire, not the ambition of a new one.

He sits back and lets the plangent notes of the choir wash over him. He hears the sound of the wooden door behind him creak open, the patter of delicate steps. He doesn't stir, hogging the pew all to himself. He remembers the preciousness of solitude he hoarded at St Edmund's during his childhood, the delicious few seconds away from the clutter of institutional life. Every morning, afternoon and evening trapped within the routines and rhythms of homelessness, the absence of domesticity haunting every hallway. Ever since – on trains, aeroplanes, pews and benches – there has been a luxury in selfishness.

He feels his composure sag as the latecomer's presence hovers beside him, accompanied by a hushed whisper, a nod towards the emptiness to his left. He nods reluctantly, tucks in his legs to let her through. As he does so, he catches a split-second of her face as she passes, before she arranges herself on the space beside him. His attention to the singing is broken. He risks another confirmatory glance to his left, beginning to memorize the geography of her face: the wide blue eyes, the dip of her cheeks, the smooth texture of her skin. Then the hair, the shimmer of jet-black. A smile that seems without vanity.

Vine turns his gaze back to the choir, the music feeling more strained than only moments earlier. He begins to feel scratchy and annoyed with the world. He is sick of this old routine, letting himself believe in the illusions. He prides himself as the realist who can only ever be surprised by hope, treasuring the shop-worn and the imperfect as a hard-won badge of maturity. The music is his only lapse, able to enjoy the symmetry of their voices.

He doesn't risk another glance but just stares intently forwards. The choir remains a blur, the fellow audience members a smudge of colour. It has happened so many times before. They progress through to the grand finale of the 'Hallelujah' chorus, after which reality will, inevitably, intrude. Merely the dull thud of departure or strained small-talk, the glimpse of a wedding ring, perhaps, or throwaway darts of husband, home and family.

As the clapping starts and the singers beam merrily, Vine waits. He has decided to let her speak, if at all, not to puncture his cynicism without due provocation. In the previous hour he has imagined her voice to be everything from Sloane archness to slangy girlishness. When she does eventually speak, he is undone by the tone, an intentness in the speaking.

'Sorry about squeezing past you like that,' she says. 'I missed my bus. Didn't think I'd make it.'

'Don't worry,' he replies, finally able to permit himself a closer look. With the music stopped, he has nothing to hide behind. He is beguiled by the quiet warmth of her eyes, the resonance of her voice, each element so at ease with the other. Her skin is white without being pale, soft and voluptuously smooth. Her cheeks reddish from the rain outside, lips faintly dewy. Her coat is a bluish check, a gold necklace beneath losing itself in the baggy folds of her scarf. She tucks a strand of hair behind her ear, and Vine scans her hands for any sign of a ring. But they are gloriously bare.

'Do you come here often?'

'Probably more than I should. How about you?'

'Only for Handel,' she says. 'Once they start on Beethoven, I lose interest.'

'Very sound.' He is about to stop, to shut himself up and nod, when he spots a look in her eyes that persuades him to continue. 'Everything after that is missing something, I find. Hard to describe . . .'

She nods. 'Yes, I know what you mean. It loses its logic somehow, doesn't it?'

And there is a quality so neatly wrapped in the way she says it that he feels his last defences drop. He is beyond the point at which he will be able to forget her. There is something too memorable to the fit of her, the alchemic effect of her smile. Whatever happens now, he knows she will stay with him, lodged as part of his history. Of what will be, or what might have been. Factual or counterfactual.

'Solomon,' he says.

She smiles, the first draft of an expression that Vine knows he will parse for years, and says softly: 'Rose.'

## 13

As Vine stepped off the 12.37 train from Paddington to Oxford, he realized how little it was possible to know of those who dominated your life. He remembered an exercise in class once where the teacher had asked if anyone knew the names of their great-grandparents. Not one person had put their hand up, almost making up for the rash of embarrassment he felt whenever questions of parentage were raised.

He knew Wilde had been at Westminster and Christ Church, Oxford, with temporary residence at a crammer that was always glossed over in the official version. It had been Westminster, rather than Eton, because some mutton-chopped forebear had once tossed a coin, and every member of the lineage had continued the tradition since. Christ Church, Oxford, because Cambridge was full of roundheads with their Bunsen burners and their maths books. The Wildes were always a family of cavaliers and politicians.

Oxford was crisp and brittle, far from its summer-varnished best. Cornmarket Street would be heaving with crowds, Broad Street a similar huddle of human traffic crawling past the Bodleian. If Wilde had got in over his head, Vine knew the secret would lie in his past somewhere. And one person could help him find it, the person who had recruited Gabriel Wilde to the secret world: Dame Angela Turnbull, Emeritus Professor of Middle Eastern Studies and former Warden of Merton College, an inveterate storyteller and raconteur with hollow legs and a ticklish laugh. The final interview.

Vine followed the sign for the taxi rank and asked for Merton College when his turn came. He checked his phone and saw an email from Turnbull: 'Much looking forward to lunch today. Mr T has commandeered the Jag for his midday fling at the doctor's surgery. Bike means I might be a minute or two tardy. Please forgive. A.'

The taxi snaked into Merton Street, bumping over the cobbles. He paid the driver and then dipped his head under the stone archway and walked into the porter's lodge, two men in branded t-shirts chatting behind the desk.

'Here to see Professor Turnbull,' he said.

One of the porters nodded. 'Just arrived. Should be outside on the bench, I think.'

Vine opened the door out into the main quad and saw Turnbull perched on the bench, peering intently at a copy of the *Guardian*.

'Professor Turnbull?'

'Ah! Mr Vine, what a delight,' said Turnbull, rising from the bench and folding the paper under her arm. She looked just as Vine remembered her, often sighted passing through the halls of Vauxhall Cross locked in conversation with Newton. Her hair was still lavishly combed, the face grooved with lines.

She led on as they crossed over the quad and through to the Fellows' Dining Room, a large, rectangular space with a long table dominating the middle, twenty or more chairs set out on either side. There were plenty of murmured greetings as Turnbull grabbed a plate and began inspecting the various dishes. Once they had piled their plates high, Turnbull beckoned to the two seats at the far end.

The conversation flowed easily to begin with. Turnbull talked at length about her new book, an encyclopedia of global terrorism ('I haven't told a soul yet, not even my editor, in case I give him a heart attack,' she whispered), the privations of the lecture circuit and the difference between British and American universities.

It was as they moved on to coffee that she said: 'So, tell me, Mr Vine . . . your email was deliberately mysterious, I presume to avoid the attentions of Cheltenham. Though, perhaps, I can imagine the cause of your invitation.'

Vine caught the curious glint in her eyes. He recognized it as an echo of Newton, the same narrowing of the lids, the theatrical pause before the *coup de théâtre*.

He was just about to speak when Turnbull got there before him: 'Something about the Head of Station in Istanbul . . .'

'So you know?'

'Nothing more than rumours, of course. I still have my ear to the ground on some of these things. When the name popped up recently I thought it rang a bell. One of the best students I ever knew. Greats and then Arabic. Quite a feat.'

Vine looked down at the dwindling band of fellows at the far end of the table. 'I'm right in thinking you recommended Gabriel Wilde for the Service?'

'Yes. The Service was desperate for Arabists at the time. We'd spent so long funnelling new graduates from the Russian department that some of them had forgotten other disciplines existed. It was the start of the new war. From the first tutorial I had with him, I knew Wilde had what it took. Perhaps even become Chief in due course.'

'Were there any issues during the vetting period?'

Turnbull tilted her gaze up at the ceiling, burrowing further back into her capacious memory. 'Two things, if I recall. While his father's side of the family were as blue-blooded as you get, his mother was different. Wilde's father had met her when he was trying to flog expensive legal services to the Qataris. She was from a family of financiers with more than a few questionable links to Gulf financing of nuisance groups around the Middle East.'

'Funding terrorism?'

'Never quite put in those words back then, but amounted to the same thing. It was her brothers, mainly. They had fingers in a lot of pies. Financed some charities that were used as cover to channel funding to jihadi groups. I had to liaise with the City regulator of the day to iron it out. Eventually, it was cleared. Though they were his uncles. His mother had died when he was much younger, which put the problems at one remove. All in all, I think there was pressure from the high command.'

'Pressure to do what?'

'Clear him. Grade him Persil-white and allow him through.'

Vine felt a fizz of tension. 'From who specifically?'

'The fifth floor. Mostly Newton as Director of Training, though Cecil took a keen interest as well. The Service was woefully short of Arabic speakers. We had lots of product coming in from assets in the Middle East, but not enough people who could actually make sense of it. It was the golden age of multi-culturalism. The Service was meant to be opening up. To have rejected someone of Wilde's obvious abilities because his maternal family actually happened to live in the Middle East, with all the incidental ties that entails, was not just misguided, but positively criminal.'

'So he went through.'

'Yes,' said Turnbull. 'He was given STRAP 3 clearance and allowed through to the Fort for training.'

'And the second issue?'

Turnbull paused, longer this time. Vine felt he had touched something, a long-trapped nerve. Turnbull sighed, pushing her coffee cup away. 'While here, Wilde made a potentially unfortunate connection with a radical don in the Faculty of Oriental Studies called Mohammed Ressam, long since dead. Ressam used to have several select students – the brightest of the bright – for extra tutorials, a discussion group of sorts nicknamed by staff the Prophets.'

Vine felt his throat tighten.

Turnbull continued. 'In the late nineties, Ressam published a book called *The Spirit of Revolution*. Bar-room Islamism, inspiring those with a dream to take action against a corrupt West.'

'What happened?'

'Someone in the college called the police and had Ressam's rooms searched. They found radical literature smuggled in from Pakistan. Audio recordings too, sermons from names associated with al-Qaeda.'

Vine inched forwards in his chair. 'And Wilde was part of it?'

Turnbull didn't look at him, staring away to her right. 'Not quite. They were the usual bunch of suggestible undergraduates. Wanting to put the world to rights. But I saw an opportunity all the same. Part of my job has always been to keep an eye out in the university. I had fitted up Gabriel to be my star recruit. When Ressam moved to Christ Church and began holding these events, I wanted to try Gabriel out, let him earn his spurs. Common practice then, always had been. I would file any interesting observations, send them back to Whitehall. That was that.'

'So Wilde began spying on Mohammed Ressam?'

Turnbull turned her eyes downwards. She sighed. 'Yes. Did a damn good job too. One of the reasons we got the arrest. MI5 were very grateful, even tried to poach him.'

'And the Prophets?'

'There were a few associated with the group from numerous colleges. From Christ Church it was mainly just Gabriel and a PPE-er, frightfully bright as well. Cartier. Since entered Parliament for her sins.'

Vine glanced up. 'Olivia Cartier was a confidant of Mohammed Ressam?'

*I first got to know Wilde when I joined the Intelligence and Security Committee.*

Turnbull looked at him. 'Confidant may be too strong. But she knew him.'

'I interviewed her a couple of days ago. She said she first met Wilde when joining the ISC.'

Turnbull smiled, chuckling to herself. 'That sounds like Olivia. She was quite a politician even then. Speaking at the Union tomorrow, apparently. A performance I am quite content to miss.'

Vine couldn't help himself. 'You don't think there might be something in it?'

Turnbull shook her head. 'I doubt it. It was just student inquiry, nothing more. Not enough to stop her passing positive vetting, anyway. This was all pre-9/11, of course. Hardly anyone had heard the name al-Qaeda, let alone knew anything about it. Now she probably just doesn't want the papers knowing and kicking up a fuss. Spoil her chances of becoming a minister in the next reshuffle.'

'And what happened to the Prophets when they left?'

Turnbull twitched at her napkin, folding it neatly into a square. 'The Twin Towers happened,' she said. 'Suddenly the world changed. And people had to find new ways to rebel. Just as they always have.'

# 14

Vine watched the stooped figure of Professor Turnbull shuffle away towards Fellows' Quad and then made his way out of the porter's lodge and on to Merton Street.

He rubbed at his eyes and tried to get himself to think clearly. He thought again of the news about Wilde's family background and the group at Christ Church, the Prophets. There was no way he could get an unbiased read on Gabriel Wilde now. The evidence was clouded with judgement. If you looked too deeply into anyone's past, perhaps skeletons could be found and motives inferred.

He began walking in the direction of the High Street, wrapping his hands in his coat pockets, happy to lose himself in the cloistered feel of the street. He needed time to think. The three original hypotheses presented themselves again in his mind. The empirical data was emerging, but it was messy; as yet, it couldn't be tamed into any sort of geometric elegance.

It was the distinct texture of the cobbles that jolted him out of his thoughts, the uneven surface making it harder to disguise the fall of the shoe leather. Vine listened again closely. There was a faint echo coinciding too neatly with his own walking pattern. He was alive to it instinctively. He listened for a third time. There was definitely another rap of sound, not in sync but clumsily trying to disguise itself, a beat off the pace. Vine didn't slow down, careful to maintain the same steady tempo, body language looking relaxed. He needed the watcher to lapse into complacency.

Vine carried on, veering away from the direction of Christ Church. Instead, he angled his way up Magpie Lane. It was much narrower here, the anorexic paving dappled with greyish light. He could sense the watcher tailing him, hanging back just a fraction.

Just as he was about to turn left on to the High, Vine kept straight on, trying to work out who it could be. An embassy watcher, perhaps. Or worse, a freelancer, all rules redundant.

Now he risked a look behind, glimpsing a smudge of mussed hair, a black t-shirt and crumpled linen jacket worn over light denim jeans. He didn't linger, the glance almost unnoticeable. But he had enough for an ID if he ever needed one.

Vine pressed forwards up Catte Street. As he reached Broad Street, he checked again for any splash of t-shirt or jeans. But he found nothing.

Only one thing was left. He saw the turning to Turl Street and moved across, seeking cover behind a slow group of Chinese tourists on the opposite side.

He risked one more look behind him. No one had yet followed him. He waited.

Ten seconds later, the watcher emerged on the left, scanning the street for any sign, leaving himself exposed from behind. Vine didn't need long, just enough time to approach, lock the man's hands together and press him against the wall. He leaned in close to the man's ear.

'Who the hell are you?' he whispered, still twisting the wrists. He took a closer look at the figure in front of him. He had a scruffy crop of mud-brown hair, droopy eyes and a scatter of stubble under his chin; gym-fit, though trying to disguise it through a shabby dress sense. 'Who are you working for?'

He waited for an answer. But none came. Vine twisted the wrists round until they were almost at breaking point.

'Follow me again, and I'll break both of them.'

There was one final twist and a high-pitched scream of agony. But Vine was already away.

## 15

Pret was rackety with customers. There was a constant push through the heavy glass double doors, excavating the remains of the snack collection.

Vine sat in the corner, nursing a medium filter. He looked down at the copy of the *FT* on the table and pulled it towards him again. He finished reading a feature piece on the seventieth anniversary of Presidential Proclamation 2714, signed by President Truman in 1946 as the formal end to all hostilities in the Second World War. A joint US–UK commemoration service was scheduled soon in the Palace of Westminster, and the piece had some juicily anonymous quotes from the Speaker's Office grumbling about interference from the US embassy over security arrangements. He flicked through other stories – a junior energy minister resigning, another scandal in the City, more bitter rows over Brexit – and then turned to the comment section. He felt a hit of unease as he scanned the headline and quickly read the first few paragraphs of the lead op-ed, splashing the pages with drops of coffee:

## WHY THE BRITISH GOVERNMENT MUST APOLOGIZE TO AHMED YOUSEF
Valentine Amory QC MP (Chair, Intelligence
and Security Committee)

It is only in times of crisis that our true character emerges. And so it is with national character as well. When the going gets tough, do we retreat into scapegoating, or unite together to find collective solutions?

With the Middle East still in turmoil, it is no surprise that the ongoing case of Ahmed Yousef has caught the public imagination. Born in London, and educated at UCL and Yale, Yousef was building a successful career as an academic. Then his life changed for ever. During a routine research trip, Yousef was detained and questioned by British intelligence, accused of aiding and abetting Islamist groups participating in the Syrian civil war. He was denied basic rights and kept in custody. Only hours after being detained, he was found shot . . .

Vine folded the paper and pushed it away. He quickly drained the rest of his coffee. He looked at the other drinkers clustered around the tables, couples picking at croissants and sandwiches. Once, he had almost pitied them, stuck in the ruts of a humdrum existence. He had cherished secrecy, the notion of an elect using their talents in the service of their country. In some part of himself, he still did. But now, just occasionally, he felt the opposite. The last few years of his thirties were slipping from his grasp, hurtling him towards the no man's land of middle age. Normal existence seemed like a promised land he was now never destined to enter.

He relished the last gulp of caffeine, then left and strolled along the King's Road, lingering over phrases from the article he had just read. He could see it happening already. Ahmed Yousef was being integrated back into normal life. He had come to symbolize something more than himself, reincarnated as a cause.

Just before he reached his house, Vine's mobile began ringing. He answered it instinctively.

'Hello?'

There was a faint clearing of the throat followed by a slur of sound.

'It's Newton,' said the familiar voice. The tone was shakier somehow, thinner and breathless. 'I've been doing a spot more research after our conversation. I think I may have found something. I'm travelling back to Paddington on the last train. Best not to speak on an open line. Meet me there at 11.45.' There was a pause. 'If I'm right, this changes everything . . .'

# 16

Vine scanned the platform concourse again, mind fuzzing with irritation after the near three-hour wait since Newton's call. He looked at the time on the departure board to his left: 11:55. It had been over ten minutes since the 11.44 from Cheltenham had arrived, and there was still no sign of him. None of this made any sense. His words had been quite clear.

*This changes everything.*

He tried to staunch a growing feeling of unease. The station was empty at this time of night. The scene was starting to be overtaken by mops and buckets, cleaners roaming freely around the platforms. The last barista headed for the exit. A paunchy middle-aged man sat behind the help desk, chest hair bristling up the gap where his top button should have been.

'Can I help?'

'The 11.44,' Vine said. 'That came from Cheltenham?'

The man gave a sluggish tap on the keyboard in front of him and nodded.

'Are there any others due in on the same line tonight?'

'No. That was the last.'

He should have been here. Vine checked his phone again and refreshed his emails. There was no message. Newton was punctual. He would have called ahead. Vine hovered for a moment before starting to follow the signs for the taxi rank outside. Was he just being paranoid? Newton could be a drama queen, injecting every hiccup with far-reaching conclusions. Perhaps it was nothing. He had been hauled in for official business and forgotten to call ahead. There were any number of plausible explanations for his failure to appear.

But it would be good to be sure. Vine took out his mobile, found Newton's number and rang it. After ten or so burrs, it went to voicemail. Vine hung up. Newton's phone was on. He would be busy.

It was just as he reached the taxi rank that he decided to try a second time. After four burrs, there was a crackle of sound at the other end.

'Hello?' It was a different voice: terse, male and official sounding.

'Sorry,' he said. 'I was trying to get hold of a friend. Must have dialled the number incorrectly.'

'Can I ask who's calling, sir?'

It was the 'sir' that confirmed it, the knot of dread in the pit of his stomach. 'I was due to meet my friend this evening,' said Vine, sidestepping all questions about his identity. 'He hasn't showed up. I'm just trying to find out if he's OK. Do you mind if I ask who I'm speaking to?'

There was a pause, a mental scramble for appropriate words. 'PC Harding, Transport Police.'

Vine froze, the trickle of passengers becoming a blur around him. 'What's happened?'

'The owner of this phone was found dead at Cheltenham train station earlier this evening, I'm afraid. Looks like a heart attack. Can I ask for your name again, sir . . . ?'

But the question came too late. Vine was already slipping off the plastic casing of the phone and inching the SIM free. He didn't turn or check his tail. Instead, he ignored the taxis and walked on alone. The SIM was vanished in the first bin, the rest of the phone in stages.

Soon he was losing himself in the corners of the evening. All other thoughts receded in the face of the new reality. Vine walked on until his legs threatened to give way beneath him, content for the darkness to swallow him whole and never let him free.

# PART TWO

## 17

Chester Square seemed so different at this hour, empty and funereal.

It all felt surreal somehow. Not only the thin, gruel-grey mist, but the thoughts that were occupying his every minute. Was it possible? Vine desperately tried to separate his own gut feelings of hatred towards Wilde from an objective assessment of the evidence. But he knew such disinterested-ness was beyond him. The facts all led to one conclusion: Wilde's maternal family in Qatar, the association at Oxford with Mohammed Ressam, the vocal disdain for US and UK foreign policy after the Arab Spring. Now Cosmo Newton dead. He was numb at it all.

He neared the house and paused for a moment. If the police were treating Newton's death as due to nothing more than natural causes, there would be no need to divert immediate operational resources to round-the-clock surveil-lance of his home. Once the information had churned its way through Whitehall, the order would go out to post some-one on the door while they waited for the pathologist's confirmation. But, until anything was flagged, Newton's death would be treated as a tragedy, not a crime.

Vine knew that gave him a limited window of opportu-nity. He looked around, checking to make sure he wasn't being observed. He could still hear Newton's voice on the phone, the sense of dramatic urgency in his tone: *this changes everything*. Whatever Newton had been working on, there had to be some evidence of it here. Newton had been schooled in Moscow Rules, trained in the habit of a fallback. That was the only hope Vine had left.

He forced down a ghoulish feeling as he walked up to the front door. He had completed one lap of Chester Square. There was no immediate sign of a police presence.

He took out two gloves from his pocket and slipped them over his half-frozen fingers, trying the door handle once. But it was locked.

He removed an old field kit from his jacket pocket and then swept the area again quickly to make sure he wasn't being watched. He crouched down further and began attending to the lock. A minute later, he felt it give.

He checked the street for a final time. There was still nothing. He eased the door open quietly and found himself entering the familiar dark porch space. A reddish dot pulsed on his right next to an alarm pad. Vine stepped across and keyed in four digits – 1791, the year of Mozart's death. He watched as the light blinked once more before falling blank.

He turned to the surrounding view. There was an array of musty-smelling coats hanging to his left, mud-scabbed boots in an untidy row beneath. He stopped for a minute, waiting to register any other signs of movement. He listened for a creak on the stair or rustling from one of the rooms. A dull throb of silence met him.

He moved forwards through the house. He tried to summon any sense of when Newton had last been here. He was into the main hall now, the staircase to his left, the kitchen on his right.

Vine quietly moved through the rest of the ground floor. He checked the kitchen once and saw several coffee mugs piled by the sink, yet to be washed. The kitchen table was bare, cupboards all closed.

He left the kitchen and began padding up the stairs, careful to dull the creak. The main room on the first floor was fustier still. There was a chipped bookcase groaning with hardback volumes, an ancient TV showing few signs of use and a dusty brown sofa busy with faded cushions.

Vine walked up to the bookcase and began sorting through the various volumes. What could he expect to find? What was it Newton had meant?

*I've been doing a spot more research after our conversation. I think I may have found something . . . If I'm right, this changes everything.*

Vine started taking out random volumes from the bookcase and flicking through the pages, half-hoping to find a note falling out. He looked again on the sofa and around the TV, trying to see if there was a book Newton might have read recently, something he could have used in case the worst happened.

He left the room and began treading up the second flight of stairs. This was a part of the house he had rarely seen before. Vine glimpsed a bathroom ahead and then a bedroom on his left. He cast a glance into both, saw nothing but a half-used tube of Colgate and old editions of *The Times* crossword. He reached the end of the hall and pushed at the door of the last room.

He flicked on the ceiling light and saw a wooden desk with an anglepoise lamp facing him. The floor was stacked with piles of paperback books, pages fanning out with a yellowish bulge. This was Newton's secret study, the official version on the first floor merely a decoy for unsuspecting visitors. Vine picked his way between the piles of books, trying to reach the desk. It was typically analogue, with two chipped fountain pens and then stacks of formal writing paper. Vine began picking up sheaves, looking down at the knobbly texture of the pages.

He put down the writing paper and began sorting through the other items on the desk. There were more pens and Post-it notes. A letter from the Royal Society of Arts was neatly folded on the right, a copy of *The Times Literary Supplement* likewise on the left.

He was just about to leave the desk when he decided to finally check the right-hand drawer. He tugged it open, expecting to find the space stuffed with tattered sheets of paper or scrappy folders moulding at the edges.

Instead, there was just a single item. It was a brown envelope, lying face down at the bottom of the drawer. The seal had yet to be fastened, as if Newton had been on the cusp of sending it. Vine reached down and picked the envelope up. He turned it round and saw the wording on the front, composed in Newton's trademark scrawl.

It read simply: *For the attention of Mr Solomon Vine.*

## 18

Vine kept up a steady pace down the Strand. As the speckled grey of Charing Cross station rose into view on the opposite side of the road, he stopped, looking up at the slanting Coutts logos like bookends to the glass front of the building on his right, three flags fluttering busily above his head.

He glanced down at the small gold key in his palm again, feeling the jagged edge press against his skin. It was the only item he had found in the envelope – Newton's last will and testament. With Newton dead, it was perhaps the only means he had to find the truth. The JIC laptop was useless now, unable to sneak into the system under disguise, a gradual narrowing of options.

He walked inside. He took the escalator and found himself in a spotless reception area, a mix of glass and polish, the percussive hum of heels on the glossy flooring. At the desk, he produced the key and was asked to wait. Drinks were provided and he poured a cup of filter coffee, looking at the envelope again and feeling sadness gnaw at him. In the unforgiving light of day, none of it had been a dream.

Ten minutes later, he was guided through to a viewing room, decked out with corporate niceties. The door sighed closed. Vine looked at the cameras in either corner. He wondered what would happen if he grabbed the box and ran. By this point, the Whitehall machine would have started putting appropriate measures in place, a police guard stationed outside Newton's house. A forensic team would sweep the premises. Vine had been careful to leave no trace. He just hoped he had been careful enough.

He looked down at the safe deposit box, and then back at the gold key. What had Newton left him? And why? Was this related to the cause of Newton's death? All of which begged the larger question: was the heart attack merely a cover for something far more sinister?

Vine paused for a moment. Then he slotted the gold key into the safe deposit box and turned. He heard the click as the lock gave way. He clasped the sides of the box and gently tilted the lid upwards, trying not to upset the contents.

At first, he imagined they had the wrong box. It seemed so unremarkable, merely a single dull-green cardboard folder. Paper jutted out at the top, the whole thing kept together with the aid of a rather soiled elastic band. He picked it up, undid the elastic band and opened the cover.

Inside there were just two pages. The first was empty except for a smattering of handwritten words; the second was more formal, typed and ordered, the whiff of officialdom.

Vine closed the folder and eased down the lid of the safe deposit box. There was a form beside the box, which he filled in. Then he walked outside and asked for a bag to take away the material. Minutes later, one of the manicured assistants walked through with a custom-designed bag engraved with the Coutts logo. Vine slipped the file into it, fastened it closed and handed the form back. With a quick check of the bag and another of his key and registration form, he was allowed to leave.

He was thirsty again. He walked back up the Strand, took a left to Aldwych, past the Waldorf on to Drury Lane. The

Delaunay was quiet this early in the morning. He found a table tucked away in the corner, ordered an orange juice and a full English breakfast and then inched the file out of the bag. He checked the restaurant, noting the camera positions.

He opened the file again. The layout was trademark Cosmo Newton. Newton had been the last cold warrior, unable to stand the management speak and corporate jargon, the lamentable PowerPoint presentations and team-bonding exercises of modern-day Whitehall. Newton worked through mountains of files and paper, unable – or perhaps unwilling – to change.

The first page of the file simply had three words on it, all written in black ink. Vine tried to decipher the letters:

MIDAS
Hermes
Caesar

Vine read the words again, checking to make sure he hadn't missed a letter.

He turned the page and then stopped, looking down at the second sheet of paper. TOP SECRET was emblazoned across the header. It appeared to be part of an interrogation transcript, dated 5 January 2016.

*I know a secret . . . A secret that changes everything . . .*

Vine shook off a feeling of déjà vu and began to read:

CSIS: You say you have heard information from others?
AY: I'm saying that I know for certain that there is a mole somewhere within the intelligence services. I know this for a fact and am willing to help the British government with

their investigations if they provide unconditional immunity from prosecution.

CSIS: Tell me more about what you heard.

AY: I need first to have confirmation that the British government and the Prime Minister will provide the immunity I seek.

CSIS: So you are telling us you have information about a mole within British intelligence?

AY: I am willing to help the British government with all the information on condition of guaranteed immunity. That is what I am telling you.

Vine turned the page over, hoping to find more. But the other side was blank. He looked back to the text and saw Newton's scribbles in the margins. Next to the mention of 'intelligence services', he had annotated: 'MI5? MI6? GCHQ? DI?'

He glanced back down at the transcript and began to read the final line.

CSIS: And what name does this mole go under?

AY: His codename is Nobody.

## 19

*2012*

Her flat is everything he expected it to be: ordered, precise, and yet somehow beguilingly individual. She has guarded it closely, always keen to meet at Wellington Square instead, claiming her place is small and cramped, unfit for company. Far from feeling rebuffed, Vine flatters himself that he can see beyond the excuses. Both of them are private people, content with their own company. There is something almost courtly about the way they behave around each other, watchful and polite. Others may burn themselves out on drive-by emotions; they are happy instead to let their guards drop slowly, trading confidences with care.

Vine takes a packet of cigarettes out of his pocket. He lights one and watches the smoke funnel out, then remembers the task he has been set. The kettle rumbles to a boil behind him, and he begins to scatter instant coffee in the bottom of the mugs before rattling around the fridge for milk. Rose is still changing, so he decides to display his talent for domesticity with a bold exploration for coasters. As the coffees continue to steam in front of him, he pulls out a drawer with cutlery, a second full of folded tea towels, another cupboard crammed with cereal and bowls, yet another filled with wine glasses and mugs. He looks around the rest of the tiny main room, the sofa at the furthest point on his right with a small flatscreen TV, and a desk straight ahead.

He checks that there is no sound from the hall, and then walks over to the desk. It is clear on top, free of the usual clutter. There are two drawers on the left. He pulls the first one out and finds it full of cardboard folders, TAX scrawled in biro on the top folder, fringed by elastic bands and paper clips. He bends down to pull out the second drawer but finds it jamming slightly. He looks closer and sees a small keyhole at the top. It has been locked in a hurry, the catch not quite holding. He casts another quick glance behind him, then tugs at it harder, yanking the drawer fully out of its slot. Inside is another collection of domestic confetti, stuffed here in order to preserve the illusion of neatness: a half-empty packet of printer paper; another folder with the title FLAT RENTAL INFO; a clear plastic wallet with what looks like a university certificate. Just as he is about to push the drawer back, jolting it into place, a smaller item flutters to the floor. He reaches out and picks it up. On the back is scrawled the words 'Pakistan 2005'. He turns it over and finds himself staring at a much younger-looking Rose. She is casually dressed with a backpack and a bandanna tied around her forehead, flanked on either side by what look like beaming members of the same family. Snippets of a house are just visible in the background.

Vine ignores the open drawer for a moment and continues to stare at the photograph. He inspects each detail, wondering what it is that surprises him. She has talked vaguely about her past, entertaining him with tales of Harvard, her legal training, gossip from the Attorney General's Office. But that is not it, somehow. There is something different about the way she looks, a beautifully weightless smile. For the first time Vine feels oddly jealous, realizing that he has never seen that smile first-hand; eroded, perhaps, by time or circumstance.

He is about to replace the photo and slide the drawer back into place when the door opens behind him, creaking slightly.

She doesn't say anything at first, moving beside him and crouching down on her bare feet, hair still wet from the shower. 'What are you doing?'

He can hear the faintest edge in her voice, trying her best to mask it. He feels embarrassed suddenly, as if he has broken an unspoken rule between them, snooping on her like this.

'I was trying to find coasters for the mugs,' he says. He looks at her for a moment and can see the struggle in her face, unease crinkling her brow. Then her face softens, and her lips are forced into a smile, the moment of discomfort banished. 'A prize-winning first and you can't find the coasters?'

'They never taught us that on the Tripos,' he says. 'Unforgivable, really.' Just before they move on, Vine nods towards the photo. 'You never told me you'd been in Pakistan.'

She doesn't glance at the photo, just stares straight at him. 'You never asked. I spent a year out there after Harvard, volunteer work.'

'Who are the other people?'

'The family I lived with. They practically adopted me. Grandmother, parents and eight children. An entire cricket team.'

'Do you still keep in touch?'

Her smile fades slightly, eyes dipping away from his, spotting something on the kitchen counter. 'Is that coffee over there meant for me?'

Vine nods, turning away to slot the drawer back into place and letting Rose direct him to the cupboard where the coasters are kept. They sip at their drinks in silence for a moment, existing without the need to fill every second.

Still he wonders when that missed beat of surprise will fade. He can't imagine a time when the musical depth of her voice will dust over into the everyday. Nor the peculiar charm of the incidentals: the way her hair threatens to curl at the merest sign of rain; the habit of massaging the lobes of her ears when thinking; even the volume of her silence when annoyed, radiating polite aggression. He would trade none of it.

Today, indeed, she seems anxious, looking around the flat as if trawling for external support. Eventually, she breaks the silence. 'Though while we're on the subject of confessions . . . there is something I need to tell you.'

'I'm intrigued.'

'You have to promise not to be angry with me.'

'I promise.'

'It's about my work. My new job.'

Vine experiences the first real tug of unease, covering for it by stubbing out his cigarette. 'A new job?'

'Yes.' She pauses, then says: 'I'm still working as a lawyer, just not quite the same type any more.'

Vine doesn't answer at first. He has suppressed this doubt so well it feels almost new. 'So you've been lying to me?'

'I'm afraid that appears to be the case.'

Her expression has changed. The unease of moments earlier seems to have given way to something lighter, freer.

She moves closer. Her voice is hushed to a whisper. 'It seems I've been picking up all sorts of bad habits from you.'

Vine feels himself smile with surprise as the words leave her mouth. All his rehearsed evasions suddenly feel fake and brittle, like leftovers from a past life. The pitch of anxiety dims. 'You've lost me.'

She nudges her toe against his leg. 'A Foreign Office analyst, with a flair for mathematics, who struggles to name a single civil servant in King Charles Street.'

'Perhaps I'm just not the sociable type.'

'Perhaps.'

'And a member of the Attorney General's Office who now never answers her phone during the daytime.'

'Bravo, Mr Holmes.'

He can see now what her smile means. To be with her, he will have to be without his secrets. He will have to surrender to this new world without reservation. 'How long have you known?'

'I've always had an inkling . . . You?'

He longs to admit that he has been without suspicion, allowing himself to trust. But paranoia is too much part of who he is, a muscle memory.

She pauses and takes another sip. 'There's just one other thing.'

He feels dizzy with the flow of revelation. 'And what might that be?'

'Well, technically, you see, the legal adviser in the Director-General's Office is only ever meant to tell their spouse.'

'Ah.'

'Which presents something of a dilemma.'

Vine nods. His heart thuds unsteadily against his chest, throat clamping tighter. He has thought about a situation like this too many times. 'And it's a good job, is it? Not one to give up.'

'Very good. Extraordinary, in fact.'

'Well . . .' he says, trying to feign calm. 'It would be a shame to ruin it on account of a technicality.'

'A real shame.'

'If only there was something we could do to rectify the situation.'

'If only . . .'

He stares down at her. Despite himself, he feels seized by a sudden desire to grasp the opportunity before it fizzles back into the everyday. He is momentarily sick of caution, of watchfulness. The world around them seems to lose definition. The echo of voices and cars outside melts away. There is only the two of them, together forming their own self-sufficient universe, if just for a moment. 'There is one way that springs to mind . . . though it comes with conditions.'

Rose raises her eyebrows. 'Such as?'

'Till death us do part.'

'Though I hear intelligence work can be deadly.'

'There's always hope . . .'

'Lots of foreign travel.'

He realizes that he can't bear the thought of a day not looking at her, not waking up beside her, feeling her touch, the scent and expressions that make up this new life. He has broken his vow. He has become dependent on another human being.

'. . . so what do you say?'

She moves her hand up from his chest, tracing the map of his face and flattening the worry lines on his brow. Her

palm is hot. The tips of her fingers feel like fire on his skin.

She leans forwards, hovering at his lips and narrowing her eyes as if deep in thought. 'I think I say yes.'

## 20

It was an inconspicuous place to die. Vine looked at the crumbling white front of Cheltenham train station and felt the unreality of it all grip him. Why had Cosmo Newton ended up breathing his last breath here? He tried to imagine Newton walking down this street and taking in the same view. The station would have been almost empty, the surroundings puddled with the honeyish glow of streetlamps.

His immediate thought was that it must be related to GCHQ. The Doughnut, as the main building was called, was hard to miss. Signs dotted the town centre advertising the direction. Buses branded the name across their sides. Among the creamy Regency buildings with their air of muted gentility, the rash of wire fencing and armed patrols was impossible to miss. As Chair of the JIC, Newton was a regular visitor. Signals intelligence was embedded in virtually every British espionage and military operation across all corners of the globe. Was this part of some routine work assignment? It was possible. But somehow it didn't feel probable.

He walked on, through the car park and into the station. The lines from Newton's folder repeated themselves in his mind: *I know for certain that there is a mole somewhere within the intelligence services . . . His codename is Nobody*. And then that other clue from the transcript, the name obscured by the title: *CSIS*. Chief of the Secret Intelligence Service, MI6. In a stroke, so many things made sense. Yousef had divulged his great secret personally to Alexander Cecil. Vine could hear Cecil's voice on the phone that day in Istanbul ordering him to let Yousef free. Yousef's secret had been all too real. The knowledge was weapons-grade, more than enough to secure immunity from prosecution. If it was even an approximation of the truth, it could corrode the very foundations of Vauxhall Cross. It was what every Chief most feared: a double within their own ranks.

He had taken the coach down for greater anonymity, so paused now at the ticket machine and bought a single to Paddington, before passing through the barriers. The station was smaller than it looked from the outside. A short bridge lay directly ahead of him towards the second platform. There were two flights of stairs to his left, leading down to the first platform. Vine had half-expected to find the place filled with cordons and busy with fluorescent police jackets. But it looked like just another day. The speaker overhead crackled with the arrival of the next train to Bristol Parkway. Two train guards chuckled behind him; car doors slammed in rhythm.

They weren't treating the death as suspicious. That was the first obvious conclusion. If anything more had been done – and, as yet, it was still conditional – it was professional enough to fool a preliminary inspection by medics. Vine had received the news just before midnight. The reports still hadn't put a name to the body. If Whitehall's lawyers had anything to do with it, the unfortunate passenger would remain eternally anonymous. Newton would never have been foolish enough to advertise his identity. As Chair of the JIC, he didn't merit any personal security detail, unlike the Chief of MI6 or Director-General of MI5. To the initiated, he was part of Whitehall's institutional memory, schooled in the forgotten arts of Moscow and East Berlin.

To the outside observer, he had the faintly distressed air of a retired don.

Vine had used the same burner phone for both calls. It had been pay as you go, bought with cash. It was virtually untraceable. If the police ever did begin a fuller inquiry they would try and track the number. But Vine didn't want to get snagged by officialdom yet. If there was something else going on here, he needed the freedom to find out what.

The only data he had to work with were the time of Newton's first call and the sketchy details from the news reports online. Newton had called at 9.02. Local media reported that medics had arrived at Cheltenham train station just before 10. That suggested the incident had occurred within a one-hour timeframe, sometime between 9 and 10 p.m.

Vine walked down the flights of stairs to platform 1. The platform was empty and grey, speckled with chewing gum and hollow coffee cups. Vine walked through the emptiness to the middle of the platform and crouched down on his heels. He inspected the edge of the platform, noticing the debris of tape that had festooned this area only hours earlier. So this was where he had died, an old man tumbling forwards on to the tracks. Vine didn't move for a moment. The breeze whistled around him, nipping fiercely at his face. After a respectful pause, he took in the immediate view.

He spotted a single CCTV camera above the doorway to the station café. It was positioned almost exactly in line with the spot. It appeared as if Newton had chosen the angle with a calculating eye to make sure everything was recorded for posterity. But Vine knew that would be another false lead. The cameras within all regional train stations linked to classified sites – GCHQ, Menwith Hill, Porton Down –

had stopped recording years ago. It had been a favourite tac-
tic of the PLA and GRU to hack into the insecure CCTV
feeds to try and assemble an accurate picture of government
employees. Members of each service regularly used the train
station, the one place they all passed through which wasn't
wrapped in security. The feed had puttered out a decade ago.
There would be no joy there.

Newton would have known that too. Vine stood up and
drank in the rest of the station. Cosmo Newton had arrived
at around nine o' clock, having discovered something that
shed new light on the disappearance of Gabriel Wilde. It
was obviously of strategic importance, given his reluctance
to speak on an open line. It had to be something that was
connected with the information he had left behind in the
safe deposit box, a thread that linked Yousef's revelations
about a mole codenamed Nobody with the other words
written on the sheet of paper – *MIDAS, Hermes, Caesar*.
Newton would have had an almost preternatural awareness
that he could be followed. If this was more sinister than a
heart attack, there was no way he would have been caught
off guard. Age had made him sharper, alive to every shade
of danger.

The track was to the right. Further across lay platform 2.
Straight ahead was the long expanse of uncluttered concrete.
The long-stay car park stood beyond a fringe of scrubby
grass to the left, sectioned off by a metal railing. What would
Newton have done? This was a man who trained at the height
of the Cold War. He had been one of the last to be inducted
into the full bevy of analogue tricks: secret inks, ciphers,
one-time pads, microfilm. His great boast was an immaculate
tradecraft, handwriting in the field that won even the enemy's
respect. That meant he always had a plan and a fallback.

Cosmo Newton wouldn't have gone to his death with an evidence trail left on ice.

Vine walked back to the start of the platform. He stood for a moment, then moved forwards. He paced his stride deliberately, echoing the rhythms of his own narrow escapes. He was a third of the way down now. Adrenaline would begin to build at this point. Thoughts started to quicken. He looked around at the options in front of him. If he were Newton, where would he go? How would he lay the clue path for others to follow? It had to be somewhere discreet enough not to be foiled by casual passers-by or police, yet obvious enough to be found.

The training manuals suggested taping files to the back of cisterns, or cleverly disguising them as trash. But Newton would know that the trash would be removed and the bathrooms scrubbed before Vine had the chance to inspect them for clues. He would have needed to find somewhere that would remain intact for long enough. Vine continued walking, scouring every inch of ground on either side to try and spot anything.

He passed the waiting room. Then he stopped and decided to go inside for a moment. The floor was still drying from a recent mopping and the seats had been spritzed with cleaning fluid carelessly wiped off with a cloth. Vine looked for anything Newton could have used to disguise a document or note, though he saw nothing. He crouched down and peered around the undersides of the seats. But the tradecraft seemed too inelegant for Newton. He would have known he only had moments to live. A trained operative was hustling him. Trying to engineer something in this room would have taken time. The pattern didn't fit. It was too fussy.

Vine left the waiting room and continued down the platform. He passed the toilets and then stopped outside the rickety door to the station café, creaking it open and stepping inside to the warmth. The café was a small square with four wooden tables bunched down the middle and a counter up ahead. A stand with newspapers was on the left, rows of drinks and packaged sandwiches lining the rest of the wall.

Vine took a moment to imagine Newton walking in here. He would know he had just seconds to execute his fallback and ensure that Vine could disinter the trail and continue. Vine walked in the direction of the counter and then saw the shelving on his right. It was different from the newspaper stand. This was a riot of gloss and colour, loud weeklies screaming at him from their front pages. There were three rows, each one getting progressively noisier. The bottom hosted the dustier titles like the *Spectator*, the *Week* and *New Statesman*. Row two moved into fitness and lifestyle magazines: *GQ*, *Good Housekeeping*, *Vanity Fair*. The third exploded with headlines: *Closer*, *Reveal*, *OK!*.

Vine imagined Newton reaching this spot and removing the product from his jacket pocket. The criteria for the fallback was much the same as any dead drop: somewhere unremarkable, hiding in plain sight. Vine scanned the titles again. Newton would have had to pick a title that would last the week at most, if not longer. The title couldn't be so popular it risked being snapped up by the first commuter to arrive for their morning coffee. That discounted the top row. The second row could be a counter-intuitive choice, yet risked being popular enough to be bought quickly. The paper type was wrong as well. The pages were too thick and shiny. Any product hidden there would be painfully apparent.

The right title needed a newspaper texture, large enough to effectively disguise another document but without the popularity of a broadsheet or tabloid. Vine thumbed through the better-known magazines until he reached older weather-beaten titles at the back. He inched one of them out of place and looked down at it. He thought back to Newton's study and remembered the publication on top of the desk: *The Times Literary Supplement.* It met every requirement: the paper, the rectangular shape, the space inside.

Vine turned to make sure the barista wasn't glaring at him. She was tidying up the row of drinks and sandwiches. He began flicking through the pages. Part of him wondered whether he had spent too long immersed in the footnotes of the secret world. Was this absurd? Was it not possible that Cosmo Newton had simply died of a heart attack, staggering forwards on to the tracks as his body gave way? He could hear all the arguments, and yet he kept flicking. He had nearly reached page ten and was about to close the paper and return it to the shelf when he stopped.

He saw a jaggedness pushing through from the next page. He turned to it slowly, part of him sure he would find nothing more than a flyer or flimsy piece of advertising.

Instead, he found himself staring at a neatly folded piece of A4 paper. He reached inside and carefully drew it out like a precious object that could shatter at any moment. He controlled his breathing and unfolded the sheet slowly so it didn't tear. He looked at the middle of it and felt a respectful smile pull at the corners of his lips. It was a printout of a map with directions trailing down the page. This was Cosmo Newton's final act on earth, providing a route for others to follow.

But there was only one word that Vine really needed to know. He read it again and then tucked the piece of paper into his jacket pocket.

He had his next destination. It was known to only a select few in the corridors of Whitehall, tucked away in a leafy Cotswold village. Officially it didn't exist, hoarding anonymity like a virtue.

BUCKLAND (MOD).

## 21

The satnav pulsed ominously, the digital brain of the vehicle tipping into incoherence. The shrewish voice gave another order for a U-turn, obscured by the clank of a tractor passing on the opposite side of the road. It was soon replaced by the rustle of the trees, so different from the whines and rattles of a city.

After two further repetitions, the taxi driver jabbed the off button. The screen fizzled blank. Vine asked the driver to stop at the next right turning and then eased back into his seat and tried to banish the thought of Cosmo Newton undertaking a similar journey. The words from Newton's file came to him again: *MIDAS, Hermes, Caesar.*

He had tried crunching all possible permutations again, but still had nothing. MIDAS, Hermes and Caesar were all classical allusions, though two of them were Greek and only one Roman. He thought of Wilde's copy of *The Odyssey* again and Ahmed Yousef's revelations of a mole codenamed Nobody. Somewhere within that riddle lay a truth that Cosmo Newton had discovered, a truth that was potentially fatal. Yet, so far, Vine could only see the cipher, taut with hidden meaning.

The taxi stopped, and Vine got out and paid. As he watched the car leave, he removed the printout and stared again at the different colours winding their way across the page. Buckland was straight on down the narrow lane in front of him. He walked on, the path narrowing as he snaked further into the village. As the procession of cottages began to thicken, he saw a sign saying MINISTRY OF DEFENCE – RESTRICTED ENTRY in bold white letters, pointing to the right.

The building was originally a manor house, requisitioned by the government during the Second World War and taken over permanently by the Ministry of Defence in the fifties. As Vine continued down the thin country lane, there was no obvious sign of security. The whorls of wire that guarded GCHQ or the subtle barriers outside Thames House and Vauxhall Cross were replaced instead by a simple pair of black iron gates. There was one member of Special Branch out front. This was not a place visited regularly.

Vine tucked away the map and reached into his jacket pocket as he slowed his pace. He knew this was the moment he could be found out. Newton had authorized a JIC card for him which would gain entry to a place like this. But, as with the laptop, it would have been officially de-authorized as soon as he was declared dead. Vine was relying purely on the fact that the Special Branch officer would only require a visual ID rather than running it through any wider checks. If they connected this with his visit to the train station, questions would start to be asked about his involvement in Newton's death. He had covered himself as best he could, but the possibility pinched at him now. He was skirting the edge of something here, amorphous and indistinct, but dangerous. If Newton had stepped on anything toxic to those in Whitehall, there was no limit to what they might do to keep that secret quiet. They had the full might of the state at their disposal.

He calmed his breathing, drawing out the JIC card. Then he began the approach. He kept his gaze level, posture casual. She would only run further checks if she spotted any obvious symptoms of guilt. He must look like he belonged.

The Special Branch officer took the card and gave it a bored glance. Her head seemed to remain tilted downwards for minutes on end. Slowly, her left hand began twitching in the direction of the radio clipped on her belt. Vine waited for her to reach for it, could already imagine the tread of others closing in around him. Once again, he wondered what Newton had stumbled upon. What secret had he found out? What if they had already picked him up at Cheltenham and simply tagged him here? There was a chance all this could be a trap, the quietness designed to lure him in before they struck. For a minute, Vine found his eyes taking in all feasible exit routes. He could feel his muscles tense, readying for a possible escape. Newton had been here the previous day. Now he was dead. Vine wondered if he was condemning himself by picking up his trail.

He watched carefully as the officer's hand continued to hover over her belt. There was a screech of noise from the radio, but she ignored it. Finally, she looked up and nodded, handing back the card and waving him through.

The iron gates began to pivot backwards. Vine felt his heartbeat slow as he started to move forwards, careful to keep an even stride. The car park was relatively clear, just a sprinkling of dusty SUVs. He crunched across the gravel and then made his way inside, a last flash of the JIC card as he was buzzed through the security barrier.

Buckland was Whitehall's secret library, a classified version of the National Archives at Kew. It was the resting place for hundreds of thousands of secret files dating back to the early fifties. It covered everything from the Ministry of Defence, MI5, MI6, GCHQ and the Joint Intelligence Committee, spanning the entire length of the Cold War and beyond to the present day.

The collection was housed across a sprawling campus. The central nervous system was a circular-shaped room packed with banks of computers and some of the starrier effects on display: contingency plans signed off by Number 10 on what should happen in the event of nuclear war; old plans for emergency evacuation of the Royals should Buckingham Palace come under attack. Vine made his way through the room, trying to acclimatize. He had often heard of this place but never been. Looking at the rows of yellowing pages and files, he could imagine Cosmo Newton losing himself here for days. It was a paradise of paper, full of the heady smell of thumbed pages.

He tried to put himself in Newton's place now. Where would Newton have gone? What was he trying to find here? MIDAS. Hermes. Caesar. The first word was the only one capitalized, traditionally denoting the name of an operation. Newton was pedantic about these sorts of things. He wouldn't have made a mistake on such basic matters of orthography.

Vine took a seat at a computer station and used the mouse to summon the screen to life. He knew there was a chance that what he was about to do would cause alerts to be flagged across Whitehall. Armed police could be waiting for him when he tried to leave the building. But he had no other option. He had to find out what Cosmo Newton had been searching for just before he died, some clue that connected with the information about the Nobody mole and shed new light on Gabriel Wilde's disappearance. He decided to eliminate the most obvious answer first, typing in MIDAS and waiting for any results to come up. Three did. He inched forwards in his chair, wary at such easy results. He scrolled down to the first one. As he looked at the date, he felt his spirits sink: MIDAS – 4 April 1947. He clicked on the link, and a photo of a mildewing document filled the screen. The type was scratchy and poor, but Vine made the effort to try and decipher it, scanning through a preliminary report on navy manoeuvres.

He clicked off and scrolled down to the next two. Both were from 1951. Vine clicked on both and read them through. But there was nothing usable there. Newton had always been sceptical of the military. Spying was his life.

The problem with trying to pick out a pattern was the overwhelming volume of data. He needed to narrow the field to have any hope of success. He reduced the search criteria to exclude MoD archives, and then began searching through for any synonym he could think of that Newton might have used: GOLD, TREASURE, BOUNTY. But still nothing came up.

Next he tried a different approach. Though military operation names were now generated by computer, many spooks still indulged in picking their own. They were the signatures of a successful case officer. Whoever ran a department would brand their operations with a recognizable sequence – the names of famous battles in the Civil War, say, or the names of characters from Greek mythology. Vine narrowed down the search criteria further to just the MI5 and MI6 files and began trying out various other names: OLYMPUS, ATHENA, ZEUS . . .

The first two produced an empty screen. But the last pulsed with a single hit. Vine clicked on it and saw the strapline at the top, subtly different from the others. CX/ LANGLEY/GROSVENOR SQUARE. He clicked on the file, but a box came up: TOP SECRET/STRAP 4. He noted down the reference number and then consulted the nearest site map.

Archive 311AB was in the basement, a foul-smelling place noisy with the sound of drains gurgling overhead. The light was poor, one of the bulbs long since extinguished. The entire area was bathed in a coppery fuzz. Vine began working his way along the shelves until he found the reference number for ZEUS, teasing out the box and taking it across to one of the viewing tables nearby. He checked to see if there was anyone else around, but he was alone. He opened the file, scanned the first page and then began flicking hurriedly through the rest.

The entire file was heavy with redactions, the majority of the text blanked out. One of the only identifying marks on the paper was a date at the top of the first page: 9 August 2009.

But that gave him the gossamer-thin thread he needed. He had a vague timeframe. From that he could begin to gather enough evidence to form some sort of pattern. He began working back through the other boxes on the shelf, discarding any that didn't share a classical name as a reference point. Soon he began amassing different names: POSEIDON, APOLLO, HECTOR . . . All of them were dated between 2009 and 2011. All of them originated from MI6 but had been copied into Langley and the US embassy in London. All of them, more importantly, had been redacted to within an inch of their lives.

It was nearing the two-hour mark when he finally saw the confirmation he needed. The page was a wall of scrubbed-out text, a deliberate dead end. He didn't yet know where it led, or what the implications were. But he finally had evidence, removed from the computer database but still – whether through accident or intent – buried here in print form. He read the date and the word again.

2 September 2011.

*MIDAS.*

Parliament Square was alive with noise, a tangle of vehicles expiring with frustration. There was the silent flash of camera-phones and the rustle of umbrellas outside Westminster Abbey. Civil servants streamed from the faceless glass of the government buildings on Victoria Street. Behind them all, Big Ben chimed seven o' clock.

Vine continued on until he reached the Westminster Arms. The post-work rush had thinned, with just a desultory few drinkers milling around the ground floor. He navigated his way down to the basement and ordered a pint of Spitfire. Huddled in one of the booths was a small gathering nursing a variety of drinks. The rest of the space yawned empty.

Vine found a secluded spot at the opposite end and tried to focus his mind. He could feel sadness threaten him now. The rush of adrenaline at finding Newton's document and the file had begun to fracture. He was left instead with the ache of knowing that Cosmo Newton was truly gone. It was the plight of orphans to accumulate substitute parents and Newton had always been his. Vine could still hear every echo from that room in Trinity where Newton had propelled him into this world. It was Newton who had educated him in the laws of the Whitehall jungle and taught him how to survive in the field.

*MIDAS, Hermes, Caesar.*

Ignorance scratched at him, the pieces still refusing to cohere into any sort of order. Ahmed Yousef had told Alexander Cecil that there was a mole within British intelligence codenamed Nobody. That much he knew for sure. Somehow that connected with an operation – or perhaps a series of operations – called MIDAS, conducted with CIA involvement in 2011. All the evidence suggested that connecting those two empirical details had led Cosmo Newton to a breakthrough on the night he died. The urgency in his words had been clear: *I think I may have found something . . . If I'm right, this changes everything.* Newton had left a fallback in the safe deposit box to allow Vine to carry on his investigation if he was unable to.

But, so far, the trail ended there. Everyone allowed into Buckland was graded STRAP 3 or above, which meant most files could be read without redactions. The fact that the MIDAS file was scraped clean of detail was noteworthy. It could mean many things: Langley could have insisted upon it, either at the time or retrospectively to protect a live asset; it dealt with an internal counter-espionage issue; or it involved some sort of black ops work, the remit of JSOC, the SAS and the SBS.

Vine looked at the words in Newton's file again. Nobody was the name of the mole; MIDAS was the name of the 2011 operation conducted with the CIA. But what about the remaining two words – Hermes, Caesar? MIDAS was in capitals to denote the name of an operation. There was a space, and then Hermes and Caesar were grouped together in the middle of the page. The surrounding data suggested they were therefore related. But how? If they weren't the names of operations, what other function did they perform?

Vine sipped distractedly at his drink, trying to shake off the sadness now and retreat into pattern-solving. There had to be some reason that Newton had left those two words close together. The gap suggested they weren't directly related to Operation MIDAS, but logic dictated that there would be some connection to both MIDAS and the Nobody mole. The two names could be for assets, but codenaming an asset with such an obvious classical echo – MIDAS, Hermes, Caesar – would be clumsy tradecraft. Even the showiest case officer would insist on something unrelated to try and insulate the various parts of a single operation against detection.

Vine rolled the words around his tongue again – Hermes, Caesar. He wondered if there was something more literal he could read into them. Hermes was the messenger god and a staple of Greek myth; Caesar was the aspiring autocrat who secured his place in the history of Western literature with a mere three words.

Vine slowed his breathing and allowed his unconscious to work. The pattern would be in there somewhere, a logical inference that would allow him to build his way up to the correct answer. What was Newton alluding to? What buried reference was he urging Vine to see? Newton was steeped in the double-speak of the intelligence world, a meta-language swirling with threads of connection that only those fluent in the dialect could spot.

Vine was about to take another gulp of his pint when he had an idea. He drew out his phone, another burner. One connecting thread began to suggest itself. Hermes was the messenger god. That meant communication and the delivery of messages. Caesar's name had been put to other uses in the intelligence world, most famously with the Caesar Cipher – one of the oldest methods for confidential communications ever known. The final clue was personal. Great tradecraft rested on subverting expectation. Newton had always been an avowedly analogue spook. Vine wondered now if that was his final cover, curating the legend to serve another purpose altogether. It was a long shot, but the only logical path he could yet deduce.

The Gmail login screen loaded. Vine typed in hermes@ for the email handle and then Caesar for the password. He pressed the sign-in button and waited for the screen to stutter with incomprehension.

Instead, the buffering gave way to the familiar sight of a Gmail account. But it had one major difference.

There were no emails in sight.

# 23

## 2013

The invitation is inevitable. Despite Vine's best attempts not to divulge his newfound happiness, Wilde has been nibbling at the edges of knowledge, teasing out a confession about a woman, then a description, finally a name. Once the details are known, Wilde has talked of little else. 'Catch of the century, Sol,' he proclaims. 'And here's us all thinking you were secretly scoring centuries for the other side.'

Rose has to work late on Friday, so Vine picks her up from her flat in Vauxhall at a dreadful hour of Saturday morning. Everyone else is still warm in their beds as they hum their way through the deserted roads.

'So seriously, Solomon' – he marvels again, the only person who insists on giving his name its full due – 'give me some tips. What's he like?'

Vine stares ahead at the road, the tuneless procession of grey. He tries to distil the essence of Gabriel Wilde. 'He's the last romantic,' he says, 'no practical sense at all. And people always mention the charm.'

'Anyone on the go at the moment?' she asks.

Vine glances across at her. 'Last I heard it was an actress of some kind, I think. Before that, it was one of the secretaries at the office. Before that, the daughter of a political grandee.'

'Which one?'

'Not sure. Something to do with the environment.'

'So I should lock my door tonight.'

Vine smiles. 'Might be an idea.'

As they leave the motorway and begin shuddering along side roads, Vine feels the intimidating might of the country close in on him. The feeling doesn't leave as they reach the sign for Broadway Manor, bumping across from the road on to the long stretch of gravel path that wends its way towards the house. The house has a cream-grey front with rows of mullioned windows, the entrance bordered on either side by fluted pillars. Today there is the residue of a recent event, a scatter of used coffee cups and paper plates, a marquee nearby flapping loudly in the breeze.

Standing on the gravel driveway is Wilde himself. The swoop of black hair is cinematically rustled, the air of disordered charm in full flow with the weather-beaten Barbour jacket, claret-red cords and scuffed sandy brogues. Vine parks the car, turns off the ignition and feels himself relax as Rose gently rests a hand on his knee.

Wilde is making his way across the gravel to meet them. He wraps Vine in his usual instinctive hug, like a politician smothering a crowd.

'On time as ever, Sol. And this must be the divine Rose? The man barely speaks of anything else. He's becoming quite a bore on the subject.' He breaks away to peck at Rose's cheeks. 'Though now I can't say I altogether blame him.'

'That's Gabriel for hello,' says Vine, remaining watchful, all too familiar with Wilde's guileless intimacy. 'Did I hear mention of breakfast?'

Wilde looks up at the sky and rubs his hands. 'In good time. We haven't worked up our appetites yet. Not quite the weather for a walk, I know, but we might catch a few minutes before those clouds do their worst.'

After a forced march through fields and across lawns, they retire to the library for breakfast. The old library is a magnificent football-pitch of a room with bookcases lining the walls. Wilde scoops up a box of matches and lights the fire, the flames elbowing their way upwards.

Vine stares at the frosted wedding-cake ceiling, the rich blue of the walls and the oaky depth of the bookcases. He walks over to an eye-level shelf nearby and fingers an edition towards him. He looks at the spine: *A Mathematician's Apology* by G. H. Hardy. He has read this book more than a dozen times and has three brownish and thumbed copies, treasured since Cambridge. He remembers a phrase that has followed him through the years since: *A mathematician, like a painter or a poet, is a maker of patterns.*

The door eases shut. Wilde thuds down a large teak tray. Steam spirals up from three cups of tea. A serving dish in the middle overflows with sausages, pieces of bacon and brown toast clumsy with butter.

Wilde sits down. He sees Vine's book on the table and embarks on a long-running joke. 'Ah . . . let me guess. Hardy. One of the novels or the poetry?'

'Mathematics.'

'Bloody hell. Puts us all to shame.'

'Some of us more than others,' says Vine.

Wilde laughs and looks at Rose. 'I don't suppose Sol has ever happened to mention that he was a Senior Wrangler at Cambridge?'

'Gabriel.'

'Cricket blue, as well. Double century and a five-wicket haul against Oxford. Had his shirt framed, I think.'

'Shut up . . .'

'*And* an Apostle. All sorts of dubious male friends, which it's probably better we don't go into now.'

'Control yourself, Wilde.'

'Touchy bugger too, come to think of it . . .' Wilde grabs a piece of toast, then lies back on the sofa with his feet outstretched. 'Now, Rose. I've picked up most of it from Solomon, here, but I could do with a recap. The best legal brain of a generation, so he says. Harvard, a spell doing your bit for the world in Pakistan, legal training and then whisked away as intelligence counsel for the Attorney General's Office. Now a sister-in-arms across the river.'

Which, Vine recalls, is how they segue into the facts that haunt his professional life – the chaotic aftermath of the Arab Spring.

'Makes you think, eh, Sol,' says Wilde, slurping at the remains of his tea. 'Rose here snaffling homegrown baddies, while we go on helping the Americans radicalize them abroad.'

'Solomon is very pious on talking shop,' says Rose, smiling at Wilde. 'He never tells me anything.'

'Sounds like Sol,' says Wilde. 'Always has something to hide.'

As they carry on talking, Vine feels the first ripple of unease. He tries to shrug it off. It is ridiculous. And yet it has skirted his thoughts ever since this trip has been planned. The tales of Gabriel Wilde's conquests are legion. There have been rumours of a recent scandal involving the wife of an ambassador, while the ghosts of girlfriends past haunt the corridors of Vauxhall Cross. As he watches Wilde and Rose talk now, Vine feels a familiar nausea in his stomach.

He is snapped out of it when Wilde leaps up suddenly from the chair and begins pacing the floor of the library.

'You know, I've always wondered what it must be like to be in the middle of a revolution. Fighting for freedom, democracy . . . storming the barricades.' Wilde wanders over to the mantelpiece by the fire. Above it is a small portrait of a woman, the detail of the painting drowned out by the lavish frame.

Vine laughs. 'Not planning for a run at Parliament, now, are we? Sir Gabriel Wilde, ninth baronet. Saviour of the nation.'

Wilde remains where he is, eyes still taking in the portrait. 'Stranger things have happened, Sol. The three of us against global terror. Sounds about a fair fight.'

'Not sure I've got the ancestry for it.'

'No, I've always had my doubts. Your semi-criminal youth.'

'Of course you have.'

Wilde turns to Rose. 'You've heard about Sol's life on the streets, have you, Rose? Told you where all the bodies are buried?'

Rose smiles. 'Why do you think I agreed to marry him?'

'My thoughts exactly.'

Later, as Rose and Wilde go to begin the washing-up, Vine retraces his steps. He looks at the portrait more closely. It is one he has never seen before. The woman in the painting looks Middle Eastern and impossibly exotic, yet jarringly familiar at the same time. He is about to move closer when Wilde is suddenly drawing up next to him.

'Always told it was slightly rude to stare, Sol,' he says, before smiling, the usual Wilde charm dispelling any hint of unease. 'My mother. She died when I was eleven. I was sent to boarding school straight after, didn't see my mother's family again. What they call an English education . . .' He falls silent for a minute, before continuing. 'Though, I must say, you have landed yourself a gem with Rose.'

'You think so?' he asks. Somehow he craves Wilde's approval more than he thought he would; the nearest to family he has, able to bestow some sort of blessing.

'Gold, Sol, pure gold,' he says, resting his right elbow on the ledge of Vine's shoulder. 'Not often you get a first-class mind in the same body as a demon for the washing-up. Quite remarkable . . .'

Vine smiles and turns back to the painting. It is only the next morning, lazily touring the library again before they depart, that he realizes it has been taken down and replaced with a different portrait of the same size. Quietly spirited away, somewhere out of sight.

# 24

Cosmo Newton had harboured one final secret. As Vine brought up the account on his computer, savouring the hush of Wellington Square, he couldn't help but admire the old man. The legend of the analogue spook had been so convincing. Vine had heard the rants many times, Newton confessing plausible ignorance to anything remotely digital. He had even circulated the rumour that he had all his emails printed out at the Cabinet Office so he could go through them by hand. All of it had been a lie – one last act of shape-shifting.

Vine moved the mouse to the drafts folder and clicked on it. GCHQ and the NSA could only monitor what was sent through the ether. Unless operating in a covert action capacity, they couldn't intuit communications that never left an inbox. The trick was simple: create a joint email account, and then communicate by saving new drafts. No email was ever sent, avoiding the possibility of being tapped. It allowed anonymous communications between two individuals both equipped with the login details for the same account.

The drafts folder had three drafts saved, each one acting as a ghostly chain of correspondence never actually sent. Whenever a participant had a new message they simply added to the previous version and saved the draft again.

Vine paused for a moment, trying to rationalize the possibilities. As Chair of the JIC, Newton had access to all the latest encryption technologies being developed at GCHQ. The only reason he would resort to an anonymous Gmail account would be if he was working off the grid, corresponding with someone he was unable to talk to through official channels. But Newton had always taken a dim view of whistle-blowers or those who deliberately betrayed the code of the secret world. Somehow Vine couldn't quite absorb the idea of Newton ferrying documents to a journalist, or conducting an affair on the side. He looked to the pages from Newton's safe deposit box again. If Hermes and Caesar were accounted for as the email address and password, then that just left two words: MIDAS and Nobody. Somehow this anonymous email account must relate to Newton's investigation into one or both of those – the operation and the mole. But how?

He turned back to the screen and clicked on the earliest draft, saved on 25 February. The first thing he noticed was the different typefaces. One of the correspondents had written in normal type, the respondent in italics. Vine scrolled further down the message to see if there was any other distinguishing typographic mark, but there seemed just to be the two. That suggested there might only be Newton and one other person using this account, a simple two-way conversation rather than a group of them.

He looked up to the top of the page. Each new line was a reply to the one before, the meaning of it creeping downwards. The first line was in normal font. Vine could hear Newton's voice behind it immediately:

We must establish some basic protocols. The most important is if you are being forced to type under duress. To signal that to me, change the font you write in to Georgia.
*Agreed. You're sure this is secure?*
As good as we can manage. I take it the package arrived?

*Yes.*

More may arrive at some point. They will all be marked personal.

*Do we ever meet?*

Not for the time being.

*So how does this work?*

Protocol is simple: check this account each night at 7 p.m.

*Fine.*

There is much to discuss. More soon . . .

Vine read the exchange again. Newton's impeccable trade-craft was at the fore, establishing basic protocols first before any further discussion was launched. Vine looked at the third paragraph again: *I take it the package arrived?* The most obvious explanation would be something delivering the handle for the email address and the password to the other correspondent. And then there was that curious question: *Do we ever meet?* That one comment alone widened the possible correspondents to an almost unmanageable field. Most patterns were solvable by containing the data sets; but if the correspondent was someone outside Newton's social circle, the suspect list could be endless. The only empirical giveaway was the timing: *Protocol is simple: check this account each night at 7 p.m.* That line at least suggested that they were operating in a similar time zone, even perhaps within the same country.

So who was this mystery correspondent? And how could they be related to either the MIDAS operation or the Nobody mole? The prose was terse and deliberately colourless: *Agreed. Yes. Fine.* It did everything it could to sidestep the uncon-scious indicators of temperament and personality. Though the mystery correspondent seemed anxious, the firmness of response suggested some awareness of similar situations. There were no slips or idiosyncratic verbal mannerisms. Whoever they were, they seemed used to being watched.

Vine closed the first draft and moved on to the second one, hoping it would contain something to shed more light on who the mystery correspondent could be, and why Cosmo Newton was contacting them.

As he did, he heard a burner mobile buzz, the sound snapping him out of concentration. He fumbled for the device, unlocked it and then thumbed the message open. There was only one line. Two words he had been waiting to hear ever since that day in Istanbul.

*It's happened.*

## 25

The taxi squealed to a stop outside Guy's hospital. Vine paid the driver and then ran inside the main entrance, careless of the surprised looks as he made his way to the bank of lifts. He checked his phone again to see if there had been any further message from Becky. The lift doors pinged open. He entered the lift, pressed for the third floor, doing everything he could to quell his frustration as he waited for it to hum upwards.

*I know a secret . . . A secret that changes everything . . .*

This could be it. Finally, Ahmed Yousef would begin to pay for what he had done. The truth would be known and logic restored, the identity of Yousef's attacker confirmed.

Vine slowed his pace as he entered the corridor, determined not to give himself away at this last moment. He pushed through the set of double doors and reached Ward 9. He scanned the way ahead for any sign of police, but there was no one. He walked forwards and glanced in the direction of Yousef's room. The view was unrecognizable, just an empty bed, the covers and sheets neatly tucked and secured.

Vine checked his phone again. Becky must be around here somewhere.

He texted her: *Where r u?*

A message pinged back almost instantly: *Can't speak here. Outside.*

Vine pocketed the phone and then took one final look back at the empty room. Ahmed Yousef would have been transferred when he woke up, shifted to another part of the hospital straightaway. But he would be conscious enough to be questioned, the truth wheedled out of him at last.

Vine retraced his steps back to the lift and out through the main reception. He waited uneasily in the cold, scanning the surroundings for any sign of Becky.

She emerged two minutes later, a thin zip-up hoodie wrapped hastily around her bony frame. She looked thinner in the evening gloom, the spindly architecture of her face more prominent in the half-light from the hospital windows behind her. She had her hands stuffed into the hoodie pockets worn over her uniform, sloping towards him reluctantly.

Vine stepped forwards, trying to interpret the graze of suspicion on her face.

She didn't look up. Instead, she inspected the scuffed ends of her shoes, head bowed. 'I shouldn't have texted you,' she said, her voice thin and whispery.

'What do you mean?'

She was breathing heavily now, her head twitching round as if she were being watched. Vine tried to follow the dart of her eyes, glancing at the windows for any sign of surveillance.

'You shouldn't have come.'

His excitement started to dilute, unease growing in its place. It was hard to believe this was the same person who had texted. 'But he is awake? You said in your message that it had happened.'

She stared up at him. For the first time, Vine saw the shake in her eyes, the tremor on her lips. 'I was wrong,' she muttered, moving her legs to regain some heat, staring back down at the ground. 'It was all a mistake . . .'

Vine felt any hope of seeing Yousef evaporate, just the slow grind of half-understood predictions. Desperation began creeping into his voice. He tried to calm himself. 'But you can't have been . . .'

She shook her head and moved closer, still scanning around as if someone were listening to every word they spoke. 'I can't do this,' she whispered. 'I wish you'd never asked me to do this . . .'

'Why?' Vine said, his voice louder now. 'What's happened?'

Her breathing was quicker, face trembling. 'Who the hell *are* you anyway? They asked me about anyone, told me to keep away . . . I can't do this any more. I'm sorry, but I can't . . .'

Vine was fidgety now. 'Come on. I'm sorry I raised my voice. I'll wait until the end of your shift. All I need you to do is tell me what you know. As you have done before. Nothing different. There's no danger to you in this.'

She was shaking her head, tears oozing down her cheeks. Her voice cracked as she tried to bottle them back into place. 'You don't understand . . .'

'What?' said Vine. 'What don't I understand . . . ?'

*There are more important things going on here than you can possibly imagine* . . .

She could barely get the answer out, lost in a haze of tiredness and fright. 'They told me to alert them if I ever saw you again. You've been lying to me, haven't you? You've lied to me all along . . .'

PART THREE

## 26

Together they could have done it. With two, any numbers could be duped. Vine would have veered off right, Wilde left. They would have divided the hostile force, then begun segmenting each section further. Soon they would have only one or two directly on their tails, while others branched off to cover exits and entrances, and others still were keeping guard at previous locations where there had been a definite sighting. Once they'd finally shrugged off their direct pursuers, they would go underground for days. Weeks sometimes. Vine could feel the legacy of all his near escapes in his shins now, worn down by years of foreign soil under his feet. Yes, with two of them they would have shredded these streets.

But working alone was different. There was no way to split the hostile force in two from the start, meaning you had to then fragment twice the number of hostiles. Meets and dead drops were timed for the busiest moment of the day, always in an area that was reliably crowded. You needed alleyways and narrow streets, bustling markets and wedges of people.

The streets around him were too quiet. The hour was wrong. And he still had no read on the number of hostiles there might be.

He knew he had taken a risk going to the hospital at all. But none of this was making sense. Who had told Becky his real identity? A team from MI5 or MI6? Or was this something else altogether, a false flag operation by the ISI, SVR, Mossad, even CIA? Ahmed Yousef had spent years in the company of some of the most renowned terrorists in the world. Any number of countries would relish the chance to question him, given the opportunity.

As soon as Becky had said the words, Vine had turned and started walking. There was every possibility they were using her to draw him out and give themselves a chance to bring him in. His first move was counter-intuitive, making straight for an entrance next to the Shangri-La hotel and into the queue for the lift. He felt the doors close around him now. He had checked his surroundings as he left the entrance to Guy's hospital. There was no way of knowing how large the team might be. If this was a full A Branch op from Thames House, there could be anywhere up to a dozen plainclothes stationed around the area. He thought back to the watcher trailing him in Oxford and wondered whether they had been monitoring him ever since his suspension, waiting for him to arrive at the hospital and use the evidence against him in court.

A Branch were good, though mainly culled from the police. They were efficient and methodical, but had never developed that extra gear that came from doing this under mortal danger. No matter how intense the pressure felt on the streets of London, it couldn't compare with Jerusalem, Riyadh or Tripoli. Every muscle locked into rhythm now, his senses heightened. He had allowed himself this risk only because he was sure he could get himself out of it. He still was.

The lift began to whirr up. As soon as the doors opened at level 33 of the Shard, Vine knew he would have a matter of seconds to act. He tensed now, rehearsing his strategy. As the doors pinged apart, he disguised himself behind the huddle in front. He had scoped this place before he recruited Becky, just for such an eventuality. He took a second to acclimatize to the geography of it again. There were cloakrooms straight ahead, a desk where guests could leave coats and belongings on his left and then the entrance to the restaurant further up on the right.

Vine quickened his pace as if heading straight on and then dipped left. This next piece of choreography was the most essential. He waited until the attendant at the desk turned, and then shrugged off his dark-blue jumper and let it fall to the floor, while simultaneously scooping up a long overcoat from a rack nearby and a brown cap hanging from the adjacent peg. By the time the attendant looked back round, Vine was already at the emergency exit leading down to the service entrance on the ground floor.

As he treaded noiselessly down the endless flights of stairs, Vine listened for the sound of any movement behind or in front. If a watcher had spotted him entering the lift, they would now be spilling out on to the restaurant floor.

Vine began taking two steps at a time. There was still a chance A Branch could have operatives placed outside, but it would be too difficult for any watchers to track him by his facial features alone. They relied on the generic markers of clothing, height, weight and stride pattern. Two of those he could alter, first with the costume change and second with a subtly altered gait, helping confuse them further.

He reached the end of the staircase now and eased himself through the double doors ahead. He angled his face down and continued at a reasonable speed through a series of snaking corridors until he found himself in a patchily carpeted hallway leading to the exit. He reached the door and checked for any obvious watcher mistakes: newspaper pages being reread, monotonous body movement, a finger unconsciously drifting towards an earpiece.

He saw two possible hostiles in a position that gave them a reasonable sightline. He waited another minute until a couple strolling down the street moved in front of him.

Vine used the opportunity to shadow them towards the row of taxis outside the Shangri-La. With the vehicles blocking the watchers' view, Vine escaped to his right and began walking down St Thomas Street.

It was too risky taking a taxi so near to the Shard in case A Branch had planted one of their own as a driver. Instead, he walked on for several minutes, waiting until one emerged from the opposite direction on Borough High Street. He hailed it and, with one final scan of the area, disappeared inside.

'Chelsea,' he said, holding two twenty-pound notes and slipping them across to the driver. 'Take the scenic route.'

## 27

There was something calming about routine. Masks were dropped for a second, all artifice redundant. Up ahead, a cleaner was inspecting the bins, trussing up bags fat with stained cups and wrappers. Vine sipped again at his takeaway Starbucks filter and dipped into the McDonald's carton, chewing down the last of the lukewarm fries.

He crunched the carton in half and drained the rest of the coffee. He was tired and weary of the procession of disappointment. But it was more than that. He had hoped to stare Ahmed Yousef in the face. He had wanted justice and revenge. But, far more importantly, he had wanted the truth. Now order seemed eternally splintered, chaos taking its place.

As he stood, he tried to resist the sharper fears that suggested themselves. He knew he had been reckless recruiting Becky and visiting the hospital while the investigation continued. It was enough for him to be chucked out of the Service. Guilt began to percolate through him. Would they try and get to him via her? Either way, all contact would now have to end. Deep down, Vine knew he had used her. She deserved better than to be tarred with his own disgrace.

He scanned down the street and memorized the vehicles he could, then started the walk back to Wellington Square. He checked around for any remaining signs of physical surveillance. There was one figure near a pub on his right, loitering with a pint in his hand; a woman was walking her dog up ahead. Behind him, he caught an elderly couple shuffling down the street. He knew the tricks. There was no end to potential paranoia. The more innocuous they looked the more dangerous they could be. He was almost sure he had shaken off the watchers from the hospital, careful to duck every camera he knew of in the area. But if they had a full team on him there was still a chance they could have picked him up somewhere. There was no way of ever knowing for sure. Instead, the suspicion metastasized inside of you, killing off all healthy thoughts until you were left with nothing but a lingering dread.

He was sick of the vigilance. As an act of defiance, he removed a pair of earbuds from his pocket and slotted them into place, trying to fake some kind of normality. He tapped on a Radio 4 podcast, catching a section on the Syrian civil war, Valentine Amory's voice reaching out to him: *The truth is that no country is truly immune from the dangers of the secret state. I believe that Ahmed Yousef could have been any one of us: an innocent man harassed by unaccountable forces within the intelligence world. All of us fighting for his rights as a citizen must take the strongest possible stand against this secret tyranny.*

Vine considered what new plans Amory could be hatching now, before quickly changing to Handel's *Music for the Royal Fireworks* and trying to calm his nerves. *Secret tyranny.* All he could think of as the dark shape of other cars fizzed past him was Yousef awake, walking these same streets, haunting his every move.

He kept a close watch on other vehicles, changing his pace and taking odd diversions, anything to flush out a tail. But, as far as he could tell, he was clean. No one had followed him back from the Shard. He looped round Wellington Square twice and then let himself relax another fatal fraction as he unlocked the front door, realizing he was too restless for sleep.

Instead, he made his way into the library and towards the safe in the far corner of the room. He crouched and entered the six-digit passcode and waited as the door clicked open. From inside, he took out the thick volume Gabriel Wilde had sent him. He carried it over to the leather reading chair beside the window and began flicking through it again.

He felt all the fragments of this case needle him. He recalled Ahmed Yousef's body in the interrogation room in Istanbul, waylaid by an invisible attacker; Newton's final message at the train station before his body was found sprawled on the train tracks, and the truth he had discovered that supposedly made sense of everything; the transcript of the interrogation between Alexander Cecil and Yousef about the mole within British intelligence codenamed Nobody; the blanked-out file on the MIDAS operation; and, finally, Gabriel Wilde's disappearance, a life vanishing cleanly without trace.

Somehow, in some way, there was an underlying logic here which he still couldn't quite grasp – the MIDAS operation connecting with the identity of the Nobody mole and the fate of Gabriel Wilde.

Vine put down the book and moved over to his desk. He reached for the box by his side and started unwrapping a new MacBook Air, routing it through a pay-as-you-go dongle, knowing it was more than likely that GCHQ would be all over his old computers. Familiarizing himself with the feel of the laptop, he began searching for any news items about a body found at Cheltenham train station; nothing, however, appeared beyond the preliminary reports he had already read. Officialdom had swooped, a D-Notice hurriedly issued to the press. But what did that mean? Could this all be far bigger than paper trails and redacted files? Were things returning to the days when intelligence officials could be silenced on home soil? The world was more unstable than ever, meaning there was every chance that Newton could have been taken out for reasons much loftier than whatever investigation he was pursuing off the grid. Newton had spent a lifetime hoarding secrets and enemies. Who was to say one of those enemies hadn't returned to settle an old score? Not for the first time, Vine wondered if he was looking in entirely the wrong direction.

He shut down the MacBook and poured himself a large measure of Scotch. Then he stood at the window and tried to still the current of his thoughts. The harder he tried to fix the pieces into a pattern, the more impossible the task would become. The key was to let the evidence build until the pattern seemed to evolve naturally, slowly denying all other hypotheses.

He downed the last swirl of Scotch and placed the empty tumbler on the side-table. Then he picked up Wilde's copy of *The Odyssey*, glancing over the inscription, still sure that there was something else buried there. He had tried teasing apart all possible connotations in the words, yet the meaning remained as elusive as ever. Something about that last line still didn't make sense.

*Take care of Rose for me . . .*

He was about to return the book to the safe when a page fell open near the middle. Vine began to scan through it, idly rolling the lines around his tongue. The leather cover was prim and solid, and the pages felt luxurious to the fingertips.

It was such a handsome volume. Of all possible books, why would Gabriel Wilde send him this?

He looked back up at the top of the page and then stopped, feeling a wave of tiredness mix with the effect of the Scotch, momentarily numbing his reflexes. He closed his eyes and looked at the line again, sure he was imagining things. But there could be no doubt.

He cursed himself for being so dismissive. His world was logic, patterns, proofs and theorems. Though he could fluke an answer on art and literature, he had always been in no doubt about Wilde's greater depth of expertise. There was only so much time on earth to read, and he had concentrated his powers elsewhere.

But as he stared at the line again, he wondered if that would now be his downfall. He began to try fitting the line into context. The passage revolved around arguably the first black ops mission in recorded literature. Odysseus is trapped in the cave of Polyphemus. Faced with certain death, he pioneers an escape through a textbook act of misinformation, lying his way to freedom.

As Vine read the line again now, he could feel the first suggestion of a pattern fix into place. It was far beyond logic. It was an act of flawed humanity – a boast, a taunt, a confession. From the riddle of information and names, a truth was starting to emerge, helping everything else fit into a new kind of order, a truth that Cosmo Newton had only fully grasped before he died. Gabriel Wilde was assuming the mantle of the first secret agent. Like Odysseus, he was proclaiming to the world a truth about who he really was.

For when asked for his name by Polyphemus, Odysseus replies: 'My name is Nobody'.

# 28

For some reason, he always remembers the flowers. At Heathrow, there was someone setting up a flower stall at the arrivals gate, one man with his row of brittle bouquets.

'Any red roses?' Vine asks, trying to juggle his wallet amid the plethora of luggage.

'One bunch left, I think,' he says. 'Someone special, is it?'

'Yes,' Vine says. He realizes for the first time he is not saying it ironically, feeling both pleased and compromised at once.

He is a week early and he will surprise her. There have been no texts as forewarning. He will just show up at the door and see the look on her face and the dance of surprise in her eyes. He has called in a favour and rolled some leave time together so he can have an extended break back in London debating with Rose what to do next. There are so many details to fix: a date for the wedding, a venue, a guest list. And then the reality of life beyond. Should he try and get another job in the private sector, one that doesn't involve so much travel, allowing her to stay at Thames House while he earns some proper money?

Yet, as Vine collects the flowers and wheels his suitcases out towards the taxi rank, he realizes how much he has come to enjoy these details. During every interminable meeting, every new horror he is faced with, he has treasured the calls with Rose. Amid the squalor of life on the frontline, she is a reminder that there is something worth fighting for.

He waits for a taxi, gives the address of Rose's flat in Vauxhall and then sinks back. He wants a proper bath, to watch good TV and to relish the comforts of his own bed, of his own fiancée. A few weeks away from the agonies of conflict and he will be ready to face it again, be able to view footage of convoys blown up, soldiers with limbs missing, the tear-stained faces of grieving families. But for now he cherishes the illusion of peace.

He gets the taxi to drop him off a few minutes away, savouring the walk, inhaling the smell and the chirp of voices and the calm of it all. He debates what he will say when he sees Rose, the shock of surprise on her face and the delights of the evening that await him.

He turns left, back rigid from the load of the rucksack and hands sore from dragging the too-heavy cases behind him. The monotony of a sleepless flight aches at him now.

Taking out the key Rose has given him from his jacket pocket, he unlocks the front door and forces his way in with the cases. He treads lightly up the stairs to the first-floor flat, careful not to make too much noise and eliminate the element of surprise. Once up, he pauses before knocking.

He stands, feeling his heart juddering hard, the adrenaline breaking through the tiredness from the flight. Feet are heard, then a voice, or voices. He wonders for a minute if she has workmen in, the landlord finally sending someone to fix the ceiling light in the main room. The sound moves closer, the door swishing open.

He looks up, smile at the ready.

There – hair still wet from the shower, towel in hand, blocking the door of the flat – is the unlikely figure of Gabriel Wilde.

## 29

Vine stood motionless for a second. It had been staring him in the face all along, and yet he had missed it. He looked at the line again and then repeated Ahmed Yousef's words from the transcript in Newton's file.

*I know for certain that there is a mole somewhere within the intelligence services . . . His codename is Nobody . . .*

He thought back to his own interrogation with Ahmed Yousef. He had been so sure he had seen Gabriel Wilde's car drive away from the compound on the CCTV screen. Yet what if it had all been an illusion? Wilde was meant to be the only one on duty that day, handling the interrogation alone. He must have panicked. Once the truth about the Nobody mole was exposed, it would be the beginning of the end.

He looked down at the copy of *The Odyssey* again, the inscription charged with a fresh energy.

*Dear Solomon,*

*In case we don't meet again, I want you to have this. All wisdom lies in this book. Take care of Rose for me.*

*Yours,*
*Gabriel*

The words made a new kind of sense. The first line confirmed it: Gabriel Wilde had known exactly what he was about to do, the snatch job executed to fool the world, every detail of the crime scene planned with forensic precision. Now the book contained Wilde's final confession and boast.

As Vine felt the first part of the pattern begin to cohere, his thoughts turned to Newton's body on the tracks. Even Wilde wouldn't be foolish enough to smuggle his way back into the country he had betrayed so thoroughly. If Newton's death was suspicious, where did that leave him? Moving over to his desk and picking up his jacket, he thought back to his interview with Professor Turnbull at Oxford and the Prophets group at Christ Church. He plunged his hand into the right-hand pocket and felt his fingers shape around crumpled card.

He took it out and stared again at the decorative portcullis symbol. There was one part of this that was still shrouded in mystery, perhaps the key to finding out the truth about Newton's death. Outside the system, Vauxhall Cross wouldn't give him the time of day. Only one contact still had access to the product he needed, the poisoned chalice of the Parliamentary Private Secretary. He had to try and find out more about Operation MIDAS and probe for any further links with the Prophets group at Oxford.

Vine got out his mobile and opened a new email account he had just set up, tapping out a quick message.

Olivia,

Forgive the intrusion, but we spoke recently about Gabriel Wilde. I've been keeping my ear to the ground, and I think I may have some news for you.

Yours,
Solomon Vine

He added the address and pressed send. Then he pocketed the phone, poured another measure of Scotch and waited.

## 30

Despite the busyness, Central Lobby nevertheless remained hushed, an almost churchy quality to the silent statues guarding each corner. From the Chamber to their left, MPs darted out, clutching papers and trailing staff. Faces Vine vaguely remembered shuffled towards the entrance to the House of Lords on their right, features obscured by tufts of snowy hair and tinfoil skin. A BBC reporter was pacing back and forth nervously with his earpiece in, ready to deliver his verdict straight to camera.

Olivia Cartier led on as they moved through the East Corridor and into the Lower Waiting Hall, then right towards the Pugin Room. The CCTV cameras here were subtle but visible, Vine noting the exact positions. He wondered now whether an analyst in Cheltenham was getting a flag on his facial recognition software. Physical watchers like the team around Guy's hospital worked for intimidation these days, rattling a suspect and forcing them into easy errors. Tabs could be kept largely through digital means. Despite his precautions, there was no sure way of evading the blinking eye at every street corner. Did they already have an active file on him? How much had they clocked and what would they do with it? They wouldn't play their hand immediately, but bide their time instead, watching and waiting.

He tried to dismiss the thoughts as Olivia moved towards a table in the far corner and ordered tea for two. It was quiet, only one other party on the opposite side of the room sipping at an orange juice and mineral water. Vine enjoyed the heavy colouring and golden shimmer, the sense of solidity to it all, like some sort of establishment copyright, echoed across the grander quads, colleges and dining halls of England.

'So . . . it was good to hear from you,' said Cartier, crossing her legs and gesticulating with her finely decorated teaspoon. 'I was very sorry to hear about Cosmo Newton's death.'

Vine nodded, still feeling the reality of the words press on him. Cartier's tone was calm and measured; the gossip in Whitehall must still be of a heart attack, an accident of some kind. 'Yes. Very sad.'

'Given the previous conversation we had about Gabriel, I hope it's slightly better news. One hears all sorts of rumours. His file was, well . . .'

'You've requested to see Wilde's file?'

'Probably not something to admit,' she said, quickly brushing the indiscretion aside. 'So is this better news?'

Vine placed his cup down. 'Not exactly,' he said.

Cartier uncrossed her legs and shuffled forwards in her seat. She looked at Vine, before finally sweeping the room to make sure she couldn't be overheard. 'You haven't discovered any operation Gabriel was conducting, then? Anything that might explain things? Have you talked to Cecil?'

The four words from Wilde's book continued to bellow at him: *My name is Nobody.* If Wilde really was confessing, then he would have others in place to help him with his cause. People he knew and trusted, their friendship of a decent vintage. Vine could still hear Professor Turnbull sitting in a room similar to this, merrily ripping apart Olivia Cartier's account of her own history. Was it possible that she was involved; had, in fact, been quietly playing him all along?

'No,' he said. 'Why?'

'The Defence Secretary got a briefing yesterday from the Director of Global Operations at Vauxhall Cross. The National Security Council is thinking of raising the threat level from *severe* to *critical*. They've been picking up more chatter from Islamist cells about another attack on London, some major financial or political target.'

Vine didn't betray his surprise. 'You think it might be somehow connected to Wilde's situation?'

'You tell me,' said Cartier. 'But Number 10 is nervous.'

'And the attack itself?' said Vine. 'What does Defence Intelligence make of it? You must liaise quite closely on behalf of the Secretary of State.'

Cartier laughed. 'Defence Intelligence doesn't like political interference, that's what they make of it. But I like to keep my contacts fresh, people I knew when serving on the ISC.'

'You have contacts in all three services?'

Cartier was still sitting forwards. 'Yes. But a very good one in MI5. Makes sure the Secretary of State isn't getting set up by the top brass.'

Vine couldn't help but feel himself drawn in by Olivia Cartier. She had a magnetic confidence to her, almost an imitation of Wilde. Each anecdote was plotted with storyteller precision.

'What has your contact told you?'

Cartier wiped something from her eye, shifting slightly in the seat, as if nervous about what she was going to say. 'The working theory is sometime in the next few weeks. For all we know this isn't just coming out of the usual places any more. If this is IS or AQSL opening up another front in Western Europe, we may have to consider military action again.'

Vine nodded. He tried to concentrate on the present and stop his mind spinning. 'And do you think that timeline is credible?'

Cartier tamed a loose wisp of hair back into place, then relaxed into her chair again. 'Doesn't matter if it's credible, does it? If it's even plausible, we have to be seen to act. The key question is what happens after an attack. No one wants more names recited at the start of PMQs. Number 10 will do anything to avoid that.'

Vine looked around the room and saw that the two other drinkers had left the table and were paying at the counter. He knew his next question would be a futile one, but he had to ask it all the same. 'And does your contact at MI5 have a name?'

Cartier smiled. 'A good politician, like a good spy, keeps her counsel. For their sake, as much as mine. I know what you lot are like. But I make no apology. We either have an informed democracy, or we don't. It's that simple.'

Vine reflected her smile in acknowledgement. All the while his mind hurt with questions, still unable to see how all the strands might connect. Some part of him wasn't sure they ever would.

The room was now empty apart from the waitress rearranging cutlery at the serving counter to their right. 'Going back to our previous conversation, I remember you saying you only got to know Gabriel Wilde when he was seconded to Whitehall liaison.'

'That's right,' said Cartier.

Vine didn't take his eyes off Cartier's expression, dissecting every flicker. He kept his voice steady. 'I was under the impression from someone else that you'd been at Christ

Church, Oxford together? A don called Mohammed Ressam. Some sort of mutual connection.'

Whatever else, he had to admire the sheer nerveless confidence of Olivia Cartier. If she was acting, it was an Oscar-worthy performance: a dawning realization in the eyes, lips curving into another half-smile, a hand brushing casually through the hair. 'I'm rather ashamed to say that I spent most of my three years debating at the Union . . . But, no, if you say so, I'm sure that's correct. Always thought Professor Ressam was a bit of an odd character, to be honest.' Her phone started buzzing. 'My next appointment, I'm afraid. The diary is crazy today. My PA must be trying to track me down.'

Soon they were walking back to Westminster Hall. Vine glanced around and noticed the space was buzzing with workmen slipping down a doorway on the right, banishing the throng of tourists. A notice had been placed at the bottom of the stairs: NOTE TO MEMBERS: WWII COMMEMORATION PREPARATION – PLEASE EXCUSE TEMPORARY DISRUPTION.

As they reached the steps down to St Stephen's Entrance, Cartier turned to him. 'You know, I almost forgot,' she said. 'There was one final thing my contact said. Apparently the word is that all this has to do with that poor chap who got tangled up with your lot. The one Valentine Amory's so concerned about.'

Vine froze. 'Ahmed Yousef?'

'Yes,' said Cartier. 'I don't know the details. But my contact is certain it's all somehow connected to Yousef.'

## 31

It was quiet on the Circle line back to Sloane Square, the usual assortment of freelancers, tourists, students and the retired, wearing school-trip smiles. Vine ignored them all as he emerged from the station and walked back towards Wellington Square. Irritation seemed to consume his body. He closed the door and headed straight for the wine rack, removing two bottles of red and drinking from the first as he treaded up the stairs.

He let the rest of the day dissolve in a funk of wine and cigarettes. He checked the cricket scores, then his trading position, pleased to find he was still up on the week.

He picked up his battered copy of *Tristram Shandy*, always the perfect book for moods like these. Only after several hours did undiluted frustration begin to energize him. He felt a whole-body craving for some form of mental release. There was one slip that Olivia Cartier had made, a slip he could use to his advantage now.

She had mentioned trying to read Gabriel Wilde's full file. As a security-cleared MP, a former member of the Intelligence and Security Committee and PPS to the Defence Secretary, she would have the right to see it. So far, Vine felt like he had reached an impasse. If Wilde was the Nobody mole Ahmed Yousef had mentioned in the transcript, how did that connect with the MIDAS operation in September 2011? Newton had left both those names behind in the safe deposit box for a reason. Somehow the truth lay in the connection between the MIDAS operation and Wilde's position as the Nobody mole, a truth Newton had only glimpsed properly on the night he died. To answer that question, Vine knew he had to get his hands on Wilde's full file.

Flush with the drinking, he went upstairs and exhumed his best suit, one of the first fitted Savile Row pieces he had ever bought. He took a taxi to Oxford Street and purchased a new phone and SIM card, then sat in a branch of Costa near St James's Church and used the free wi-fi to download PDFs of the Parliamentary Estate, debating how to go about breaking into the most famous collection of buildings on the planet.

From the maps and his recent experience, he knew his best shot was through Derby Gate, the most lightly guarded entrance of all with one sleepy police box nestled alongside the back of the Red Lion pub. The entrance at Portcullis House was the most heavily guarded, followed by 1 Parliament Street and St Stephen's. Derby Gate it would have to be. He clicked off and began flicking through the websites of various MPs. He started compiling details for his legend, learning how to inhabit the character and speak the language, pulling trivia from various different figures to tailor the disguise he needed.

In case the authorities later tried to ID him through tracking his movements on CCTV, he walked back to Victoria and began some light counter-surveillance, losing himself in the concourse of the station. Then he took the Victoria line to Oxford Circus and doubled back to Green Park, before taking the Jubilee line to Westminster. By the time he emerged from the Parliament Street exit at Westminster station, he was confident he would delay anyone scrolling through the tapes.

He approached the Derby Gate turn from Whitehall and the sight of the Red Lion pub, the hardened members of the parliamentary drinking corps packed noisily on the pavement outside.

It was the perfect time for a simple distraction exercise, straight out of the Fort handbook. Unexpectedly, he felt a trace of anxiety settle on him, like a bruise midway through healing. It had been a while since he had done this properly and the cost of a mishap here could be fatal. He rubbed his palms dry and tried to shrug off the effect of the booze.

Then he started. He elbowed his way among the groups and spotted a foreign trade contingent clustered on the pavement, on to their sixth pint of London Pride. All it took was two moves: the drink was spilt with the left hand and the first punch simultaneously swung with the right. He ducked out as the shock gave way to recrimination and more punches started flying. A flutter of concern spread from the other drinkers on the pavement, the policeman only stirring from his booth when one man fell to the floor.

As the policeman began physically restraining two inebriated bureaucrats from further lunges, Vine took the opening. He disappeared through the heavy iron gates and vaulted over the metal barrier only ever lifted in the event of the Prime Minister walking across from Number 10, then scurried past the overweight time-servers in the security booth on his right. Both were laughing. There was the crackle of the TV in the background. They were oblivious.

He found himself in a deserted car park with the two flights of stairs to the back of the Norman Shaw South building ahead. He calmed his breathing and paced his stride.

This was the moment to test the first part of the plan: the strength of his legend. It was a convention that doorkeepers in the Palace and the police memorized the faces of all 650 Members of Parliament, never asking for their passes. Vine had duly created another legend for himself while sipping his coffee – Sam Henderson, MP for East Norfolk, first elected in 2015, recently voted on to the Health Select Committee. It wouldn't fool anyone with a computer, but it would get him out of a tight spot with a tired police guard.

He walked on, seeing one police officer, then another. He strode past without flinching, daring them to insubordination. If he could survive this, he was through. He waited for the pause, the throat-clearing, the request to see his pass.

Both nodded. Neither asked him for anything.

Timing was key to the plan working. The Palace was alive at night Monday to Thursday. From Thursday evening to the weekend it died a slow death, MPs wheeling their cases out to the Tube and back to the constituency for a long weekend of visits and engagements. The Diplomatic Protection Group tasked with guarding the Palace shed half its number. If he could ever get away with this, it was now.

He walked up the two flights of steps into Norman Shaw South and along the tiled entrance. His chest was still thumping, a film of sweat on his forehead. A voice told him this was wrong. He should turn back now, lessen the possible charges if he was caught. The press would have a field day. Parliament was itchy about its independence. Any suggestion the intelligence services were snooping without permission would cause panic in the corridors of Whitehall. What he was about to do was reckless in the extreme. Yet he kept going, through another doorway and up a winding staircase seemingly without end.

There was no other sound. He didn't stop moving until he reached the fourth floor. With every turn, he expected a door to creak open behind him, a rush of voices and questions. But there was just more silence, dead and tuneless.

He walked along the main corridor until he found Room 406 near the end. Now he was beyond the point where he could turn back, too far in to escape his decision. He ducked down and checked for any signs of light underneath the doorframe. But there was nothing. Olivia Cartier would surely have left by now, back to Kensington ready to put in a long Friday trying to increase her majority. He checked the two offices either side. The lights were off too. It was perfectly still. There was nothing but the dull red blink of the TV monitor in the hall.

He allowed himself a second of thought before he made his final decision, waiting for any new sound. Then he stepped back, tensed his upper body and charged forwards. With a surgical thud, the door gave slightly but held fast. Two tries later, it opened, springing forwards with a sudden lurch and throwing him head-first into the room.

He regained his balance and stayed motionless for a second. Had anyone heard him? The building wasn't equipped with motion sensors or any form of advanced inbuilt security. He waited for the scrape of approaching footsteps, sweat oozing from his forehead to his neck, dripping into the collar of his jacket. He turned and found himself looking round a barn-like office peering across the Thames. Allowing his eyes to fully adjust to the darkness, he saw four desks spread throughout the room and a variety of chairs that leaked foam. He shouldn't be here. And yet, somehow, he still couldn't leave.

He would give himself no more than five minutes. Pushing the door closed, he took a deep lungful of air, his brain threatening to cloud over. He had to keep moving.

He worked his way round to what he presumed was the PA's desk with the spray of pens and Post-it notes. Turning on the PC, he began sorting through the various sheets of paper nearby. Every few seconds he paused, the rattle of the old windows in their frames sounding ominously like movement. He forced himself to continue. Minutes later he spotted a single A4 sheet with KEY CONTACTS written in a bold title across the top.

The A4 sheet listed everyone's email address and phone number. Vine turned the page over and saw with relief a scrawl of loopy blue biro: USERNAME (jenkinssd) PASSWORD (sept2888). The Lenovo PC jolted to life. He replaced the CONTACTS sheet and typed in the username and password. Once in, he loaded up Outlook and checked through the account. The inbox showed not just the PA's account but a main MP address as well. As he began scrolling through, he could already hear the list of charges: breaking and entering, illegal surveillance, espionage against his own government. The evidence would be laid out clearly, the fruit of days spent tapping his every move and conversation, the judge gleefully weighing up sentence.

Vine refocused his attention on the screen. There was an array of press releases and diary appointments. He had hoped that it might be linked into another email account used for Olivia's personal correspondence. But there was nothing.

He looked at the round white clock on the wall, watching the minutes slip away, knowing he couldn't stay here much longer. And yet all this couldn't be for nothing. He scanned the other desks, picking his way through piles of magazines, press cuttings, headed stationery and envelopes. He was getting careless of the sound now, feeling his breathing become heavier. The drink was pulling him down. He had to keep sharp for just a few more seconds.

He walked over to the desk closest to the window at the end. It was tidier than the others with a bookshelf behind. This had to be Olivia's desk for constituency work, odds and ends when waiting for a vote and too tired to bother dragging her way back to the Ministry of Defence. The desk was ordered, dusty at the edges but clear of paper. The PC wasn't switched on, pens and photos cluttered either side. He turned and tried to battle free of disappointment. Then he saw the bag on the green sofa by the mini-fridge near the coat hangers at the entrance.

He cursed himself and the drink for not spotting it earlier. It was a nondescript shoulder bag, roomy enough to haul around files and papers for constituency work.

A sound echoed outside, like a door creaking. He paused, waiting for a second noise – a cough, the scrape of shoe leather on worn carpet, the sound of a voice.

Then he moved towards the bag and zipped it open. Inside, he found three files fat with paper. He pulled them out, reading the labels on the top of each: CASEWORK, KENSINGTON ASSOCIATION, PARLIAMENTARY. He flicked through the first two and found nothing more than email printouts and draft flyers. Next he reached for the Parliamentary folder, knowing there was a chance that any further clues could be hidden in here. Surrounded by phalanxes of armed police, it was all too easy for many MPs to be careless with operational security.

Vine flicked through lists of votes and messages from backbenchers until he found one note tucked away at the back, dated the previous day. He unfurled it carefully. It was on headed notepaper from the Prime Minister's PPS and sent with a compliments slip through the internal parliamentary postal service.

He opened it fully and began to try and decipher the spidery hand:

*Olivia,*

*PM asked me to arrange a meeting. Needs to be in person. Late tomorrow (Thurs) looking best, before she heads off to Chequers. Commons Office, not Number 10. Slightly delicate – about an application to see a file? – so instructions not to text, email or phone.*

*Yrs,*
*EW*

Vine paused on the last sentence: *application to see a file.* Surely it had to be the file on Gabriel Wilde. He took out his phone and snapped two photos, then stowed it back in his pocket.

His reflexes slowed for a minute as he tried to analyse the implications. By the time he began to consider the full weight of the other sentences – *Late tomorrow (Thurs) looking best . . . Commons Office, not Number 10* – the sudden drumbeat of sound outside had already grown too near. Vine willed it to be his own paranoia, evaporating on closer inspection. But the sound was unmistakable: a rhythmic tap of movement, building slowly.

There was a fatal semi-second delay in reaction, the booze gumming up his reflexes. He barely had time to replace the note or the folder before he heard the door being shoved ajar. Light pitched through from the hallway. Olivia Cartier's voice, newly returned from serenading the Prime Minister, sounded behind him.

There was a moment of astonished silence, then an accusatory bleat of shock: 'Vine . . . what the *hell* are you doing here?'

## 32

The Fort training manual treasured one clear principle. Running was a last resort. The adroit move as an intelligence officer cornered in hostile territory was to scope the surroundings – elegant tradecraft usually dictated this was done well before any operation – and then try and talk your way free. The cover story had to be watertight and the explanation fluent. If that failed to work, the second option was to seek cover as a member of the British Diplomatic Service and invoke the power of the embassy and the threat of inevitable geopolitical upheaval. Only the most self-confident of FSB and MSS recruits wanted to claim responsibility for sparking a diplomatic incident and incurring the wrath of NATO. Only if either of the first two moves were impossible did you think about a third – trusting your legs to outrun a bullet.

As Vine assessed his options now, he tried to remember these lessons. But he knew they were no use. It was not so much the act he had committed, but the implications that would be drawn. He was already on the brink of expulsion from Vauxhall Cross. Continuing Newton's quest off the books would be considered intolerably bad manners; breaking into the office of an aide to one of the most senior members of the British government would be borderline treason. It could be shaped into evidence for any number of maladies – a psychotic episode, a nervous breakdown or, worse still, potential evidence of working for a foreign power, smuggling secrets as an agent in place.

There was a split second as Olivia Cartier reached for the light switch behind her. Vine had already discounted the idea of trying to escape via the windows that panelled the right-hand wall. Behind him was a door that led directly into another large open-plan office. But it would be bolted shut now, and the effort to unbolt it would allow Olivia time he didn't have. If he wanted to escape from this, he knew there was only one option.

As he saw her attention flicker momentarily towards the light switch, he moved. There were only a few metres between them, allowing him to reach the door handle in three steps and bundle into the hallway in another two. The light was better here. He had memorized the floor-plans from the PDFs and let his mind skim the possibilities. The distance was less important than spotting the gap in security. Norman Shaw South was on the edge of the Parliamentary Estate. The Derby Gate entrance he had come in was the most sparsely guarded, but the crowds outside the Red Lion pub would be able to spot the exfil more easily than the arrival. The main Portcullis House entrance, meanwhile, was limited to passholders.

That left two options. The 1 Parliament Street exit would be the shorter, but it meant navigating the echo-chamber of Portcullis House and then the potential snare of the police monitoring station near the Parliament Street doors. One glance by the DPG guard on duty, and the doors could be locked automatically.

So to the final option. As Vine dipped left, he visualized the rest of the route in his mind. There were four flights of stairs down to the ground floor of Norman Shaw South, then a further flight and a walkway across to the right-side entrance to Portcullis House. That was a simple swing door, not limited to passholders only. Straight ahead lay the second most dangerous part, an exposed line straight ahead to the escalators that purred downwards to a glassy exit on the left functioning as a hidden thoroughfare directly into Westminster Tube station. There was a chance it would have one member of the Diplomatic Protection Group still patrolling it. But it was a risk he would now have to take.

Once clear of that, Vine would have free passage down the tunnelling of the colonnade straight ahead into New Palace Yard. Though there would be a sprinkling of security, he could pass as a Member of Parliament for long enough to clear the barriers directly outside the entrance to Westminster Hall. The last part would be the riskiest. Westminster Hall was a barn-like space, riddled with DPG guards further on in Central Lobby. The one slice of luck he needed was space enough to disappear right through the wooden doors of St Stephen's Entrance and out in the direction of the House of Lords.

As he reached the final flight of stairs at Norman Shaw South, he tried to calculate how long it would take to send an alert to all DPG guards currently in the Palace. During the day, the lines would be continuously staffed, any message relayed with pinpoint speed. But he had to hope that the time of night would work in his favour. The DPG guards would be lured into complacency by the hour, Olivia struggling for an extra minute or two to locate the lead officer on duty. An extra minute was all he needed.

He knew there was no time to question the plan. Speed was the only thing that would save him, trusting the bureaucratic sludge of alerts and authorizations to slow down any response. He flew through the double doors towards the side entrance to Portcullis House and then gently slowed his pace.

There was a chance he could encounter a member of staff still packing the place up for the night.

As he entered the main atrium of Portcullis House, Vine glanced left then right. It was empty apart from one figure at the far end steering a mop in circles around the floor. He made himself slow further, keeping his tread light to try and slip past without giving away his position. He kept a close watch, waiting for her to turn at any moment. But the figure remained fixed on the task. As he reached the edge of the escalator, he saw a thin trail down the figure's right-hand side. She was wearing earbuds and listening to music, cut off from the world.

He took the escalator two steps at a time, balancing his weight on the front of his feet to dampen the noise. He fastened his jacket tighter and then marched forwards at a brisk tempo, not even turning to check whether there was a DPG guard in the booth on his left monitoring any final departures for the Tube.

It was as he reached the gloomy colonnade leading towards Westminster Hall that he heard the first stirrings behind him. There was the sound of multiple footsteps on the tiled flooring above the escalator, soon followed by the crackle of a radio and a man's voice closer by asking for the information to be repeated.

Vine pressed forwards, moving to a quicker pace as he neared the end of the colonnade. Ahead he could see two DPG guards at the exit on to St Margaret Street. He began to veer right across the cobbles of New Palace Yard towards the barriers in front of Westminster Hall.

Voices spilled out behind him, the contours of the sound fragmenting down the long distance of the colonnade. Vine knew he didn't have enough time to consider a back-up plan.

He broke into a run now, vaulting over the waist-high barriers in front of him and bounding forwards towards the heavy wooden double doors leading into Westminster Hall.

He pulled the right-hand door open and spotted three DPG guards narrowing in from his left. Already, he could hear more voices from his right. The alert must have been confirmed. Every DPG guard was now looking for the suspect who had breached Palace security.

Vine slipped through the thin doorway. The acoustics of Westminster Hall were different from elsewhere in the Palace. There was no hope of muffling footsteps here, every movement reverberating with a watery echo. He could see the two flights of steps at the far end of the hall. Further up to the right was his escape – the door leading towards St Stephen's Entrance. He pelted forwards now across the deserted space, pushing his body as hard as it would go. He needed ten seconds more grace and he could do it. Once he was out on to the street, he could lose himself in the mix of cars and foot traffic up towards Millbank. All he needed was one second of hesitation on the part of the DPG guards patrolling the space from Central Lobby.

He had his foot on the first step, the door through to St Stephen's no more than a few metres away. Then the space above him began swarming with armed members of the Diplomatic Protection Group, Glock 17s prepped and ready to be used. They seemed to spill in from both right and left, bearing down on him like an invading army. Undone by drink, he had committed the cardinal sin of underestimating them. They had lulled him into a false sense of assurance, letting him through Westminster Hall unscathed so they could regroup and corner him at the end.

The silence was shattered by a volley of barked orders. For a moment, Vine remained standing where he was, a part of him entranced by the thought of four or five shots being slugged into his system. It would be a better way to go than spending the rest of his days in exile or rotting for his sins at Her Majesty's pleasure. But as he saw the trigger finger of the lead DPG officer twitch slightly, Vine found his legs folding obediently, his knees cracking on the hardness of the stone floor, his hands raised behind his head and then the heat and bustle of other bodies crowding him into submission.

There was the pinch of handcuffs being applied, and then a jolt of pain through his body as he was hauled to his feet. Outside, his senses were assaulted by the skirl of blue police lights.

As he was jammed into the back seat of the waiting car, he turned and caught Olivia Cartier standing outside the doors to Westminster Hall. She had her arms folded, silently watching the scene play out.

Before he had a chance to read her expression, the car drifted forwards and then accelerated away, shrieking through the darkness.

## 33

The cell mattress at Charing Cross police station was lumpy. Vine held his head in his hands, terrifyingly sober. The place hadn't seen a cleaner for weeks, reeking of alcohol and sweat. He realized, looking around, that he was no longer protected by the all-forgiving embrace of Vauxhall Cross. There would be no nods and winks on matters of national security. No plainclothes men having quiet words with the Commissioner. He was an outcast, as good as a private citizen.

He needed a gulp of fresh air, to get away from the stale smell of this place. Instead, he lay back and closed his eyes, the time seeming interminable, minutes as heavy as days. As his head rested against the mattress, the interview replayed in his mind. The blinking eye of the recording machine, the sour smell of the detective inspector with three-day stubble, the rickety table.

'You say you knew Ms Cartier?'

'Not really, no. I've met her twice.'

'Twice?'

'Yes.'

'And why did you first contact her?'

Vine paused. He found himself suddenly aware of all the ways his answers could be interpreted. What had once seemed like common sense was now fanged with doubt. 'I was following up some leads on a friend of mine.'

The DI stifled a grin at this point. 'Following up some leads?'

'Which is not how it sounds.'

'How do you think it sounds? Like you're some sort of private detective?'

'Not quite.'

'What are you then?'

Vine had been forced to sign a document when he arrived: name, occupation, address.

'Says here you're an analyst. Foreign Office. Very grand. Why does an analyst need to follow up leads with a Member of Parliament?'

Vine was tired of the half-truths. 'You don't understand.'

'Enlighten me . . .'

Vine folded his arms and leaned back in the seat. To hell with it all. For years he had been governed by an intense fear of what he was about to do, abided by the strict rules of Service secrecy. But loyalty had found him on the scrapheap. He owed them nothing.

'I'm waiting . . .' said the DI.

'The truth is I'm not an analyst from the Foreign Office,' said Vine. 'I'm an intelligence officer from the Secret Intelligence Service. I was consulting Ms Cartier on a matter of national security.'

The DI's grin widened. 'Wonderful. A petty criminal and a fantasist. Not what you usually get on the night shift, I'll tell you that.' He signalled to the PC by the door.

Vine felt a mounting unease as he was ordered to stand, handcuffed again and led away. Back in the cell, he addressed the back of the departing PC: 'Call Vauxhall Cross. They can confirm.' As the cell door shut on him again, he realized with a shudder that they might not.

*A petty criminal and a fantasist.* Vine wondered whether that would now be his epitaph.

# 34

*2013*

There is something about the night that hides sins. But now, in the first hopeful hours of a new day, the city seems to revitalize itself, to suggest this one could be different. Soon it will evaporate, of course, the dawn rising and shattering the illusion of newness. It will be a day like all the others, spoiled by the wrong temperature, the clouds heavy with intent. Yet the moment is enough, thinks Vine, as he stares along Westminster Bridge; hinting at some nameless perfection always just beyond reach. Enough to keep the world ticking over, refreshing the quest each day.

Beneath him he can see a boat still chugging dutifully along the Thames, the wind-ruffled water frothing at the edges, a wrapping-paper crinkle in the middle. There is the odd glint ahead, a lone walker, some figure of the night seeking out the dark to cover his trail. Pale-yellow light leaks from buildings along the South Bank, casting a faintly sinister echo of a spotlight, as if any one of these figures is on the brink of exposure.

For a minute, he experiences a brief rustle of sympathy for those he has spent a lifetime fighting. The same nihilistic drive, the intolerance of boredom and the everyday. As he looks out at the humdrum picture of the city, he has an urgent desire to do away with it all, to start over. He wonders whether another day merely repeating the rhythms of life, the mindless cycle of daily chores, will be the end of him.

That the centuries-long smoothing-out of human exist-ence – the elements giving way to the cocoon of the city – is not enough. Anarchy or chaos would be better than such chlorinated nothingness.

Behind him, Big Ben chimes three in the morning. Vine knows he has no chance of sleeping, too troubled by mem-ories of Gabriel Wilde's face in the doorway of the flat, of Rose's passionless apologies. He has already filed his applica-tion for a promotion within the counter-espionage team, ensuring he roves the world. He can lose himself in sniffing out security breaches and hunting moles, patrolling the gutter of the secret world, escaping clear of all this.

He can feel the last traces of optimism fade, the old cer-tainties scab over. For now, he remains there, staring, cast out of the daylight, condemned to be a creature of the night.

## 35

Dim scenery whipped by outside, a colourless swish of activity. Though his body ached with tiredness, he felt energized as he sat staring out of the back of the Range Rover. He was no use padding around police cells or waiting for verdicts. He longed to be back in the action, to savour the beauty of logic and cold, hard reason. Back in the game where he belonged.

He must have slept for several hours at least, before he heard the clank of the cell door opening. He was bleary-eyed as he saw two plainclothes men standing outside the doorway, asking him to accompany them. For a minute he thought he was still dreaming, until he signed out at the main desk and walked past the same DI shaking his head and muttering something about going to the papers. Ahead was a black Range Rover, the back door open. As he heaved himself in and felt the dip of the leather seats, he realized for the first time that he had no idea where he was being taken.

They drove for over an hour, the roads uncluttered this early in the morning. There was no way he could be sure, but he didn't doubt that his captors were MI6, and his destination one of the many safe houses located around the country for agent debriefs and other emergency security protocol. He wondered whether the DI had told them about his outburst. He would be reprimanded, moved from suspended to sacked.

Only as the car slowed and began winding through thin, muddy country lanes did Vine realize his destination could be far more august. He began to make out the manicured lawns of cottages, the place wrapped in a medieval hush with barely another vehicle to be heard. This wasn't safe-house country; this was long-weekend territory for Whitehall barons eager to get away from the London rush.

They turned again, headed left, then indicated. It was as they stopped at a makeshift guard post outside two heavy metal gates that Vine appreciated the full importance of his dawn visit. The driver's window purred downwards, a pass was flashed, and the gates began whirring open. They taxied forwards gently, crunching over gravel, until the car stopped outside what looked like an old vicarage. Two DPG officers stood either side of the entrance, both armed.

As the passenger door opened and Vine stepped out, he knew only a handful of figures within the British state were afforded such security: members of the Cabinet with national security portfolios (Foreign Office, Defence, Home Office as well as the residents of Numbers 10 and 11 Downing Street), the Chief of the Defence Staff and the heads of the two London intelligence agencies. He suddenly felt exposed, his suit stained with sweat from the attempted escape, crumpled and tatty from the cell. It usually paid to be smartly dressed when in the presence of 'C' himself.

Vine followed his nameless captors inside the brown door, marvelling at the plush interior. A chandelier swayed above them, the hallway covered in black-and-white tiling. It looked as if it had been cut and pasted from the inside of a glossy magazine. A wide staircase wound upwards to the first floor straight ahead, while several rooms opened up on the right. From one of these came the newsreader baritone Vine had heard more times than he cared to think, deep yet with a hint of a smoker's rasp. Sir Alexander Cecil filled the doorway in the remnants of a suit, the tie long since abandoned, cuffs curled midway along his arms, right hand brandishing a lit cigar.

'Ah, the thief has returned,' he said, walking towards Vine, a semi-amused glint in his eyes. 'Let him be, gentlemen. I can handle the criminal from here on in, I think. Follow me, Vine.'

Vine saw his entourage back off, condemned to wait for further instructions. He followed Cecil through to a roomy drawing room, full-length windows covered in thick curtains, two large sofas and a weathered armchair set in front of a crackling log fire that hissed and popped in the background.

'Please, please, have a seat,' Cecil said, settling himself in the brown leather armchair and crossing his legs.

Vine sat on the far end of the nearest sofa and stared across at Cecil, remembering the last time they had met. Looking at him this close up, he could see why Newton had always resented him. The silvery mane swept back and the thespian brood of the eyes. Newton couldn't have been more different: reserved, intolerant of flamboyance, dedicated only to the facts of the case and the logic of assumptions. Cecil could back-slap, buy a round, do a turn at the Christmas revue and bring prime ministers and presidents into his confidence. Newton would grow itchy at poor questioning, irritable at flimsy reasoning. Cecil had ascended to be 'C' himself, no doubt soon to be elevated to the peerage and, when the moment came, a glowing obituary in *The Times*, memorial service at Westminster Abbey and eulogies from the brighter lights of the political establishment on either side of the Atlantic. Newton, meanwhile, had died still hunting down a lead, his passing garnering little more than relieved sighs from the few who had known the sharper end of his tongue. Such, as Newton would have said, was the way of the world.

Vine tried to remain calm, not give away any sign of unease. He could still hear Cecil's voice on the phone that day in Istanbul.

*There are more important things going on here than you can possibly imagine . . .*

Here, now, Vine felt a curious mix of emotions. He had been naive to ever think he could leave this life behind.

'So . . .' said Cecil, at last. 'You have been busy, then, haven't you? Running secret errands for Cosmo Newton, chatting up former contacts. Fergus Goodwin and Olivia Cartier. Cease and desist, I see, doesn't seem to be part of your vocabulary. Now breaking into one of the most highly guarded buildings in the world . . .'

Vine cursed himself for being surprised as Cecil reeled off the list in that languorous drawl. The knowledge of secrets was the currency of this trade. He thought back to the watcher pursuing him through the streets of Oxford, and the team at Guy's hospital. Cecil had been shadowing him all along.

'I've been using my skills where they are wanted,' said Vine. 'You didn't really give me much choice.'

Cecil laughed, raising his eyebrows. 'Fair enough, I suppose. Not that I had many other options. The world is changing, Vine. We are no longer fighting a battle solely against the enemy, but against ourselves. The thirty-year rule, Valentine bloody Amory and his tribe at the ISC. Make one wrong move and we might not even have an intelligence service in ten years' time. The pressure on me to act was enormous, from all sides of government. I did what I thought was best.'

'You did what you thought was politically convenient.'

'I often find them to be the same thing . . .' He leaned forwards, taking another puff on the cigar. 'So, tell me . . . what is it you think you know?'

Vine debated how much to say. He thought back to Newton's file, Ahmed Yousef's accusation of a mole inside British intelligence codenamed Nobody and Professor Turnbull's information about the Prophets group at Christ Church. He looked up at Cecil and saw the expectancy in his eyes. There would only be one chance to say it.

'I think Cosmo Newton was right to follow up the Yousef lead. There is a mole somewhere inside MI6.'

Cecil's face puckered with distaste. 'How the hell do you know about the Yousef interrogation?'

'Newton told me.'

Cecil looked almost beyond anger, shaking his head as he stared across at the fire. 'The greatest threat to Western security. Cosmo sodding Newton . . . Go on . . .'

Vine resumed. 'And, as I think Newton discovered before he died, the evidence shows that there is really only one person it could be.'

'I see.'

'From what I have been able to find out, I think Gabriel Wilde has been working as a double agent for Islamist groups inside Syria. I believe Wilde is the mole Yousef talked about in his interrogation. The mole within British intelligence codenamed Nobody.'

Cecil's lips curled into a faint hint of a smile. 'Yes,' he said, looking back up at Vine. 'Yes, in many ways I suppose you're right.'

## 36

It is a warmer day, the throb of sun offset by the near-invisible splash of grey at the edge of the skyline; quiet, too, the silence only broken as the heavy iron gates open, a rusty whine in need of oil.

Vine waits for a gap wide enough for the bulky nose of the vehicle, then manoeuvres the Toyota SUV up the thin paved driveway and parks it in front of the whitewashed house dominating the view. There is no bodyguard today or polite driver. Today is beyond top-secret, sharing intelligence straight from Number 10.

He wanders up to the house and presses the doorbell. A locked briefcase rests in his right hand. He tries to staunch the jangle of nerves. The secure room at the consulate has been ruled out. Wilde's house is the only place that meets requirements.

Just as he feared, it is Rose that answers. There is something different about seeing her away from the familiar backdrop of London. She has let her hair grow longer, he realizes, accentuating the smooth marble of the forehead and those soulful sky-blue eyes. She is wearing a loose white dress, her arms and neck browned to a show-piece tan. The only hint of the elfish non-conformity he so treasured lies in the bright pink sandals, joyfully scuffed at the edges.

'Solomon,' she says. Her voice is edgy. She leans towards him, and they exchange an awkward embrace.

He pulls back too soon, catching the familiar suggestion of her perfume. He is terrified of being unable to let go, unconsciously retracing the contours of her. Every time he imagines he has moved on, a comment or a reference takes him back, life since defined by her absence. 'How are you?' he says, pleased that his voice sounds reasonably authoritative. He is here on a work visit. This is not personal.

'Good, fine,' she says, ushering him in and closing the door behind them. She takes his jacket and hangs it on a nearby peg, and then leads the way. 'Busy with work, as usual. Did Gabriel ever tell you I'm now lawyering at the consulate?'

'No,' says Vine, trying to ignore the deadly implication of the last sentence. All possible communication is now run through Wilde, a subtle detachment from any suggestion of friendship. 'Enjoying it?'

'Well enough. Not particularly stretching, but it keeps me sane at least. Some pro bono work on the side which is much more interesting . . . Gabriel's just through here, I think.'

Vine tries not to pause over the interior of the house. He has never been here before to witness the full conclusion of their marriage first-hand. Yet he can't help bristling at the homely feel of it, the starchy consulate guidelines subverted by poorly drilled picture hooks defacing the walls. They move down the hall to the main room, the old-fashioned fittings odd against the modernity of the sofas and wide-screen TV, the clutter of phone chargers, iPads and laptops scattered throughout.

Wilde is repositioning a mirror, a showy attempt to make it symmetrical. He holds it briefly, waits for it to steady, then smiles as he turns to Vine. He walks across, face wreathed with his flat-pack good humour.

'Sol. Good man. Managed to dodge the nasties, did we? Didn't make the journey too eventful.'

'Just about,' says Vine, marvelling once again at Wilde's levity with it all, that odd mix of prep school and gallows humour.

'Suppose we'd better get down to business, then.' Wilde leads through to the regal polish of the dining room. There is a long oak table spanning the length of it, silvery cutlery – no doubt a wedding present – twinkling in the fluorescent heat. Wilde makes his way to the drinks cabinet and pours them both a Scotch.

'Might be safer out on the patio,' he says, 'just in case the bastards on the other side have got their headphones on.'

Vine nods and follows Wilde out on to a long rectangular patio with a flimsy table in the middle, two chairs plump with cushions. The garden is a parched collection of emaciated twigs and dehydrated flowers.

'So,' Wilde says, sitting down and taking a first sip. 'Number 10 is on the warpath, so I hear.'

Vine has spent the last few days in meetings with the National Security Adviser at Number 10. He unlocks his briefcase and takes out a plain manila folder, handing it across to Wilde. 'The National Security Council met yesterday morning. They agreed unanimously to cooperate with the Americans in providing covert action support with Langley for Syrian opposition groups.'

'How strong is the contingent?' says Wilde, as he takes the manila file and opens it.

'Five patrols from 22 SAS at first,' Vine says, watching Wilde flick through the briefing. 'Deliberately kept much smaller than usual for security reasons. If this ever got exposed, the diplomatic blowback would, obviously, be extreme.'

Wilde laughed. 'That's the understatement of the year . . . And what's our objective?'

'Two-month horizon to begin with. Mainly basic weapons training. The NSC is clear that they don't envisage the unit engaging in a direct combat mission.'

'Fascinating.' Wilde reaches the end of the file and closes it. 'Presumably this isn't all you have?'

Vine takes the file back and locks it again in his briefcase. 'No. The NSC asked me to negotiate some form of intelligence transfer, alerting you if the mission produces product directly relevant to customers in Istanbul. This is just a courtesy briefing to let you know the basics.'

'Why not just normal channels?'

'I don't trust them. Not for product of this sensitivity. There are too many people in the consulate, too many contractors and others who could gain access, even within your station. We need the distribution list kept as tight as possible.'

Wilde leans back in his chair, as if half-amused at Vine's precautions. 'So what?' he asks. 'Carrier pigeons?'

Vine ignores the smile. 'Either courier or we meet. Handover in person. Keep all trail to a minimum, do a lot of it verbally. Nothing on email, nothing digital. We think we're immune from hackers, but we're not. No one can hack into a burned paper file.'

'Too true.' Wilde downed the rest of his glass and stared at the bottom of it. 'This must have taken some planning?'

'Yes,' he says. 'It originated from Langley. The Director of Special Forces wanted to loop in Vauxhall Cross to make sure any product was passed along the system.'

Wilde nods. 'So why, if it's not too delicate a question, am I just being told about it now? This is my patch, after all.'

Vine has prepared for this and knows the answer. He doesn't look at Wilde, but just repeats it straight up. 'Need to know,' he says. 'I had to be sure that the mission was green-lit by the NSC first. It was too sensitive to risk sharing within the Office before I knew it was going to last . . . Same rules we all play by.'

'And others?'

'The usual. MoD, Number 10.'

'Of course,' says Wilde. 'Understood.'

They talk on about the wider landscape, consulate gossip, seeing how far they can revive the easy patter of their past existence. But it is gone now, Vine realizes. They can survive on grains of the deep bond they once had, an almost fraternal impression of conversation. But the division runs too deep. Wilde is bored by it, any hint of ill-feeling an intrusion on his happiness; Vine is unable to let the events of the past slip, syllables freighted with the overwhelming fact of the betrayal. They tread water, waiting for the other to leave.

It is only when Wilde makes the first move and excuses himself to the bathroom that Vine picks up the two empty glasses and makes his way back through the dining room. He stops midway. A small square hatch at the end of the room to the kitchen area is now open. Through it he sees Rose in the middle of making lunch. She is cutting bread in smooth, thick slices, the old rebelliousness tamed into a foretaste of middle age. Youth is deserting them all now.

Just before Rose looks up and spots him, Vine is surprised by Wilde returning. 'Think Rose is preparing lunch of some sort,' he says, voice loud with false brightness. His old careless physicality is restrained now, hands resting above his hips. 'Told her you probably wouldn't want to stay. Work never stops for Solomon Vine.'

Vine nods and mutters something about needing to get back. He conjures up a final parting from Rose and notices the lack of a second invitation. He heads back down the hall, trying to dampen the surge of fresh anger he feels, the bitterness so raw he can almost taste it in his mouth.

Wilde stops at the door and looks out over the pristine quiet of the scene ahead of them. It is sealed from danger behind their imposing gates and expensive security alarms, the make-believe of official living.

It was a mistake to have come, Vine realizes. He wants more than anything to get away, back to the emotionally airbrushed life he has learned to be content with.

'Do you mind if I say something,' Wilde says, at last. He caresses his jaw, as if modelling for some cosmic photographer.

Vine is stunned into politeness. 'No . . . of course not.'

Wilde nods. 'Just be careful, Sol.' He pauses, eyes dipping to the ground. 'It's not a competition, you know. We're meant to work as a team.'

Vine feels the heat oppress him. He can hear Cecil's cadences in the speech, realizes that they must still be talking frequently, Wilde forever Cecil's apprentice; wonders too if all this has just been for show, Wilde already briefed on the details behind his back. 'What are you saying?'

Wilde tries to sugar his next sentence with a further pretence of uneasiness, a shuffling of the feet and an unconvincing folding of the arms. 'I just wouldn't want to think that you were letting any of our past difficulties influence things . . .'

'You're an articulate man, Gabriel,' snaps Vine, unable to bear Wilde's courtly attempts at politeness. 'Just say it.'

Wilde smiles disarmingly. His jet-black forelock tumbles again over his brow, the casual disorder Vine has never been able to copy. 'I'm just saying that we're dealing with people here. It's not a game of chess. I know you hate me for what happened, and I'm sorry about that. Truly, I am. But it would be a terrible conclusion to our own personal situation if it ended up costing other men their lives.'

Later, Vine can never quite decipher exactly what prompts him to do what he does next.

It happens in a second. He isn't conscious of the movement of his arm or any rational decision to do it. Rather, it is suddenly done, unable to be undone. The right arm is bunched, windmilled and cracked into the lower jaw. There is the burning aftershock and the crumbling form of Wilde forced backwards and losing his footing, a whinny of pain.

There is a dreadful anti-climax and a silence so complete that only Wilde's faint groans confirm what has just occurred. A spatter of blood colours the stone steps, the ringing crack of bone on bone.

Vine stands, feeling nothing.

Then the eerie silence is broken by hurried feet down the hall. Rose fills out the view, running towards them. 'What have you done?' she shouts, breathing heavily. Her eyes are glassy with surprise. 'What the hell have you done?'

Vine can't summon any words. He is too taken aback by the jagged volume of her voice, the nameless *you*.

'I'm sorry,' he manages to mutter eventually, though he is not. He would do it again. He has filled too many hours with the ways in which he will inflict justice on Gabriel Wilde.

'Go,' she says. She refuses to pay him the courtesy of looking up. Her voice is quieter, the lack of noise like a wordless condemnation. 'Please, Solomon . . . Just leave us.'

## 37

'Cast your mind back,' said Cecil, settling into his armchair. The fire continued to crackle. Outside, there was nothing more than the light tread of the DPG officers.

By 2013, said Cecil, the storyteller baritone in full swing, the Service had just about recovered from its lowest point. The previous decade's fiasco over WMDs and the dodgy dossier was starting to drift into the recesses of Whitehall's memory. MI6 had survived almost intact, even if it had ceded ground to MI5, with its shiny Joint Terrorism Analysis Centre. But it was still in business. That, ultimately, was all that mattered.

Then the unthinkable happened. Just as things seemed to be settling down, the summer of 2013 saw the worst intelligence leak since the Cambridge Five. Edward Snowden, an NSA contractor, stole a treasure trove of highly classified files implicating the UK and US intelligence establishments in a mass surveillance programme. The leak was lapped up by the media. Almost immediately, every terrorist group around the world had first-hand confirmation that the main threat to their lives came not from bombs but their own mobile phones.

From that moment on, Western intelligence faced one of its greatest challenges yet. Every major terrorist leader on our radar vanished almost overnight. Mobile phones were ditched, and groups went back to using pen and paper. Embassies stocked up on typewriters. Even Number 10 began to forbid senior ministers from carrying their phones into Cabinet meetings. So reliant had we become on SIGINT, we faced complete obsolescence. Without a signal to trace, Vauxhall Cross was reduced to watching paint dry. Some in the Treasury would have pulled our funding without a second thought.

Whitehall went into one of its habitual panics for nearly twelve months. Old Soviet hands were hauled back in to teach new recruits what old-fashioned HUMINT was all about. All the while the civil war in Syria continued to rage. Libya descended further into chaos. Iran continued with its nuclear shenanigans despite pious utterances otherwise. And a newly militant Russia seemed intent on rediscovering its former glory.

'Then came the knockout blow,' said Cecil. 'In June 2014 there was a geopolitical first. It was what every intelligence chief had always feared, but as yet had never come to pass. A non-state actor took control of Mosul in Iraq. Not only that, the so-called Islamic State soon proclaimed the restoration of the caliphate. Every politician in Whitehall and on Capitol Hill was predicting the destruction of civilization. Not only had the intelligence community lost any hope of tracking terrorists, we were now facing the very real prospect of the end of the world order as we knew it.

'Unless we came up with a solution, Vauxhall Cross would have been mothballed by Number 10. They needed product, and they needed it now. The answer required something far more daring. It had to be something that put everything on the line, human intelligence gathering and an act of personal valour that no fragment of computer code could ever contemplate.'

Here Cecil paused. He seemed faintly nervous, as if about to cross a line with no chance of return.

'In the summer of 2014,' he continued, 'a top-secret operation – so secret it was never even given a formal code-name for fear it could be identified – was born on the fifth floor. Such was the secrecy involved that only eight people in the world were briefed on its activities. On the UK side: C, the Prime Minister, the Foreign Secretary and the Defence Secretary; on the US side, the Director of the CIA, the President, the White House National Security Adviser and the Vice-President. All MI6 protocol was overridden, with product from the operation carried straight to C and the Prime Minister. No one else in the Istanbul consulate would be briefed on it, not even the Ambassador himself. It was off the books, not ever to be considered part of open government.'

Vine felt his throat tighten. His chest beat harder. 'And what was this operation?'

Cecil breathed louder, running a hand across the prickles of stubble dotting his chin. 'Nothing less than an attempt to convince Islamist groups in Syria that a high-ranking MI6 officer was willing to turn double and pass classified intelligence and military secrets to them. That someone within British intelligence was willing to play traitor. We could pass disinformation on drone strikes and get gold in return. Repaying our debts by helping Langley with better coordinates for their MQ-9s, hence the American presence on the distribution list.'

Vine felt all his assumptions shake and fall away. He could hear Olivia Cartier's words on Wilde: *If you want my theory, I got the impression he was working on something. Something big.* He thought back to his interview with the Deputy Head of Station, Wilde's loud disgust at the effects of Western foreign policy and the note from the Prime Minister's PPS in Olivia's bag.

Suddenly, everything began to make sense. 'All of which would require a top-level Arabist, sympathy with the region, perhaps even some Middle Eastern blood,' he said, the logic of it all beginning to piece together in his mind. 'A record of once having flirted with the movement at university, perhaps even suspicion of being a practising Muslim.'

*As far as the fifth floor seemed concerned, Gabriel Wilde was untouchable.*

*There was a mat . . .*

*To wash away the blood on his hands for good.*

Cecil's voice betrayed his tiredness, the vowel sounds frayed. He nodded. 'There was only ever one officer who could perform such a task,' he said, rubbing at his eyes. 'If caught, he faced almost certain death. For all we knew, the various Islamist cells across the border might never buy it. If it went wrong, the repercussions could be catastrophic. In order to protect ourselves, it was clear that MI6 and Downing Street would deny all knowledge if he was exposed, cast him off as an actual traitor, perhaps even threaten prosecution. There are few people on earth who have the courage to agree to something like that. This was a disinformation campaign on the level of a double cross. Even fewer people so sure of their abilities that they might pull it off.'

'But Gabriel Wilde was one of them.'

Cecil raised his cigar, as if toasting the memory. 'Indeed he was.'

Vine sat back, barely noticing the force of the sofa against his body. As the truth began to work its way into his system, he felt suddenly unclean, momentarily overwhelmed by the idea of Gabriel Wilde's face, that confident humour, torn to shreds in an airless cell somewhere, welcoming the prospect of death. That single line played through his mind once again.

*My name is Nobody . . .*

His reverie was broken only by another pang of understanding, memories of his second conversation with Olivia Cartier in the Palace of Westminster: *it's all somehow connected to Yousef.* His head shot up, gazing at Cecil, who watched him patiently, as if waiting for him to reach the obvious conclusion.

'But, that means . . .'

'Yes,' said Cecil. 'Yes, it does. It means that there is only one way our troublesome Dr Yousef could possibly know there was a mole working in the region.'

'If he was, in fact, in contact with Islamist groups in Syria.'

'Quite so. Not just an academic sympathizer, but in touch with the top brass.'

Vine flicked through the list of names Cecil had told him: C, Prime Minister, Foreign Secretary, Defence Secretary. 'So Newton knew nothing . . .'

'No. And he damn well nearly blew the entire thing. Running rogue investigations even though we had put a ban on anything to do with Yousef. Fate, thankfully, intervened on our behalf.'

Vine thought of Newton's body on the train tracks, the fallback in the safe deposit box and the note buried at the station café. Was that all Newton's death had been – fate? 'So that was why you told me to release Yousef?' he said.

Cecil seemed almost annoyed with Vine's naivety. 'Yes,' he said. 'Ahmed Yousef thought he was buying himself immunity by telling us about the Nobody mole. In fact, he was telling us about our own operation and inadvertently condemning himself. We needed him out in the field to lead us to his superiors. That's why I ordered you to release him . . . It was our chance to reel in the catch of the century . . .'

Despite himself, Vine could see the reasoning. 'So . . . if this remains highly classified, why are you telling me?'

Cecil rose from his chair, stretching out his arms to regain some feeling and pacing towards the curtains. He peered out at the gravel driveway. 'Because recently we've been picking up a surge in chatter about new threats to London.'

'A revenge attack?'

Cecil closed the curtain and walked back towards Vine. 'I think that the kidnap and murder of a British double agent won't be enough for them, no matter how much publicity they get out of it. They will want to launch a retaliatory strike in the country that devised the operation. If Ahmed Yousef heads up a cell in Britain, then he is the perfect person to do it. Branded a saint by the high priests of the liberal elite, vouched for by Members of Parliament. He is beyond reproof, beyond suspicion. Who better to take revenge upon the country that dared to infiltrate your organization? Anyone who tried to stop him would be a social outcast.'

'You think a plot is imminent?'

'Yes.'

'And Wilde?'

Cecil sat back down in his armchair and crossed his legs. For once Vine thought he saw the thespian mask slip – eyes bloodshot and rimmed with grey, wrinkles decorating the mouth. Cecil looked exhausted with the depravity of the world. 'These groups have always been masters of publicity. My best guess is that they will time Wilde's execution at the precise moment they launch the attack, gaining maximum airtime and maximum terror.'

'So that is why I'm here?'

Cecil looked up at him. He fished out a white handkerchief and blew loudly. 'Now he is back in the land of the living, there is no way we can run ongoing surveillance on Yousef through official channels as we have done in the past. You are only the second person beyond the initial eight to have been inducted into the truth about Wilde, and it will remain that way for the time being. I need someone who knows the terrain, is outside the system and has nothing to lose. You are the only person who fits that brief. I can give you a small team, whatever reasonable leftover technology we have and the use of a safe house in Kensington we have managed to keep out of the gaze of the Treasury. No one knows Wilde and Yousef like you do. There is no one else I can ask, no one else in your situation. This is outside Five, GCHQ, the National Security Council, Number 10. Completely deniable.'

Vine tried to hide his sense of shock and elation at the request. He had expected an unofficial advisory role, perhaps, nothing on this scale. 'You said I was one of two to know the truth? Who is the other person?'

Cecil fixed him another mercurial stare, eyes still glinting through the tiredness. 'Rose Wilde, or Spencer as she is now calling herself, since the separation.'

'She didn't know already?'

'She knew Gabriel was doing something, never the full contents. It was too dangerous.'

Vine thought of Olivia's allusion to Wilde's marital difficulties. He tried to imagine the strain such work would put on a relationship, the sheer pressure of juggling so many selves.

*In case we don't meet again, I want you to have this. All wisdom lies in this book. Take care of Rose for me . . .*

'You're not telling me that she is . . .'

'Yes,' said Cecil. 'That's exactly what I'm telling you. She's been filling in back at Thames House. But there is no keeping her away from this. She's currently on compassionate leave. She did a lot on the legal side of this back in the day and knows this space better than most. I can't afford to let her sit silently on the bench. If we are going to stop Yousef, then I need her in on the operation. The only question is whether you can work with her.'

Vine felt hollowed out at the idea. Yet with every twitch of concern he thought again of Wilde, mutilated beyond recognition, tortured for every secret he had ever known. Now was no time for petty personal grievances.

'Of course,' he said, the lie flowing easily.

'Good,' said Cecil, getting up again and poking at the charred aftermath of a log. The room had become decidedly chilly, a bitter draught filling the space around them. 'Let it remain that way. I need a few more days to make some calls, then the safe house is all yours.'

'And what about trying to find Wilde? I presume there is something underway?'

Cecil continued staring at the fireplace, lost in his own thoughts. 'That I really can't tell you, I'm afraid. But, yes. On both sides of the Atlantic, we are doing everything we can to find him before it's too late.'

Vine felt the conversation fizzle away. The end had been signalled. Daylight was already beginning to leak through from outside. He got up and tried to move his feet to ward off pins and needles.

Cecil moved towards the door, and Vine followed him out into the hall. 'Get some sleep,' he said. 'You won't be getting much for the next few weeks, that's for sure.' He stopped, looked down at the tips of his shoes, then back up at Vine. 'I know we've had our differences. But you and Wilde were two of the best intelligence officers I've ever had the privilege to see. If anyone can sort out this mess, I know you can. Succeed in this, and miracles can happen. We can put Yousef away for the rest of his life. No more tribunals, investigations, reports. You can be back where you belong.'

'And the police charges? Breaking and entering at the Palace of Westminster?'

Cecil looked half-amused. 'We'll deal with it. A misunderstanding, that's all.'

Vine didn't answer. He just acknowledged it with a nod. It was what he had been longing to hear ever since the suspension – a way back and the chance for redemption.

He saw Cecil stare at him, as if there was one final test before he was allowed to return to the fold. 'By the way . . . when Newton died, I don't suppose he left you anything, did he?'

'No,' said Vine, without missing a beat. 'Nothing at all.' He looked at Cecil, wondering for a moment if he should tell him about the other parts of Newton's quest: the hunt for the truth about the MIDAS operation and the anonymous Gmail account. They were the only remaining parts of the puzzle he had still to solve, but parts that Newton must have thought explained the whole. Curiosity almost forced the words out, before he stopped himself. Newton hadn't trusted Cecil with the information; he couldn't afford to either. And yet the truth about the MIDAS operation haunted him still – the redacted file, the involvement of the CIA, the calculated absence from the computer database. Something had happened on 2 September 2011 that cast fresh light on the Nobody mole and Gabriel Wilde's disappearance, something that might explain what really went on that day in Istanbul.

He heard the door shut behind him and saw the Range Rover waiting to drive him back. He walked across the gravel front, trying to analyse the implications of all he had learned and all that remained cloaked in mystery.

Soon, however, he found all thoughts were colonized by one person, the memories to whom everything inevitably returned.

Rose.

# PART FOUR

## 38

It was just after rush hour, a desultory trickle of commuters and shoppers still picking their way past each other, beeping themselves through the ticket barriers. As Vine walked out of South Kensington station, he felt strangely calm. He slowed to watch the routine scenes outside the touristy cafés, walking up past the Natural History Museum and the campus of Imperial, letting the sugar-rush of anticipation claim him.

As he approached the safe house, he knew it must be an anti-climax. After what had happened, Rose had come to acquire a sort of mythic status in his mind. She was the woman who got away, carrying with her the promise of a life he had never had the chance to live. Only months after the betrayal, the newly minted Rose Wilde had left for Istanbul. Vine had spent too long encasing a version of her with regret at all he had lost. As he continued up Exhibition Road, he knew his ideal couldn't sustain prolonged contact with reality. He would be forced to acknowledge that the fault lay not in the stars, but within himself.

The house in Prince's Gardens was suitably anonymous, with similar buildings either side. It had three floors, two neo-classical pillars framing a nondescript black front door. The street was half-busy, mostly students on their way to and from lectures. It was the perfect place to lose yourself, neither dingy enough to attract attention nor lavish enough to look like anything other than the home of a high-up in the City.

Vine buzzed, gave the agreed password – 'Tennyson' – and opened the door. Downstairs everything looked normal: a spotless kitchen on the left, a laundry room with a washing machine and tumble dryer straight ahead. There was even a collection of boots and coats on the pegs for show. To the burgling or door-knocking classes, this was a house like any other.

He walked up the stairs to the first floor, where he could hear music seeping out from the main room down the hall. The door was ajar and he pushed at it. The curtains were open, though the windows were all covered with thick blinds finely tailored to the perimeters of the frames. The sepulchral gloom only served to highlight the plethora of screens and IT equipment. There were two giant screens on the wall to the right. Leading up to it were desks busy with computer monitors, most of them currently blank. Around him, wiring dribbled over the wooden floorboards. From a small pair of speakers blasted tinny strains of Beethoven's Fifth.

Hearing the tread on the floorboards, a large bespectacled man in a tweed jacket and green cords hurriedly dived to turn the music off. Having done so, he stood up and approached, moist, fleshy palm outstretched.

'Sorry for the accompaniment,' he said. 'Still trying to get the kit all set up so we can crack on at midday. Eliot Montague, nerd in residence. You must be Solomon Vine?'

'The very one,' said Vine, shaking Montague's hand. 'Anyone else arrived yet?'

'No. We're expecting the others by eleven.'

'Good.' Vine closed the door, stepped over another tangle of cables and drew up a swivel chair near to where Montague was working. 'So how did you err?' he asked, crossing his legs. 'Why have you been condemned to type code for me rather than in the thick of it at Vauxhall Cross?'

Montague adjusted his glasses. 'GCHQ, actually,' he said. 'Slight run-in with the Official Secrets Act. A few things I disagreed with during an operation, had a glass too many with a university friend from *The Times*. It was this or a spell inside.'

Vine smiled. 'I warn you, the food here will probably be worse.'

'I'll take my chances.'

'So what am I looking at?' he asked, casting his eyes round the second-hand IT equipment they would have to use. 'How close can we get to Yousef?'

Montague's eyes widened as he turned towards Vine. 'Depends how many questions you're going to ask,' he said. 'I am correct in thinking this is off the books?'

'Completely,' said Vine. 'And don't worry. Don't ask, don't tell as far as I'm concerned, though stay out of GCHQ territory as far as possible. We'll avoid trying to hack CCTV systems to begin with. But nailing Yousef is all I'm concerned about.'

'All the better, then,' said Montague. 'Plugging into the CCTV systems around his house would have been ideal, making it much easier to locate his movements. But we can establish a decent profile through other channels.'

'Anything else?'

'By this afternoon, I should have been able to do a general sweep of his digital footprint.'

'And what about the comms side?' asked Vine. 'If he is plotting something, there's got to be people he's working with in Britain. Some sort of sleeper cell.'

Montague nodded. 'Depends if they've gone completely Moscow Rules on us and are back to pen and paper. Most likely using burner phones. If I get enough time, I can trace calls. We should be able to get something at any rate.'

Vine got up and walked around the electronic debris in the room. He thought of Wilde holed up somewhere in Syria, being tortured for every secret he knew and the scale of a possible revenge attack. If there was going to be another major strike on UK soil then money would have to be transferred somehow.

'I need everything you can find me on Yousef's finances,' he said. 'Bank account, tax records, recent expenditure. See if there's anything that can't be explained. Whatever he's planning, there will need to be equipment and logistical back-up. That's the first place to start. Once the others arrive, we can try and put some surveillance on him and begin tracking movements.'

'Sure thing,' said Montague, getting up and prodding screens into life.

'And one thing,' said Vine. 'If we're found out, then we all go down. Don't advertise yourself when hacking into these systems. If anyone finds out what we're doing, prison food will be the least of your problems.'

Montague smiled. 'You haven't read my file, have you?' he said.

'Should I have done?'

'I designed most of these systems when I was at Imperial, a nice earner on the side. I know how to get in and out of them better than anyone else on earth.'

Vine turned back towards the blanked-out windows. 'Which is why I know you weren't thrown out of GCHQ for indiscretions to *The Times*,' he said. He caught a guilty frown on Montague's face. 'You were granted a reprieve from extradition by the Home Secretary. Which must mean you did something pretty phenomenal. My guess is hacked into the Pentagon's system.'

'Ah,' said Montague, all the computers now shuddering into action, the room partially lit by the glow of the screens.

'As I said, be careful. I'll ask no questions but I expect no surprises either. Do we understand each other?'

Montague nodded. 'Well enough, I think.'

'Good.' The buzzer on the intercom sounded, a shrill, nasal blast. 'I'll get it,' said Vine, wandering out to the hall and towards the handset on the landing. He stopped in front of it, praying that it would be either one of the pavement artists. But somehow he knew it wouldn't. As he picked up the phone, he felt his long-tended composure begin to crack.

'Tennyson,' she said, her voice somehow more completely hers than he remembered.

He put the phone down, pressed the key symbol and heard the door – to the past, or the future, he couldn't be sure – push open.

## 39

'So how have you been?'

Vine took a sip of his black filter coffee and wondered how on earth he could construct a satisfactory answer. He looked across at Rose, struggling to believe after all this time that she was actually sitting opposite him, alone. Up close, she looked barely changed from when he had last seen her: the hair was slightly shorter, styled sideways across her fringe; but the cheeks, lips, the warmth of her eyes caused the same flutter in his stomach as they always had. She was wearing a red dress with a black tailored jacket, more formal than when she would tramp into Thames House in a favourite baggy green jumper, the eternal student. It was different too from the expat look she had perfected in Istanbul. But she still retained that impish smile, more seductive by its very artlessness.

'I've had my ups and downs,' he said.

'I heard about your suspension and Yousef. That must have been tough . . . What happened?'

It was the question that still haunted him. Someone had set him up that day in Istanbul, someone with access on the inside. It was the one detail Cecil had refused to discuss, as if embarrassed by his own ignorance. Even four months later, Vine could still remember every detail of those moments: seeing Wilde's car pulling away, the number of cigarettes he'd smoked, the precise choreography of it all. Was it possible that Wilde had returned that day and taken out Yousef before he let slip the truth about the existence of the Nobody mole?

Had Wilde set him up in order to keep his operation alive, an operation he had given everything for?

Vine dragged himself back to the here and now. As he took another sip of coffee and felt the normality of the café around them, he was newly beguiled by her eyes. He wanted to somehow apologize again for the scene at their house, Wilde felled on the steps. But he couldn't. He found himself still unable to form the words.

'That's why I'm here,' he said, dodging her question. 'A chance to get Yousef for good. The truth will come out eventually, that's all I've got to believe. He can play the saint only for so long. If we can pin some evidence on him, then my life can get back to normal.'

They were sitting in the branch of Pret on Brompton Road, tucked away at a corner table well out of the earshot of others.

'And how about you? My problems are nothing. Cecil said he'd told you everything?'

She nodded, cupping her hands around the mug, steam drifting from the surface. 'Yes,' she said, looking out of the window. Her voice sounded far away, distracted.

Vine wondered what could possibly be going through her mind. The endless tales about Wilde's libertine existence still wouldn't change the trauma of knowing a man you had once loved was being broken piece by piece.

He knew he shouldn't pry, but was unable to help it. 'Did you have any idea?'

She looked back at him and tried to work a smile on to her lips. 'No,' she said. 'He was too good for that. I knew he was preparing for something . . . if anything, I was almost glad when Cecil told me what it was.'

'How do you mean?'

She seemed uneasy about the logic of her own assumptions. She tried to coat it with a shake of the head and a dismissive smile. 'Nothing, really. There was a point when I was worried he was about to do something stupid.' There was another tentative sip and a sigh. 'Come back to the house with a USB stick and tell me we had to run away. So few people know what it's like out there. What the threat of war can do to you. My nightmare was that one day I'd open the newspaper and see his face all over it.'

Vine delayed his next question, allowing a beat of silence. He felt his own suspicions consolidate again, refusing to disappear entirely. There was still something off, quietly inexplicable, about the book Wilde had sent him, needling at any sense of resolution. What better way for a true double agent to cover himself than volunteering for such a mission? Every possible action could be justified. Wilde could be passing all manner of secrets and Cecil would be playing the unwitting accomplice. It was a faultless disguise.

*My name is Nobody* . . .

'Was that when . . . ?'

She looked completely unembarrassed, as if she'd had this conversation too many times to care. 'Yes,' she said. 'Separation was inevitable, really. The affairs, the secrets. I couldn't stand waking up every morning and wondering if I was going to make it through the day. I wanted him to try and find a desk job back in London, perhaps leave the Service altogether. I was tired of my legal work. I wanted to come back to Thames House. But he wouldn't listen.'

Here she stopped almost completely. Her body language became frigid. Her smile was rustier, movements gummed up with some unspoken emotion. She toyed with her hair, brushing it away from her face, casting her gaze down at the middle of the table and resting her chin on her right hand.

Vine could see Cecil in his armchair relating the news about the classified operation as if it were a piece of gossip. 'There's nothing wrong in admitting you feel cheated,' he said. 'We spend our lives in a house of lies. In the end, all it does is corrode us. It stops us being able to believe that anything can ever be real. We can't believe the happiness, so we're always just left with the pain.'

She looked up at him, extending a warm hand and placing it over his. She smiled a sad, drawn smile. 'You always were the wise one,' she said. As quickly as it was offered, the hand darted back and was tucked away in the fold of her elbow. 'So . . . Yousef. Our off-the-books piece of intrigue. You're starting with the bank records?'

Her voice had changed again, flipping back to singsong brightness. He knew the agony of being exiled from the action. Perhaps being here was the only way she could cope.

'You're sure you're up for this?' he said, pushing his mug away from him. 'Given everything you're going through.'

All traces of emotion had been banished from her face. 'If Yousef is connected to the kidnap of Gabriel, then the entire British army couldn't keep me away from this operation. He may have driven me mad at times, made me sadder than I knew I could be, but I did – I *do* – love him. And I'll do anything to get him back.'

Despite himself, Vine could hear that single syllable replay in his mind again and again. He nodded and locked away the feeling of her hand brushing his across the table.

'Of course,' he lied. 'That makes two of us.'

# 40

In the following days, Vine became a whirl of restless activity, the rhythmic tick of day and night meaningless behind the thick blinds that drowned out all natural light. When he stared in the mirror of the poky second-floor bathroom, he saw his eyes had become terminally bleary. His forehead was lined and voice hollow. But on he went, drawn to the magnetic pulse of the screens in front of him, excavating files, chasing leads, churning the flurry of detail through his mind. Anything to find out more about where Ahmed Yousef might be planning to strike.

He could feel himself retreat into his usual monastic insularity, an air of prickliness descend on his mood, dismissive, cold even, as if attributing any merit to others proved weakness.

As the full scale of his insomniac life became public, he began to be aware of mutterings from the others, even catching Montague discussing it in the hall with Rose when he imagined Vine was out of earshot.

'You realize he hasn't slept for over two days,' Montague said, voice lowered to a conspiratorial hush. 'Not even a sleeping bag, or a kip on the sofa . . . I tried to raise it once, but he didn't seem amused.'

'I know,' said Rose. 'Probably better not to go there again.'

'Understood. Is there something more to this that the rest of us don't know about?'

'No,' said Rose, a certainty in her tone. 'It's just Solomon being Solomon, I'm afraid. He was always like this on operations.'

So commenced the period of waiting. It was one of the tests Newton and his subordinates used to devise at the Fort, scanning for signs of repressed daredevilry. New recruits were forced to conduct gruelling surveillance exercises on faceless houses along the English coast. The lack of point was the entire point, the brutal grind of tracking a person's movements an introduction to the reality of the secret world.

While Montague worked on fine-tuning the tech-ops side back at Prince's Gardens, Vine accompanied the two watchers – Waugh and Anderson – on physical surveillance, taking the back seat in the carousel of vehicles the team used (smart BMW, flaking Audi, battle-scarred Ford) and watched the ripple of activity from Yousef's house on Cumberland Street. Every day he amused himself with the character he was inhabiting, the theatrical flourish learned at the hands of a surveillance expert all those years ago during training. He smiled again at the codename for the mole. The ultimate task of any decent spook was always to become just another Nobody.

It was early on the fourth day that it happened. Yousef had stayed in, as he often did, buried in research work thanks to the wonders of Google Books. Then, out of nowhere, he broke his hibernation, left the house at 9.30 and got into the Astra parked near the pavement. The clothes were different. Not his usual professorial jacket and nondescript formal trousers, but casual: a bluish check shirt, jeans and slip-on footwear. He moved gingerly – inevitable after a period out of action – but with pinpoint accuracy.

'Let's follow him,' said Vine.

'You sure?' said Anderson. 'He could be a decoy, in case they think they're being watched. Try and shake us off before the real magic happens.'

Vine shook his head. 'Where's Waugh?'

'Doing the rounds on Warwick Way.'

'Tell him to keep his eyes open and inform us if anything kicks off here,' Vine said, pausing before trusting his instinct. 'Then start the engine and let's see where he takes us.'

Anderson duly radioed to Waugh, then edged out to follow the Astra.

Vine called through to update Montague and Rose at Prince's Gardens. Then he fell back into silence. They dodged through jams and made sure they kept up a good sightline on the vehicle. He relaxed slightly as the Astra turned off on to the M4, then the M5. Anderson remained silent, not daring to flick the radio on in case it disrupted Vine's train of thought. Instead, they endured the constant purr of the motorway, occasionally veering into the overtaking lane as the Astra sped onwards.

Just over two hours after leaving Cumberland Street, they took the turning for the A4018. They followed the Astra as it signalled and weaved its way towards a large car park littered with vehicles. Up ahead stood a vast glass edifice, customers trickling out laden with shopping bags.

'Off for a bit of retail therapy?' Anderson said, as he took a space far enough away from the Astra to avoid being seen, killing the engine.

'Perhaps,' said Vine, his voice toneless. 'Though if he couldn't find it in the shops in London, I doubt he'll find it here.'

'What do you reckon then? Brush pass? Dead drop?'

Vine got out of the car. He looked at the building and the revolving glass doors leading into the glow of a department store. 'Some sort of dead drop,' he said. 'Good location.

Plenty of places to lose yourself. Poor CCTV coverage. I couldn't have picked it better myself.'

Anderson shut the door, locking it with a bleep of the key. He followed Vine's lead in pursuit towards the entrance. 'How many floors do you reckon?'

'Two levels, three at most. Quiet time of day, so the only other customers are the elderly and students.'

'How long?'

'Not more than an hour. Service the drop and head back to London.'

They were fifty metres behind Yousef now. They pushed through the revolving doors into the department store, bathed in a kitschy gold. The target didn't pause, walking straight through until he emerged into the main shopping mall, an airless rectangular strip with shop windows lined up either side. It was busier than Vine had thought, the crowd a mix of the snowy-haired and middle-aged, mothers pushing buggies and jacketed men browsing the latest smartphones. There was something so greyly anonymous about such a building, the dull overhead lights, music piped through tinny speakers, recycled air with no sense of temperature. Everyone became the same, the swell of forgettable faces and forgettable clothes. The dead white light of a shopping mall was the perfect place to lose yourself.

Sure enough, the target spent the first half hour dissembling. Yousef started wandering through the aisles of a clothes shop, then wasted a bored handful of minutes in a bookshop, leafing through a cookery book with evident lack of enthusiasm. The final part of this initial period he spent perched on a stool in Starbucks on the upper floor, sipping timidly at a latte in a tall, thin glass. Vine kept up contact while scanning a magazine in the newsagents opposite. Anderson patrolled the corridor outside.

Lulled as they were by the gentle pace, they almost missed him. Anderson had finished an approach and was wearily treading back in the direction of a cosmetics store. Vine was on the verge of letting tiredness take him, stifling a yawn. It was only muscle memory, an eternal vigilance, which caught the empty seat and the haze of blue disappearing down the escalator.

Breaking protocol – Anderson leading, Vine hovering to protect his identity – Vine began pursuing. He let Yousef establish sufficient distance, then he dropped the magazine and followed. He left it to Anderson to spot the move and change into a support role while Vine quickened his pace towards the escalator to keep eyes-on.

He watched Yousef descend towards the lower floor and get off at the end of the escalator. The pace slowed. Yousef strolled over to the glassy expanse of the large Gap store window below. Then he stopped to stare at the display. Yousef looked relaxed, hands resting loosely near his jean pockets, eyes locked in a seemingly formless browse.

Vine felt his insides curdle. He quickly angled his body away from the reflection just in time and reached for the phone in his pocket, putting it to his ear and seamlessly climbing back up. He kept on walking without so much as a glance behind.

Only when he was out of the frame did he risk another look. It was harder here, the view obscured by fake shrubbery and kiosks below cluttering his line of sight.

He walked faster, still keeping a read on the ripple of shirt collar now dissolving in the sea of similar jeans, t-shirts and overcoats. Vine reached the entrance to the newsagents again. He saw Yousef stop below and conduct another lengthy session of window-scanning, then retrace his steps back down the mall.

Anderson was behind him. 'What happened?'

'He's not shopping, that's for sure,' said Vine.

'A drop?'

Vine shook his head. He was both annoyed with himself and yet quietly satisfied. It was the first concrete sign of intent, calculated tradecraft. After this, there could be no doubt that Yousef was planning something. Every move confirmed it – the change of clothes, leaving London, choosing the perfect place to draw out a tail.

'No,' he said. 'We got it wrong. This isn't a brush pass or a drop. This is basic counter-surveillance. That's what it was all for. Yousef suspects he's being followed. He was trying to isolate us so he could confirm it.'

'Did he see you?'

There was a stony silence. Anderson caught Vine's expression.

'Sorry,' he said. 'Stupid question.'

## 41

Vine nodded to a member of the security detail and slid into the back seat of the armoured Jaguar XJ, catching a waft of expensive aftershave. The door shut behind him.

'This will have to be quick,' said Cecil. He flicked through another email on his phone and then tucked it away in his jacket pocket. 'I've got half the Cabinet waiting for me at Banqueting House, most of whom think Ahmed Yousef should be given a knighthood in the New Year's honours list for services to martyrdom. What do you need?'

Vine had spent most of the day debating how to frame this, sugaring an admission of failure. 'We're running at maximum capacity but not getting anything. We've gone into every record we can and found nothing.'

Cecil was moving impatiently in his seat. 'So what do you want?'

'Step it up. Access to all public surveillance equipment.' Vine tried to keep his voice calm. 'I wouldn't ask if it wasn't vital. Unless I am allocated a larger team, then any other surveillance exercise is going to get burned eventually. This guy has spent years of his life dodging watchers. If he really is planning an attack as we speak, then it's the only way.'

'Do you have any product yet?'

'I might have something on a mobile number. But to find anything more we need a proper run at it. With only two watchers, that means a hell of a lot of changes. Eventually, Yousef will catch us. We have to get into the CCTV.'

Cecil sighed. He stroked away a crease on his shirtfront, then turned his gaze to Vine. 'There's no way I can get a warrant, if that's what you mean. As I told you, ministers would hang me out to dry.'

Vine waited. He watched Cecil's face, letting the silence goad him.

'Cover your tracks and make sure you give yourself a reason to be inside the system,' said Cecil, staring straight ahead. 'If you end up sitting in a police interrogation room, I won't be there to get you out this time. Understood?'

Vine nodded. 'Perfectly.'

He was halfway out of the car when he heard Cecil's voice behind him. The tone was different, less brash. 'And make sure Rose is fully briefed on everything you're doing,' he said. 'If something happens, we need another pair of eyes. Someone who knows their way around all the material. Team work, if you know the meaning of the phrase. I want her and Montague in the room on everything.'

Vine tried not to let any anxiety infect his voice. 'Why . . . something the matter?'

Cecil adopted his diplomat's face, an uneasy softening of the brow. 'Just politics, Vine,' he said. 'Always the bloody politics.'

# 42

Back at Prince's Gardens, he buzzed, gave the password, pushed the door open and began tramping up the stairs. There were some old leads he wanted to check again, trawling for a clue he might have missed. He reached the main ops room, saw a light on and was about to try and force himself into a display of bonhomie by asking Anderson if he wanted a drink. Then he opened the door to find Rose sitting alone in the middle of the spider's web of cables.

The room seemed vaster than usual somehow, the screens speckling the view with flashing greens and reds.

'I told Anderson to have the night off,' said Rose, holding a remote in her palm. 'I couldn't sleep.'

Vine took off his jacket and sat down next to her, the BBC News channel mute on the first big screen up ahead. He remembered Cosmo Newton's comments what seemed like a lifetime ago at Cambridge during his recruitment interview: *New modes of warfare.* This is what twenty-first century spying looked like.

'Don't you find it funny sometimes,' said Rose, stifling a yawn. 'The amount of power we have. A whole city at the click of a button.'

Vine sat back, allowing himself an inch of relaxation. 'Did you ever check anyone out?' he said.

Rose laughed. 'I beg your pardon?'

'At the start. Friends, enemies from university, family members . . .'

'A firing offence.'

'It was Gabriel's favourite trick for new dates. Get a contact at Five to find him something juicy and then slip it into conversation.'

'That sounds like him.'

'Used to scare the hell out of people.'

Rose laughed again. She pressed a button on the remote, and the second big screen burst into colour, the wall filling with the face of Ahmed Yousef, an older photo from his MI5 file, when he was under surveillance in Finsbury Park.

'Strange, isn't it?' she said. 'I know more about this man than about some of my closest friends.'

Vine crossed his legs, never taking his eyes off the screen. Yousef looked almost normal up there, professorial and disarmingly fusty.

Rose clicked to another slide, crawling with squiggles of biro. 'A medical evaluation when he returned from a spell in a Jordanian prison,' she said. 'Given the once-over by a police doctor.'

Vine could repeat the phrases without thinking. 'Numerous digestive problems, weakness in his limbs, respiratory difficulties.'

'Very good.'

'But that's not where the real interest lies,' said Vine, suddenly more alert. He felt any tiredness receding. 'The killer is the psychiatric evaluation. Most detainees come back with what could politely be called post-traumatic stress disorder. Lack of sleep, vivid nightmares, flashbacks. Some can't even leave the house.'

'But not Yousef?'

'The opposite. I've watched the tape. He is charming, polite, reasonable. He can do a passable impression of tolerance too, the actor in him. The psychiatrist actually said in the report that he was the most rational subject he had ever evaluated.'

Rose turned towards him. 'So what makes you so sure that he isn't?'

Vine looked at her. 'I'm quite sure he is,' he said, at last. 'You know once you see him face to face. His eyes, the window to the soul. He is the most dangerous sort of all – a sane man leading others to do insane things. The only questions we need answered are who he's working with to plan the attack, and where and when he's going to strike.'

'But what if he's too good? With others, we can count on them for simple errors. What if Yousef doesn't make mistakes any more?'

'Everyone makes mistakes,' he said. 'Yousef might pretend to be infallible. But he's not. We just need to keep watching.'

She didn't respond. The room was quiet for a moment, merely the dull hum of machines.

'You can talk to me, you know,' said Vine, summoning up the confidence to move the conversation away from shop talk. 'What are you thinking?'

'Just the usual.'

'Gabriel?'

'Yes,' she said. There was a slight heave in her chest. 'I can't get the thought out of my mind. What they must be doing to him. It's too horrible to think about, yet sometimes it's all I can think about . . .'

Vine could hear Newton's words float back to him: *the best we can hope for now is that they killed him quickly.*

'I don't even know what's being done to rescue him,' she said. 'When Cecil told me about the operation he just said a mission was underway. Nothing more.'

'I can talk to Cecil again if you like,' said Vine. 'You deserve to know.' He waited, trying to gauge her mood before he said more. 'You've been the victim in all of this. The least you can have is some idea of what is being done to get him back.'

She sat up, tracing a hand through her hair. 'But we both know why . . . We're both professionals. It doesn't surprise me. It's what I would do in their situation.'

Vine shook his head. 'No . . . that's nonsense.'

'You know it's not, Solomon. We both do. He was always just another chess piece in Cecil's grand game. Even if he is alive at the end of it, there's no way he won't have divulged everything he knows. No one could resist. Everything the West has done will be hurled back at him. He'll become a sacrifice for it all.'

Vine could see Cecil in his armchair, those words tumbling out of him: *it was clear that MI6 and Downing Street would deny all knowledge if he was exposed, cast him off as an actual traitor, perhaps even threaten prosecution.* He thought of Cecil in his armoured car, happy to let Wilde take the rap for his own misadventures.

And yet that twinge of suspicion recurred, unable to be silenced. What if Wilde had set this whole thing up, an ingenious double-bluff? In some part of him, Vine felt he was letting Newton down. He had yet to find any further answers about the MIDAS operation, yet to identify the mysterious correspondent on the Gmail account. Newton had been sure that those details would shed new light on the Nobody mole and Wilde's disappearance. He could see the watchers tailing him at Guy's hospital, the man shadowing him around Oxford. He had presumed they were Cecil's men. But Cecil had access to every digital resource available. He could have stitched together his knowledge of Vine's whereabouts more easily than deploying physical surveillance. What, instead, if they were acting on Wilde's orders? Vine analysed the thought, wondering if his own anger was deliberately diluting the last of his rational powers. Truth and fiction seemed amorphous suddenly, motive and inference refusing to stay still.

Neither of them said anything. He longed to hold her and to comfort her. He wanted to be free of guilt and worry, of hurt about what had happened.

'You should get some sleep,' he said eventually. 'It will be easier in the morning.'

'You promise?'

'Let me walk you home. I could do with the exercise.'

She smiled. It was a sad, humourless curve of the mouth. 'Sure,' she said. 'Just let me get my things.'

He watched her walk out of the room towards the hall before getting up and yawning loudly. He picked up his jacket and wriggled his arms through the sleeves, wondering whether tonight, at last, he might be able to turn off the thoughts and sleep. As he waited for Rose to return, he saw her coat draped over a nearby chair. It was still cold outside, so he picked it up to hold for her, an instinctive act of chivalry that made him feel suddenly self-conscious, ridiculous even. He was just about to replace it – trying to remember the exact angle across the chair – when he felt a slight protrusion from the inside chest pocket, a bump in the silky lining. His hand was moving before his brain engaged, fingers clasping round the glossy surface. Inching it out, he gently smoothed down the crease in the middle. Then he smiled.

He turned the photo round and saw the marking on the back – 'Pakistan 2005' – that he recalled so well from the day he had first seen it, tumbling out of the desk drawer when he had been searching for coasters; the day scarred in his memory by what had followed – a fluffed proposal, an even clumsier engagement. He turned it back round and stared again at that younger, happier Rose, guarded on all sides by the family she had stayed with, a generational sprawl. Her smile was even more arresting than he remembered, shot through with a giddy optimism, eyes dancing with life. It was a world away from this place, like a memory from a past existence. Kept near her now as a means of surviving the day.

He lingered over it for a moment longer, unwilling to let go. Then he refolded the photo down the crease and replaced it carefully in her inside pocket, before positioning the coat back where he'd found it. Silently – instinctively – covering his tracks.

# 43

The bar of the Royal Horseguards hotel was dotted with tables for two tucked in the corners, close enough to the main area to lose your conversation in the noise yet space enough for comfort. The crowd was the usual mix of travelling corporate suits and greyer-haired tourists beguiled by its nearness to the Palace of Westminster.

Vine and Montague took a vacant two-seater, their body language convincingly wary around one another. The waiter came. Montague ordered a glass of white wine, Vine a glass of red.

They followed the usual script – the recent cricket scores, future holiday plans – until the drinks came. Vine had been glad to get out of the safe house, quarantined for too long within the four walls. He scooped up a handful of nuts, chewed them down and then leaned forwards, voice never rising above a murmur: 'So . . . do you think we can do it?'

Montague gulped down a mouthful of wine. 'Technically, yes. I can get into the CCTV systems without too much fuss. Just a question of whether some eagle-eyed counterpart spots me. They're getting better these days. Not Silicon Valley money, but enough to recruit guys and gals who know how to make a keyboard sing. I can cover my tracks, of course, but it will have to be for short bursts at a time.'

Vine nodded. He sat back in his seat and stared down into his glass. There was a tarnished look to Montague that intrigued him, the sort of donnish melancholy that Vine felt reflected his own – scuffed somehow, as if regretting the price that had to be paid for knowledge.

Montague coughed lightly. 'The powers that be aren't rethinking, I hope,' he said. 'I doubt we would ever get this past the Foreign Secretary. Definitely not the Home Office. GCHQ and the Met are very touchy about anyone else getting into the system . . .'

Vine shook his head. 'It's not the methods that are the problem. It's the man. Yousef is a genius in the art of victimhood. If he gets any definite confirmation we are watching him, we'll have every civil liberties lobby group spamming their MP's inbox by morning. The press would lap it up.'

Montague looked as if he was almost smiling to himself. 'Well, if duty calls on that front, I've always fancied giving the hacks a bit of their own medicine. Altering a few headlines, waking the lawyers up.' He had sunk the last of his wine now, staring at the glass. 'Are we off-duty enough for a second helping?'

Vine laughed despondently. 'Be my guest.' He watched Montague scan the room for a waiter. The dance music on the overhead speakers was replaced by velvety jazz.

He was still only halfway through his wine, savouring the flavour in his throat. He suddenly felt his body give in to tiredness, the fidgety twinge of it on his muscles. The dam must break soon, he knew. Even spies could only wait for so long.

Once started on his second glass, Montague said: 'What do you think he'll do? Brush pass of some sort?'

Vine thought back to the sly simplicity of the counter-surveillance at the shopping mall. There was something that continued to unsettle him about it, a wrong note which he couldn't quite identify. 'That's what I'd do. Nothing digital, not worth the risk. Just a handover, lost in the crowds. Become a needle in the haystack.'

'Which means we'll need eyes on him for most of the day. Risk getting caught inside the system.'

'The catch-22.'

'Do you think he really is planning an attack?'

'Yes. It's the only explanation for how he's acting. The key question is, are we good enough to stop him?'

With that, Montague took another large gulp of wine, and they gathered up their coats. Vine asked for the bill and paid. At the door, he looked to his left at the grandeur of the Ministry of Defence and said, as if to no one in particular: 'Who spies on the spies? The eternal question.'

'What do we do if they find us?' said Montague, threading his arms through the sleeves of his overcoat. 'Who do we say we are?'

Vine smiled. Something else was brewing. He could almost taste it in the air. He glanced back at Montague.

*Who do we say we are?*

He flicked up the collar of his coat as they began walking down Whitehall Court.

'Nobody,' he said, at last.

## 44

'Alpha 2, do you have a visual?'

Vine looked up at the two main screens. The fuzzy image of Ahmed Yousef was always the same, a ghostly smudge. It was only a week in, and already Vine found his every thought consumed with the possible movements of the wraith-like figure in grey.

'Confirm,' said Anderson, his voice crackly over the comms system. 'Into Green Park Tube station.'

Sitting rapt before the screen, Montague tapped furiously on the keyboard, trying to summon the appropriate CCTV camera.

'Which line?' said Rose, taking the right-hand position in front of the screen, arms folded. She turned to Vine. 'Has to be Victoria. He's heading home . . . Alpha 2, which line?' she repeated.

'Doesn't look like he's getting on from platform 4. He's heading for the Jubilee line.'

'Where's he going?' said Rose.

'Keep close to him,' said Vine. He turned to Montague. 'Tube stops he could be going to?'

Montague tapped again. 'Westminster, Waterloo, Southwark, London Bridge.'

Vine felt his pulse beat faster. Westminster. After days of nothing, this could be the moment Yousef began to lead them to his target. 'Alpha 1, where are you?'

Waugh didn't answer immediately. 'Still stuck on Piccadilly,' he said. 'Tried to check out Yousef's detour through St James's Church.'

'Anything?'

'Not that I could see. Just a way to shake off a tail from Jermyn Street.'

'He's been under surveillance for the best part of fifteen years,' said Rose. 'He knows what he's doing.'

Vine tried to summon all the possible scenarios. 'OK. Alpha 2 stay close to Yousef, make sure he doesn't leave you on the station platform. Alpha 1, get back to Cumberland Street, make sure we have that covered.'

Anderson said: 'Confirm. Target heading for Jubilee Southbound.'

Montague quickly worked his magic with the CCTV cameras. Soon they were staring at a live feed of platform 6.

'Where's he gone?' Vine said. He scanned through the clumps of people waiting for the train due in less than a minute. 'Switch to one of the east-facing cameras. He must be further down.'

Montague clicked again. He cursed as the footage buffered on them. 'Sorry, this equipment is pretty bloody horrible at the best of times. I'm having problems connecting.'

Vine cracked his knuckles. He felt his chest tighten. They had about forty seconds until the train arrived. With a platform this busy, Yousef could lose surveillance easily. Alone, there was a vanishingly small chance that Anderson would be able to get an eyes-on in time to track him.

'Back up,' said Montague. The live stream from an east-facing camera further down the platform juddered into life on the screen.

'Anyone?' said Vine.

'Right at the end,' said Rose. 'Behind that group of tourists.'

The screen blurred slightly as the headlights from the train glittered into view.

'Alpha 2, target is near the end of the platform. About to board the penultimate carriage. Do you have a visual?'

The platform had descended into barely organized chaos as streams of passengers disembarked.

'Alpha 2?'

There was nothing, just the sound of heavy breathing from one of the mikes. Eventually, with a breathy rasp, Anderson's voice came through: 'Confirm.'

'Which carriage are you in?'

'Third one down. I have sight of the target.'

'Is he carrying anything?' asked Rose. It was almost impossible to tell from the CCTV footage.

'No.'

'Stay with him,' said Vine. 'Alpha 1, update please.'

Waugh's voice sounded again, still laced with a defensive edge. 'Nearly at Green Park.'

'OK. Confirm when you reach Victoria.'

Vine coughed, reaching for the bottle of Evian and downing half of it in one go. He reeled again through the other possible stations: Waterloo, Southwark, London Bridge. London Bridge was a possibility if he didn't get off at the next stop.

'How much longer approximately?' he asked Montague.

'One minute max.' Montague brought up a diagram showing Westminster Tube station on the left-hand screen. 'If he gets off the train, there are three options. He stays on platform 3 and heads towards the District and Circle lines. Or he leaves platform 3 and either takes the escalator down to the Jubilee Westbound on platform 4 or the two escalators up towards the main exit.'

Vine looked at the digital clock on the bottom of the screen. He saw the glow of the approaching train on the right-hand screen, waiting as it shuddered along the platform, inspecting the penultimate carriage for any flicker of movement.

'Alpha 2, did you get that?'

On the footage, the five-foot-nine frame of Ahmed Yousef stepped out of the train carriage and began pacing down the platform. Montague changed the CCTV feed to the first escalator.

'He's on,' said Rose.

'Alpha 2, do you copy?'

'Confirm. I have a visual. Target has left platform 3. Going up. Looks like he could be heading for the exit.'

Yousef was walking up the left-hand side of the escalator. His pace quickened slightly as he veered round to catch the second escalator up towards the main station concourse.

'Where does he go now?' Vine whispered to himself. 'Alpha 2, do you still have a visual?'

There was another pause. 'Yes. He's beyond the ticket barriers, heading out of the Bridge Street exit.'

On the screen, Vine saw Anderson place his Oyster card on to the scanner, walk through the ticket barrier and break into a light jog towards the steps leading up to Bridge Street. Behind him, Montague's breathing was becoming thicker, heavy with annoyance.

'Bear with me,' he said.

Vine stopped himself saying anything. He tried to let the anxiety subside. They had no read on the target.

'Alpha 2. Anything?'

'I can't see him.'

'Camera situation?'

Montague didn't look up. He just smashed his thick fingers harder on the keyboard. 'One minute . . . I can't do it any faster. There are some network problems I've got to work through.'

'We're currently blind on the target,' said Vine, voice scratchy with irritation. 'If we don't get something soon, we've lost him.'

'It's too busy. I can't get past the crowds,' said Anderson. 'I can't see him.'

'Damn,' said Vine. He hit his hand against the side of the table and barely noticed the sting. This was the one lead they had managed to get since the counter-surveillance at the mall, some basic residue of tradecraft. Now they'd let him go.

'Camera up,' said Montague.

Vine and Rose both stared at the CCTV picture of Bridge Street outside Westminster station. It was like looking at an ant colony, a gaggle of faces and clothing scraping past each other. Vine scanned every face he could see.

'He's not there. Alpha 2?'

'He's either gone round along Portcullis House way or right towards Parliament Street. No visual.'

Vine worked his hands up his cheeks and pressed at his eyes. The footage on the screen kept whirring, a meaningless blob of people.

'Try switching back to the station concourse camera,' said Vine.

'What are you thinking?' asked Rose. Her voice had remained calm and smoothly professional. 'He never left?'

'I don't know. Or it's a courier job of some kind. He's thrown off a tail to collect something. Then back down the entrance on the other side.'

Montague switched the footage. And then, suddenly, there he was. Yousef was making his way back through the ticket barriers and walking now down the two flights of stairs to platform 1, no obvious attempt to hide from surveillance.

'He's relaxed. He knows he's untouchable,' said Rose.

Vine stared at the insouciant stride, Yousef teasing the cameras. 'It's as if he wants to get caught.'

Rose moved closer to the screen, trying to pick out a detail. 'What's that?' she said. 'Tucked under his left arm?'

'A package,' said Vine, adrenaline coursing through him. 'Alpha 2, target is back in the station with a package.'

'Platform 1,' said Rose. 'Straight back through St James's Park to Victoria.'

'Alpha 1. Target most likely heading back to Victoria. Are you there?'

Waugh again: 'No. Just about to board at Green Park.'

'We need you at Cumberland Street as soon as possible.'

They watched as Yousef got on the train. The carriage disappeared from view just as Anderson reached the bottom of the platform steps.

'We need to see the platforms at St James's and Victoria,' said Vine.

As the Tube pulled into St James's Park, they scanned every passenger to make sure he didn't get off. Then they endured the few minutes onwards to the chaos of Victoria. Vine prayed they hadn't missed anything as the train came to a halt.

He watched as Yousef headed right towards the glow of the exit signs, going blank for a minute as he tramped up the flight of stairs in the crowded rush. They picked him up again as he scanned his Oyster and took another right towards the main exit up to the train station.

Vine stood mute as he saw Yousef's pace slow. He looked phlegmatic, shuffling with an almost inebriated calm. The camera changed to the view from the top of the Tube station.

Yousef continued through the rush of the exit from the Tube station into the train station proper, suddenly shrinking in the cavernous space of the main concourse. He was past the snaking ticket queue on his right, now moving towards the odd selection of stalls cluttering the middle, one man rattling a bucket for a dementia charity, another a phone provider luring new customers with unseasonable free ice creams.

Yousef reached the middle of the station thoroughfare. He turned his head to the right as if spotting the circular wall clock with its ponderous hands and roman numeral markings for the first time. Then he stopped.

The swirl of commuters began shaping round him, barely glancing up from their phones.

'What's he doing?' asked Rose.

'See if there's a camera there,' said Vine, feeling his voice thin. 'Zoom in if you can.'

With a few clicks, Montague summoned up a different camera and went in closer. Vine could feel his gut begin to churn as the screen was filled with the face of Ahmed Yousef staring up directly at them. There was the trademark smirk across his jawline, the fearless set of his eyes. It was as if he alone, of all the hundreds of oblivious commuters, could see the eye monitoring them all.

'Seriously, Solomon, what the hell's he doing?'

Vine didn't answer. Something was wrong. Badly wrong. He watched the odd, slow movement of the arms, inching up horizontally, scarecrow-like. With a queasy hit, he saw the left armpit of Yousef's jacket was now clear. The package he had been carrying had vanished completely.

Yousef was taunting them with its loss like a magic trick, a smile etched on the corner of his lips.

## 45

Vine loaded up the Gmail login screen and went through the familiar routine of entering the email address and password. He tried to blank out all thoughts of Ahmed Yousef and the way he had played them with the brush pass. He knew he could spend hours torturing himself trying to deduce what could be in that package. But it would be no use. Yousef was a skilled operator, fluent in the arts of unsettling an enemy. For all he knew, the package could have been nothing more than a prop. They were still no closer to having any concrete information on where Yousef was planning to strike.

Vine waited as the screen whirred into life. He had neglected Newton's investigation for too long, dishonouring the trust that had been placed in him. During all the sessions at Prince's Gardens, Vine had been unable to shelve the parts of Newton's investigation that remained unsolved, working away feverishly in the back of his mind. Deep down, he knew it stemmed from more than just a hatred of not knowing. He still smarted at the idea that Wilde would have the last word, garlanded with silent praise from Downing Street to the Oval Office. He knew it was petty, deeply irrational, unbecoming of a fellow officer. But the betrayal had buried itself so deeply, smuggled into every pore. Newton had discovered a truth that apparently changed everything on the night he died. Whatever else, Vine wouldn't rest until he knew what it was.

He clicked on the drafts folder again and then on to the second draft which had been saved on 11 April. He took a sip of black coffee, the kick of it banishing the last of the drowsiness. He leaned forwards in the seat and read through from the top, Newton's words followed by those of his mystery correspondent:

Circumstances have changed. We may not have as much time as we think.

*How so? Are you altering the plan?*

No. But I fear that my life could be in danger.

*How?*

That's not important. I do, however, have insurance that needs to be kept safe if the worst should happen.

*What type of insurance?*

Very minimal. But it could be crucial to our joint endeavour.

*What would need to be done?*

They would only eliminate me if they felt it also eliminated the evidence. The insurance must be safeguarded before that time. It would be used only in the event of my death to tell the world the truth.

*How difficult would it be to safeguard?*

The logistics would be easy. The fear factor worse.

*Are you asking me to keep it?*

I am asking you nothing. It must be your choice, and yours alone.

*And you're sure there is no other way?*

I'm sure of nothing. But time is limited. If we don't act now, the truth could be lost for ever.

*Would it be following the usual protocol?*

Yes.

*So be it.*

Good. Until then . . .

Vine clicked off the draft and sat back in his chair. So many of the phrases jostled for position in his mind.

*I fear that my life could be in danger . . .*

*. . . insurance that . . . could be crucial to our joint endeavour . . .*

*It would be used only in the event of my death to tell the world the truth . . .*

What was the insurance? What was the truth that they needed to tell the world? Something to do with the MIDAS operation or the Nobody mole? And what made Cosmo Newton think his life was in danger months before he died?

Vine laid out all the pieces of the case in front of him again: Yousef's testimony about a mole codenamed Nobody somewhere within British intelligence; the MIDAS operation that started in September 2011; Gabriel·Wilde's mission to convince Islamist groups that he had turned double; the insurance Cosmo Newton had, presumably relating to either the MIDAS operation or the truth about the Nobody mole; and the anonymous correspondent in this email account also involved in what Newton called 'our joint endeavour'. Did any of this information lead to an alternative hypothesis? Was he so blinkered by his emotions that he was twisting the facts to his own design?

Yet still that knot of suspicion refused to leave. He picked up Gabriel Wilde's translation of *The Odyssey* again now and flicked through to the line that continued to terrorize him. He could see the smirk on Wilde's face as he read: *My name is Nobody.* There were only two possible explanations. Either Cecil was right, and the Nobody mole Yousef mentioned in his confession was simply Wilde in his guise as double agent. Or Wilde had played them, using the double agent operation as a cover for what he had been doing all along. It would be the ideal mask, a classically elegant deception. Vine found himself thinking of the shooting of Yousef that day in Istanbul, the day everything had started. He had always assumed the shooter meant to kill, but the ripple effects now seemed too honed and calculated: taking him out of the action for a start with the set-up; stopping Yousef divulging vital information about the existence of the Nobody mole; and scotching any further official surveillance, freeing up Yousef to carry out an attack when the time was right. The near-miss was actually perfectly calibrated, setting in motion a plan of quiet beauty. Was that what Newton had discovered the night he died, the details of the MIDAS operation somehow providing definite proof?

Vine turned his attention back to the email account and clicked on the final draft, saved on 6 June. It was shorter than the others. He started reading.

> Did the insurance arrive safely?
> *Yes. Confirm receipt.*
> Good.
> *Does the situation remain the same?*
> Yes.
> *Should we stop?*
> No. We must go on. The truth is too important.
> *Even if the truth gets you killed?*
> It would be an honourable way to die.
> *Inter arma enim silent leges.*

Vine scanned the last line again, about to click off the draft and log out of the account. Then he paused, the words catching his attention. He had noticed it during the first scan through. But now its full importance began to hit him, the change in style suddenly deafening. The line contained only

five words, but they managed to undo the cultivated bland-
ness of the two previous drafts. It was the one mistake the
anonymous correspondent had made, a fatal slip. Vine recognized the line, summoning the last of the Latin he had to
translate it.

*Inter arma enim silent leges.*

*In times of war, the law falls silent.*

The meaning was secondary; the usage was key. It was a
single speck of data that could be used to build up the pattern, an anomaly that winnowed down the possibilities.
Identifying Newton's correspondent was still improbably
hard. But Vine had a foothold now, something to work with.

He clicked off the account and began trying to draw up a
list of the most likely candidates to use a phrase like that:
senior Foreign Office mandarins, perhaps, or the loftier ech-
elons of the legal world; maybe even a source used to the
verbal eccentricities of Westminster.

As he began jotting down names and ideas, forcing himself to think of any other possibilities, a familiar noise began
humming beside him, rattling on the surface of the desk.

He looked down at his phone, the screen alive with a new
message. As he started reading the words, he found his
thoughts immediately switching back to Prince's Gardens,
the sight of Ahmed Yousef ducking free of their attention.
He checked the number again, trying to spot any flaw. But he
knew whose number this was, every digit memorized.

A shiver ran through him, his throat tightening un-
bearably.

*The games are over. Now is the time to talk . . .*

# 46

It was madness. Vine knew it in his bones. But he felt any last patience break. They had tried ordinary channels, clinging to immaculate tradecraft in the hope it would save them. It was doomed to failure. They weren't competing with a clean skin. Ahmed Yousef was versed in the rules of the trade. Vine knew he should call this in and wait for authorization. But Yousef would never be found out by conventional means. Only by breaking the rules could they have a hope of breaking him.

Vine moved from the shadow of the street, checking his tail, making sure there was no one behind. He wondered whether Yousef had sprung some final trap, expertly reeling him in with the message. And then there was another voice, a nagging insistence as he watched Yousef fool them through Westminster Tube station, the smirk at Victoria. He thought further back to the scene at the mall, Yousef deliberately pausing within their sightline, exhibiting his counter-surveillance measures. He hadn't quite been able to pinpoint what was wrong, but now he thought he knew. There was something far too confident about all of it, as if Yousef knew for certain when and how they were watching him. The choreography was too perfect to be mere chance. But how could he possibly have been so sure?

Vine felt the shadows leave him as he walked across to the front door, his movements exposed by the dribble of toffee-coloured light from the streetlamp. He stopped, alert to any sound. But there was nothing.

All he could hear were the words from the message Ahmed Yousef had supposedly sent him a matter of minutes earlier; a final, impossible taunt.

*The games are over. Now is the time to talk . . .*

He moved towards the door, tightening the strap on his bag to avoid unwanted noise. At any minute, he expected the whirl of police cars behind him, or an alarm to erupt. But the deathly quiet continued. There was only the faint screech of a car accelerating somewhere in the distance.

He scoped the door first. He could break it down or pick the lock, but both would take time. Instead, he tried it and felt a curious absence on the other side. The door was giving.

Vine began to experience a worm of unease as he pushed the door open fully, tensed in case there was anyone lurking behind. There was a light on in the hallway, the rest of the house cloaked in darkness. He thought about calling out, then decided against it.

He continued moving and started to get a sense of the place. There were too many corners here. Any hostile could hide away while still having a clear shot at him.

He took in the layout of the ground floor. There was a kitchen, a small living room and another door leading to a utility room, perhaps, or storage. He stopped and listened for any sound, answered by an empty silence.

The ground-floor rooms would need to be checked off first, before conducting a fuller search of the house.

He waited for another second, then darted forwards. The kitchen was clear, plates piled on the bench waiting to be loaded into the dishwasher. The living room contained nothing more than a sofa, a TV propped neatly on a stand and a pile of magazines and journals stacked on a wooden coffee table. Next he checked the last remaining ground-floor door.

It was a utility room, the lights on a small washing machine and tumble dryer flashing in the gloom.

There was still no further sound, so Vine moved towards the stairs, climbing softly upwards, spotting a corridor to his left with two further doors.

The first was a bedroom, a light on the bedside table spraying the room with a dim glow, Yousef's clothes draped over the top of a chair.

He walked through and examined the en-suite bathroom, then backed out and crossed the hallway. The second door was a spare bedroom, the smell mustier, not recently used. He was back at the end of the hall, about to go down the stairs again, when the light from the small window above him changed. Headlights, probably, the finer glow showing a further door straight ahead.

Vine went towards it, gently pushing it open. The light from the window dimmed again, temporarily obscuring his view. He tried to adjust his eyes to the darkness and get a handle on the layout before him. Just as he was about to walk further in, he stopped in the doorway.

Ahmed Yousef was sitting with his back turned, lolled forwards against his desk.

Vine called out to him, inching across, reaching out a hand and pushing at Yousef's shoulder, trying to budge him awake. He began applying more pressure, forcing Yousef back to consciousness, as if rousing him from a deep sleep.

Eventually, he stopped. He slid his right hand towards Yousef's pulse, the skin flimsier than he remembered, desperate to hear the metronomic tick answer, that drumbeat of life against his fingertips.

Then, slowly, he tilted the head back, a delicate manoeuvre, as if the entire facial structure could shatter at any moment.

Blood had soaked through the shirtfront, only sparse patches of white still visible against the deep stain that had spread right down to the top of the trousers.

He took a breath, letting the pause last as long as possible. Then he forced his eyes upwards to the throat. There was a single wound, expertly done; it would have been over in seconds.

For the briefest of moments, Vine experienced nothing. There was no sudden rush of pain or anger, just a haze of disbelief, numbness circumventing his training. All thoughts and strategies and plans were temporarily annulled. He stood motionless for a moment, feeling any last pattern fall loose and scatter.

When he finally reached for his phone, he saw that his right hand was sticky with blood.

## 47

It was in the moments between reaching for his phone and dialling that he saw it. He didn't call the emergency number, but pocketed the phone for another moment. The shock was starting to fall away, training kicking back in. The temporary lapse of emotion was retreating, and reason taking its place.

Vine eased Yousef's body backwards, watching the heavy weight slump against the top of the chair. Then he looked at the desk, seeing a dull glimmer shape into an object. It was a phone — newish, with the aftermath of a box-fresh shine. Reaching over and picking it up, he saw there were finger marks on the screen, as if it had been used recently. He pressed the home button, watching it blink to life. The phone was locked. He needed a passcode or some other means of opening it.

Vine looked at Yousef's body, not giving himself time to regret his next action.

He bent down and drew up Yousef's left arm. Some part of him knew this was stupid, but he had stopped listening to that voice. There was only the case now, still a chance this might work.

Vine took the mobile in his right hand, and Yousef's left arm in the other hand. He positioned Yousef's index finger on the screen and swiped across, bringing up the initial greyish menu, news stories and other items.

Then he moved the index finger down and pressed it on the home button, praying that he could momentarily fool the phone's brain. Just as he was about to give up, the initial screen folded away and the standard array of apps began to appear. Vine thumbed through into settings and began changing the passcode so he could manually unlock it in the future, before clicking back to the main screen. He checked the Mail folder, but there was no account set up. Then he moved to Photos, Notes, and several other apps – quickly checking them off just in case.

He moved on to the Phone icon, scanning contacts and voicemail first, but both were blank, as was recent calls.

Finally, he thumbed on to the Messages icon. He paused. Where he had expected to find lots of message chains to numerous contacts, there was only one. He thumbed it open and looked up at the bubbles of words.

As he stared at them, Vine felt his body tense. The room took on an odd hallucinatory quality, his lack of sleep turning the evidence in front of him cloudy and featureless. He tried to shake the feeling off and force himself to greater mental clarity, tracking up to the top and looking at the words again. But they were still the same.

The immunity agreement was a play. They are using you as bait to track down other sympathizers. But we have mutual friends and I believe I can help you. You can't know my name and must NEVER try and contact me directly. But follow my instructions now and I guarantee you'll walk away from this . . .

Drive out of London following the M4, M5 and A4018 and follow signs for the Parkway Mall at 0930 tomorrow. Act as if you are flushing out a tail . . .

Pick up a package at the Bridge Street entrance of Westminster Tube station at 1600 today. Then head back to

Victoria and make for the exit. A further intercept will take place on the stairs before the ticket barriers. The camera on the top right of the main concourse of the train station will be monitored . . .

All worked fine. You've done your bit, and I'll do mine. I will be in touch soon . . .

There was one final message, Yousef's reply sent only minutes earlier:

The games are over. Now is the time to talk . . .

Vine looked at the number again. The digits were still the same. He knew them by heart, articulating them now to make sure there was no possible mistake. Then he turned back to the words, each syllable lurking like a nightmare. They had been deliberately planted to leave an indelible digital trail, finishing off the work that had been started in Istanbul, every one of them condemning him further.

Each incoming message had been sent from his phone.

# 48

There was a sound outside, brakes squealing at a turn. Vine snapped back to the room, a cold terror starting in his chest and seeping out through his whole body. He looked at the mobile and briefly considered what to do with it. As he had changed the passcode, and given its contents, there was no way he could hand it over to the forensic team. There would be too many questions to answer. He did another quick check around the room to make sure he couldn't spot any cameras or bugging devices. They hadn't managed to plant anything in Yousef's house yet, and Cecil had ruled out ongoing official surveillance from Thames House or Vauxhall Cross. He saw nothing.

He slipped the mobile into his jacket pocket and then looked around the rest of the room for a final time. He could feel the minutes slipping by, some distant part of him knowing he had to call this in soon. But whoever was doing this was trying to unbalance him. He had to stay focused.

There was nothing further on the desk. The rest of the room was lined with bookshelves and papers. Vine walked along the bookshelves, checking again for any further discrepancies, spotting none. All the books were shelved in alphabetical order, spines patterned with dust.

He reached the end, already attempting to concoct a cover story of sorts for when the forensic team arrived. But he could feel the weight of Cecil's words pressing on him.

*This is outside Five, GCHQ, the National Security Council, Number 10. Completely deniable.*

*If you end up sitting in a police interrogation room, I won't be there to get you out this time.*

All the pieces of this case began to fragment. He had been so sure he had discerned the pattern, tracing each empirical detail until it built into a theory. Ahmed Yousef would lead them to the answer, each action confirming his guilt. Yet now he lay soaked in his own blood, the answer evaporating once again.

Outside, Vine heard the first suggestion of a police siren. He looked down at the wine-red tongues of colour on his hands. The thought of the number beat at him relentlessly, his stomach curling with fear. He had always been sure before that he could extricate himself from any situation. But as the strange house seemed to close in on him now, he wondered whether this would be the end. Someone was toying with his mind, each strand of reason and logic disfigured into madness.

The siren – or was it sirens? – seemed to grow louder, thickening into a wall of sound. Vine cast one last look at Yousef's body and then found himself propelled by nothing more than instinct back out into the hall and down the stairs and away. He had no clear sense of geography any more, his legs seeming to move through a primal reasoning all of their own. He reached the door and felt each creak of it like a blow.

Soon he was stumbling into the fog-grey night, down narrow streets and past lifeless buildings, the world newly odd and alien. There was no way he could risk returning to Wellington Square. That was surely the first place they would look, once they had tracked his movements to the house and matched his facial profile to his file on government records. There would be no get-out-of-jail-free card to play. This had all been too well planned, Yousef merely one cog in a far larger wheel which he had been too blind, too complacent, to fully understand.

As Vine felt his breathing become ragged, he knew one thing with more certainty than ever.

These streets were no longer a refuge. There was no back-up plan or diplomatic trick to make this go away. He couldn't be vanished from here through a flight to Brize Norton, or bargained by HMG in a prisoner exchange. There were no codes, treaties or conventions to save him.

His own home had become a foreign country. One from which there might now be no hope of escape.

# PART FIVE

PART FIVE

# 49

The dregs of the coffee clung to the surface of the sink. Outside there was the muffled noise of cars slouching past, trains clunking their way free of the station.

He moved back into the middle of the room and thought about calling Rose. But the better part of him always stopped at the last moment. He was the one who had been hot-headed enough to approach Yousef directly, rising to the bait and endangering their operation. He was the one who should pay for that mistake.

He looked around now at the boxy hotel room. At first, he had been full of elaborate plans to try and get out of the country. It was his job to plan for every eventuality, and he had a fallback to escape from London if he ever needed to. He always carried a debit card under an alias to purchase the ticket for the Eurostar and had long ago memorized the street map of central Paris. By the time the police had alerted MI5, and both had coordinated with the DGSI, he could have been criss-crossing mainland Europe, before finding his way to South America.

He had been going through with that exfil plan when he decided to double back. He was never aware of a conscious choice not to escape until he found himself at St Pancras, purchasing a ticket using his own debit card and making himself visible for the CCTV cameras, before subduing one of the station guards – of a similar build and height, with a brush of sandy-coloured hair – in the station toilets and disappearing towards the staff car park, beeping a newish ocean-blue Ford Mondeo into life.

Such a textbook diversion wouldn't fool the more alert minds at MI5 for long. But it had bought him enough time to plot his next few moves, parking the guard's car in a long-stay on Carburton Street, changing into some mufti he found squirrelled away in a gym bag in the boot and then picking his way back to Victoria station with care. The most immediate priority was to disorientate the desk officer at Thames House who would be trying to rationalize his movement patterns. The last place they would rationally expect him to return, once they wasted hours churning through the passenger lists and CCTV photos from the Gare du Nord, would be near the scene of the crime. On exiting Victoria station, Vine had disappeared down Hudson's Place and on to Bridge Place before continuing straight on to Hugh Street, stopping outside a forgettable touristy hotel of the sort that littered the scrappier part of Pimlico. Years ago he had helped the owner escape deportation by intervening with the Home Office, on the understanding that if he ever needed a room no questions would be asked.

He had paid cash and was given the key to room ten on the top floor. He had immediately closed the curtains and then done a preliminary sweep of the place for bugs. Then he had slipped off his shoes and perched on the end of the bed, feeling all the adrenaline of the last few hours drain from his body. Finally, unwillingly, he had allowed himself to tip over into sleep.

From the alarm clock near the bed, he saw it was just after 6 p.m. He had been out for almost twelve delicious hours, weeks of wakefulness finally catching up with him.

He looked down at his hands and saw that the insides of his nails were still coppery. He had tried to scrub off all traces in the St Pancras toilets but wondered now whether Yousef's blood would infect him for ever. His head still ached with tiredness. He padded over to the cramped hotel bathroom, turning on the shower and letting the streams of water sluice down him, bringing him back to life.

He stayed there for ten minutes, watching as the sweat and dirt of the last two days tumbled from his body, swirling around his feet. He had done so much, seen so much, that he sometimes wondered if he would ever be clean again.

Eventually, he turned off the shower and reluctantly changed back into the clothes, feeling the texture of them cling to his skin. He found a dusty glass and let the tap run until the water turned icy, drinking down as much as he could manage, an almost unquenchable thirst. The cold seemed to jolt his system awake, lessen the chaos of competing ideas that whined like feedback through his brain. Whoever had planted the text messages, whoever was behind all this, was trying to unstitch every last thread of sanity, forcing him to doubt his own mental powers. Somehow he had to remain rational.

As he towelled his hair dry, he picked up the cracked remote from the table beside the bed and turned on the TV. He scrolled through until he found the BBC News channel, sitting through the weather and the sports news until it was time to replay the evening's headlines. They were almost through, the first flicker of relief in his stomach, when the final item stopped him. There was an old photo of Ahmed Yousef and the headline: FORMER TERROR SUSPECT FOUND MURDERED AT HIS HOME.

After a short segment in the studio, another photo filled the screen along with commentary from the anchor about an ongoing police manhunt. Before Vine had time to react to the glimpse of his own face, the footage cut away to an interview recorded earlier. He immediately recognized the figure of Valentine Amory sitting in his grand Commons office. Vine turned up the volume, edged closer to the screen, breath catching in his body.

Amory was looking in the direction of a producer out of shot, legs folded, hands resting calmly in his lap. 'Even for those of us used to dealing with the secret world, the news about Dr Yousef's death has come as a shock,' he said. 'Though, I am sad to say, not necessarily as a surprise. Some say that in times of war, the law falls silent. *Inter arma enim silent leges.* I believe that for too long the intelligence community has used the excuse of the war on terror to erode the law as we know it . . .'

## 50

He grabbed his jacket and began packing away the few items he had with him. Right at the last minute, Newton's anonymous correspondent had become careless, recycling an idiosyncrasy that could be used as an identifier.

*Inter arma enim silent leges.*

He heard Amory's voice on the TV, expertly reciting the tag. It was impossible, surely. And yet the more Vine thought of it, the more elegant a solution it seemed. Valentine Amory was a Member of Parliament and Chair of the Intelligence and Security Committee, tasked with holding the intelligence services to account on behalf of the public. He was the one person who was almost untouchable, immune from the usual tactics of the secret world. Even the merest whiff of interference in his affairs would bring down the full wrath of Parliament on Cecil and the rest of them. Who better to safeguard vital information in the event that Newton was taken out? Amory was the one man no one could touch.

Vine closed his bag and then locked the door to his room, still seeing that photo of himself flashed before the world. He knew London would be swarming with police trying to find him, Wellington Square placed under constant watch. These streets were now hostile territory. One false move and it would all be over. In addition to his role as Chair of the ISC, Amory was also the highest-profile defender of Ahmed Yousef. To approach him now would be putting everything on the line, a march straight into enemy territory.

Vine tried to ignore that thought, knowing he had no other options. Instead, he decided to make the most of the evening gloom, the last chance he might ever get to hurry through these streets.

It was raining, heavy clouds bruising the skyline. There was the rattle of a plane overhead. He wedged his hands into his jacket pockets and began pacing, sucking the air into his lungs. Then he was down towards Buckingham Palace, staring across the last of the bedraggled tourists hovering round the Victoria Memorial, the guardsmen standing motionless and inhuman as the rain worked its way into their skin.

The Mall was similarly deserted, like a film set at the end of shooting. Vine slowed his pace, craned his head up towards the sky and let the rain wash the top of his brow, relishing the icy trickle down to his nose, mouth, through the gaps in his jacket. It felt like some sort of absolution.

He walked on to Whitehall, past the statues of Haig, Monty, the bunting of Empire. Barriers were being put up on either side of the street, staff in fluorescent jackets huddled under umbrellas. A gaggle of important-looking military figures – the uniforms American rather than British – were being politely shown around final preparations for some future parade. Vine saw the absurdity of it all more clearly in the rain. What right did they all have to cling to past glory, skulk about pretending to maintain the balance of peace? He wondered whether too long in the shadows had made him deaf to common sense. Finally, as he turned left, up past the Tube station, taking his place at the start of Westminster Bridge with a direct view of the glassy front entrance to Portcullis House, he longed to be free of all of it. Of England, of history, of the peculiar strain of muddling through that allowed good people to suffer and others to walk free.

He tucked himself away in a corner and settled down to wait for as long as he had to. Just past one in the morning, he saw a thin figure with a red velvet collar and umbrella, head covered by a trilby hat, making his way out of Portcullis House. As Chairman of the Intelligence and Security Committee, and a backbench MP, Valentine Amory QC was not gifted with any state security. He was forced to carry his secrets alone.

Vine moved into view and took his final gamble.

## 51

Valentine Amory stopped, caught off guard by the voice.

'I'm sorry?'

Vine walked towards him, brushing the sheen of water from his eyes. He tried to ruffle his hair dry. 'I need to speak to you. In private.'

Amory moved forwards, voice raised against the tattoo of rain on the canopy above them. As he took in more of Vine, his face creased with recognition. 'You look familiar . . . Who are you?'

Vine kept his hands in his pockets. He knew that Amory could turn him in any second now. It was a reckless move coming here. But the clock was against him.

'I'm the man you're trying to put in prison,' he said, at last. 'Solomon Vine, trainee at Fort Monckton and former counter-espionage officer for the Secret Intelligence Service. Don't worry, the pleasure's all mine.'

Amory stepped backwards and turned in the direction of the dwindling police contingent inside the glass doors behind him. Any moment now, Vine knew, everything could be over. His entire future depended on the next action of the man in front of him.

'You have every right to turn me in,' said Vine. 'But, before you do, hear me out. I didn't kill Ahmed Yousef. I was set up, just as I was in Istanbul four months ago. There is something far bigger going on here. Cosmo Newton knew it. Since his death, I have been trying to figure out what that is. You used an anonymous email account to send messages to Newton without ever meeting. Newton, for whatever reason, trusted you with information to be kept safe in the event of his death.'

Amory's glance had pivoted back round from the police to Vine, face torn with confusion. 'How do you know all this?'

'Newton left me a file in a safe deposit box when he died. In it he wrote down the login details for the email account. He was trying to lead me to you. He also wrote the word MIDAS. I believe that the truth about the MIDAS operation is the key to everything that has been going on. And I believe you know where I can find the last bit of information I need.'

The lights had turned red, and the green man glowered at them. The road was almost deserted, but Amory used the diversion to dart forwards, his umbrella flapping in the breeze. They reached the other side, Amory trying to establish distance as he hurried over Westminster Bridge and away.

Vine started to follow, feeling an irrational surge of hope. Amory hadn't alerted the Diplomatic Protection Group officers stationed inside the entrance to Portcullis House. There was still a chance this could work.

'I know Newton gave you the insurance,' said Vine, his voice cutting through the rain. 'I just need to know what the insurance is. Whatever it is, it could be the final clue that makes sense of everything that's been happening. Newton's death, Yousef's death . . . all of it.'

The figure in front of him stopped. He turned slowly, the annoyance on his face softening. He walked back to Vine and pursed his lips. 'You're asking me to help someone who is currently a fugitive from the law? Someone who is suspected of murdering a man I have been actively defending?'

Vine opened his bag and slowly drew out the first sheet of paper from Newton's file and handed it to Amory. 'This is the paper,' he said. 'The paper Newton entrusted to me. All I'm asking is for one more shred of loyalty to him. Help me find the missing piece of Newton's puzzle and you will never see me again. Once I've looked at it, you can even hand me in. But something awful could be about to happen. Something far bigger than Ahmed Yousef or Cosmo Newton. The information about the MIDAS operation could be the only thing that can stop it.'

Amory dipped his head and sighed loudly. A gloved hand removed a speck from his eye as he returned his gaze to Vine. He handed back the sheet of paper. 'How long were you waiting out here?' he asked.

Vine frowned. 'Several hours.'

'Ah.' He twitched at the top of his trilby and straightened one of his brown leather gloves. 'Then I take it you haven't yet seen the video?'

Vine stopped. 'The video of what?' He felt the damp clasp of his clothes against his body, every bone convulsed with cold.

'The British hostage, in a prison uniform, about to be executed.' He shook his head. 'If you really think this is connected, then I suppose we don't have much time.' Spotting an approaching taxi emitting a yellowish gleam, Amory raised his arm and waited for it to stop.

He opened the door and looked back at Vine. 'If we're going to talk,' he said, 'we can at least get somewhere dry.'

# 52

The footage played on constant repeat: Sky News, CNN, BBC News. The bedraggled face of Gabriel Wilde in an orange prison uniform kneeling in front of the camera. Behind him, a man in a balaclava held a knife to his head and ponderously repeated a prepared script. Vine translated the Arabic himself: 'For too long the British government has attacked us. This man has been part of that work and must suffer the consequences. If the British government makes another attack on us, we will be forced to seek further vengeance. To the British Prime Minister we say one thing: if you value the life of your people, you must leave our lands.'

Vine pressed the mute button, allergic to the medieval flourish. He knew he would never be able to fully forget the sight of Gabriel Wilde's face scabbed with blood, the deadened way he stared at the camera. But he couldn't afford to let emotions skew reason. The video was designed to provoke an immediate physical reaction in an audience, to let the heart override the head. There would be no better way to discount yourself from suspicion than staging a hostage video, burgling instinct and sympathy. As Vine peered at the screen again, he was more convinced than ever that the whole thing was a play, a stunt, a warm-up, ensuring the forthcoming attack obliterated all other news stories on both sides of the Atlantic. This was far bigger than any of them had ever realized, Ahmed Yousef only the lieutenant to a much greater plan.

He felt sick and shivery, the effect of the hours of rain beginning to seep through his body. He took the towel and rubbed it against his head, working out the worst of the moisture.

He placed the sodden towel to his right, sank back into the cushiony warmth of the sofa and thought of Rose. He wanted to call and hear the sound of her voice. But still something stopped him.

The door opened. Valentine Amory was newly changed into a pair of burgundy cords and a dark-blue jumper. He saw the footage on the screen.

'I presume you know who that is,' he said. 'One of ours?' Up close, Amory's voice was fruitier than Vine expected, the demotic varnish put on for the cameras. Curls of silvery hair flowed back over his head. His face had a brownish tan to it, as if he boasted some exotic ancestry or spent half the year in the south of France.

'Yes,' said Vine. 'Head of Station in Istanbul.'

Amory picked up the single sheet of paper from the coffee table, the one Vine had shown him on Westminster Bridge. 'This is Newton's handwriting, I take it?'

Vine nodded. Amory unfurled it carefully and reached for his reading glasses. He read it once, then again, lowering his glasses when he finished.

Vine took a sip of brandy and felt it banish the spine of ice running through his body. 'The insurance Newton mentioned in the email account. I presume you have it?'

Amory folded the piece of paper. He placed it delicately on the coffee table and then took off his glasses, rubbing them on the bottom end of his jumper. He nodded. 'This way,' he said.

Vine followed, into the hall and right up the stairs. There was a glimpse of a bathroom, then a bedroom. Straight ahead was a locked wooden door. Amory took out the key from his pocket, opened it and switched on the light. Inside stood a vast study, dominated by a broad oak desk and two leather armchairs.

Amory shut the door, locking it again as a precaution. Then he turned to face Vine, doubt still written across his face.

'Before we go any further,' he said, 'I must ask one thing. I need you to tell me everything you know. Right from the very beginning.'

## 53

Vine nodded, still taking in the room. Behind the large desk was a portrait of Amory in his Commons office, the grandeur of the portcullis sign on the green-leather chair complementing the blaze of colour from his purple socks through to his Old Etonian tie.

Amory poured two drinks, handed one to Vine and then took the armchair on the left and waited. Vine continued to stand, happy to pace as he talked. He had never divulged the full story to anyone. But he had no one else to turn to. Any moment now Valentine Amory could still pick up the phone and call the police. Vine knew he had one chance to make his pitch convincing.

'It all started four months ago,' he began. 'I was a senior member of MI6's counter-espionage team, spending most of my life on planes travelling between different embassies. My schedule had changed unexpectedly and I found myself in Istanbul. When I arrived, word reached me that Ahmed Yousef, who was on the National Security Council's Most Wanted list, had been detained. The Head of Station, Gabriel Wilde, was about to conduct an interrogation, and I joined him. It was largely fruitless. Yousef was too practised to be fooled by any of our tricks. But his own pride began to trip him up. He kept boasting that he knew a secret that would secure his release.'

Amory's expression was unmoved, his eyes beady and inquiring. 'Did he tell you what this secret was?' he said.

'Not at the time, no. Midway through the interrogation, we were called away by the RMP guard on duty. They are instructed to only interrupt a live interrogation if contacted either by the Ambassador or directly by the switchboard at Vauxhall Cross, so I knew it had to be something important. Gabriel's wife, Rose, had called earlier as well, and he had to leave for some domestic emergency. So I took the call alone.'

'What was the call about?'

Vine had reached the end of the room, and started turning back. 'It was Cecil himself, telling me that I had to release Ahmed Yousef immediately.'

'Did he tell you why?'

'No. He didn't give a reason. I tried to question it, but he refused to elaborate any further. Gabriel had left, so I decided to take some time outside to collect my thoughts. But not before I made a crucial mistake. I ordered the RMP guard to turn off all the CCTV cameras.'

Amory didn't react, just a vague tilt of the head upwards. Vine could see why he made such an imposing committee chair, forcing a witness to strain for reaction. 'Why?'

'Somehow I realized I couldn't obey the order,' said Vine, trying to recall his own internal logic. 'Whatever secret Yousef knew, he thought it was enough to get out of jail free. I was well aware what he was capable of, and I couldn't face letting him back on the streets. I thought I could keep him for further questioning and blame any CCTV issues on a power cut.'

'And instead?'

'I was outside for twenty minutes. When I returned, Ahmed Yousef was on the floor of the interrogation room. He had been shot. Blood was everywhere. I ordered an emergency medical team and then asked the guard to find out who had been in the building. He checked and returned to say my card had been used.'

Amory looked more intrigued now, the lawyer in him stirred by contradictory evidence. 'Despite the fact you were outside the whole time?'

Vine nodded. 'Yes. Someone was trying to set me up. The only evidence against me was my card and my order to disable the CCTV coverage. But, together, it was more than enough. I was immediately suspended from duty.'

Amory took another languorous sip of his drink, letting the information settle. 'Which is when Cosmo Newton recruited you for a spot of private enterprise?'

'Three months later, I got a postcard from Newton asking me to meet him in St James's Park,' continued Vine. 'He told me that Gabriel Wilde had disappeared from his post as Head of Station. Blood had been found at his flat in Istanbul, and it looked like a kidnap. He said Cecil was acting oddly, closing ranks. But Newton suspected something else was wrong. He asked me to go and interview some of the key people Wilde knew: Olivia Cartier, his old don at Oxford and his Deputy Head of Station who was back for some annual leave.'

'Did you find anything?'

Vine could hear the words from those interviews, phrases that had jostled for position in his mind ever since. 'I found evidence that Wilde's behaviour had changed in the run-up to his disappearance. He had become very vocal in his opposition to US and UK foreign policy; there was talk he had converted to Islam. He had even been a member of a group called the Prophets at Oxford. Just as I was gathering all the evidence together, Cosmo Newton called me to say he had discovered something. Something that changed everything. He asked me to meet him at Paddington station that night. I went, but he never arrived. That was the night he died.'

Amory shifted in his seat, crossing his arms and bowing his head, as if deep in thought. 'What were his exact words?'

Vine knew them by heart, each one etched into memory. 'I've been doing a spot more research after our conversation. I think I may have found something. I'm travelling back to Paddington on the last train. Best not to speak on an open line. Meet me there at 11.45 . . . If I'm right, this changes everything.'

'This changes everything?'

'Yes.'

Amory nodded. His expression still gave nothing away. Vine couldn't tell whether he bought it.

Eventually, Amory asked: 'Did you have any idea what he meant?'

'Not then, no. But I knew the Whitehall machine would crank into gear before too long, so I immediately went to his house to see if I could find anything that might shed more light on what he'd discovered. In a drawer in his second-floor study, I found an envelope addressed to me. Inside was a gold key for a safe deposit box at Coutts bank on the Strand. The safe deposit box contained two documents. One was a single sheet of paper with three words in Newton's handwriting: *MIDAS*, *Hermes* and *Caesar*. The second sheet had the transcript of an interrogation from January this year between Yousef and Cecil. In it, Yousef offered information about a mole codenamed Nobody working inside British intelligence. In exchange, he wanted guaranteed immunity from prosecution.'

Amory got up from his seat and began pouring himself another drink. 'So you figured out that Hermes and Caesar were login details for the Gmail account?'

'That part was relatively simple,' said Vine. 'You just had to know how Newton's mind worked, the play on associations. Hermes was the messenger god; Caesar gave his name to the Caesar Cipher. It was the two other words that refused to make sense. So I tracked Newton's final movements before he died, finding a fallback at Cheltenham train station which led me to Buckland.'

Amory smiled. 'Whitehall's secret gem.'

'Yes. There I found a redacted file on the MIDAS operation dated 2 September 2011. It had been deliberately scourged from the computer system, but someone had forgotten to burn every paper copy. One of them still existed. Newton must have been checking it out on the day he died.'

'And the identity of the Nobody mole?'

Vine moved over to the empty chair and drew his bag to him. He opened it and eased out the copy of *The Odyssey* that Wilde had sent him, feeling the weight of it in his hands. 'The more I investigated, the clearer it became that the Nobody mole could only be one person – Wilde himself. His maternal family had been involved in financing groups linked to Islamist activity. He had been a member of the Prophets at Oxford. His behaviour had changed dramatically recently. And this arrived with an inscription from Wilde himself. To reach me when it did, it must have been sent just before he disappeared.'

Vine handed over the book to Amory, who put down his glass and began carefully flicking through the thick pages.

'There was one line in particular that I was sure confirmed his guilt,' said Vine.

Amory had already found it, tucked away near the middle. 'Book nine. Odysseus speaking to Polyphemus,' he said. 'My name is Nobody.'

Vine nodded. 'I thought it was Wilde trying to taunt me, a boast about his defection. But I needed more evidence. During a conversation with Olivia Cartier, she indicated that she had access to Wilde's MI6 file. If there was suspicion of him being a double, I knew it would most likely be in the file. So I broke into the Palace of Westminster and tried to find out if she still had it. But I was caught and arrested by the authorities. That was when Cecil hauled me in himself.'

Amory handed the book back and scooped up his drink. Vine had expected a frown at this point, the MP bridling at the overreach of the secret state, storing the information away to use at a later date. Instead, there was a look of mild appreciation. 'Impressive feat.'

Vine placed the book back in his bag and closed it again. 'Cecil inducted me into a top-secret operation he had been running with Downing Street and the White House,' he continued. 'After the Snowden leak and the rise of IS, Cecil had launched a daring HUMINT play to try and persuade Islamist groups in Syria that Wilde was a double agent, willing to pass on product from MI6. Actually, he was passing on disinformation, helping Langley better target their drone programme and take out senior commanders in the field.'

'So Wilde was the Nobody mole. But working for us all along?'

'Cecil put together Yousef's testimony about the Nobody mole and Wilde's top-secret operation and decided they must be the same thing.'

'But you're not sure?'

'It's one theory.'

'If true, though, everything you'd found was cover?'

Vine started pacing again, somehow unable to remain still. He had feared Amory would shop him to the police immediately, or recuse himself because of his work on the ISC. But he was still there, still listening. Vine allowed his initial doubt to fade, replaced by the slightest hint of optimism.

'Yes,' he said. 'Wilde needed to make it look like he was an actual defector. Hence letting people see him with a prayer mat and the exaggerated disdain for Western foreign policy. It was part of building his legend. But it had another effect. Ahmed Yousef had always denied he was an active Islamist agent, merely an academic supporter. But, by telling Cecil about the Nobody mole, he appeared to be inadvertently condemning himself.'

Amory returned to his seat and took another slow sip of his drink. 'I see. The only way he could know about a mole within British intelligence was if he was in collusion with Islamist groups.'

'Exactly. Cecil assumed Yousef was talking about his own operation. So while Cecil agreed to give Yousef immunity from prosecution, he was actually making another play. Cecil could use Yousef as bait to identify every Islamist agent and sympathizer on our shores, buying his way back into full favour with Number 10 and restoring MI6 to its former glory . . . until the events in Istanbul changed everything.'

'Almost overnight, Ahmed Yousef became a martyr, a symbol of state oppression.'

Vine debated how to frame his next sentence, before deciding against diplomacy. 'Suddenly, MPs like you were writing op-eds and appearing on TV demanding an inquiry. Cecil's grand plan to use Yousef as bait no longer worked. In the teeth of a scandal, there was no way he could get ministers to sanction official surveillance of Yousef any longer.'

Amory had finished his second helping. He reached over and placed the glass on the corner of the desk, then swivelled his attention back to Vine. 'So he turned to you?'

'He commissioned a small team to mount an off-the-books surveillance operation. Following Wilde's unmasking, Cecil believed there would be a revenge attack, using Yousef to carry it out. It was the perfect situation. Yousef was now beyond reproach. There was no one better.'

'Until his death complicated things?'

'Throughout the surveillance, I felt something was wrong, but I could never pinpoint exactly what. He seemed too certain that we were watching him. Then, out of nowhere, I received a message directly from Yousef himself. It said simply: *The games are over. Now is the time to talk*. We had made no progress with surveillance, so I went round to his house on Cumberland Street to confront him. I wasn't sure what I would do. But when I got there, I found Yousef had been taken out. Worse still, I saw messages on his phone that explained everything we had tracked him doing: the counter-surveillance measures, the brush pass in the Tube. All of them had supposedly come from my number. Yousef had been nothing more than a decoy, distracting us from the real preparations for an attack. And someone was trying to finish off the work they started in Istanbul, taking me out of the picture by framing me for Yousef's death.'

'They wanted you to run.'

'Yes.'

There was silence for a moment. All Vine could hear was the soft thrum of cars on the street outside, the odd snatch of conversation. He had to pray that Amory believed him, despite everything.

Amory nodded again, still refusing to exhibit any direct emotion. After a pause, he said: 'So tell me . . . why you?'

## 54

Vine didn't answer at first. He looked at Amory, saw the studied blankness in the face, the former barrister in him adept at wheedling out inconvenient truths. 'Whoever is behind all this is planning something,' he said, at last. 'Something big. And they know that I could stop them.'

'But why you specifically?'

It was the question that continued to needle him. The set-up in Istanbul, Wilde's translation of *The Odyssey*, the messages on Yousef's phone – all of it had been calibrated for him, anarchy undoing reason. 'My role in counter-espionage for a start,' he said. 'Then my connection with Newton.' Vine paused, wondering how much he could risk sharing with Amory. He couldn't let emotions appear to cloud his judgement, yet it was pointless denying the obvious. 'And something more personal as well . . .'

'Personal?'

'I think Gabriel Wilde is behind all of this.'

'But the video . . . ?'

'The video is a fake. I'm sure of it. We trained together and worked together. We shared the same goals, the same aspirations, even loved the same woman. He won her, and he's now trying to bury me for good. It is the perfect act of deception. Wilde can pretend to be what he has been all along. Every indiscretion is forgiven, every betrayal sanctioned by the fifth floor. Wilde is Nobody. But he isn't working for us. He's working for them. He always has been.'

'And what about MIDAS?'

Vine stopped pacing, the question rooting him to the middle of the floor. Expressing the thoughts out loud, he was more convinced than ever that the evidence trail could only lead back to Wilde. But there still wasn't enough to prosecute. It was a blend of gossip, assumptions, inferences and speculation. He needed proof, something that gave Wilde motive and means.

'In the file he left for me, Newton included the page with the word MIDAS on it and the transcript about the Nobody mole,' he said, at last. 'Somehow he must have thought that the two were connected, one shedding light on the other. The truth about the MIDAS operation has to be the smoking gun that nails Gabriel Wilde. It's the only explanation.'

Amory didn't respond at first. He was rubbing his palms against each other, emitting a soft, powdery rasp. 'And the possible attack? You said Cecil thought something was being planned?'

'Cecil told me there had been increased chatter from Islamist cells since Wilde's disappearance. He thought there would be a revenge attack on London because they'd found out about the deception operation. Wilde wanted us to think that, of course, to concentrate on Yousef and miss the bigger picture. It was all working perfectly until Yousef broke the protocol, contacting the sender directly. I got the message, and so they switched to a back-up plan. Frame me, get me on the run, render me powerless to stop whatever they are planning. The timing of the hostage video will be for a reason. It's a warm-up for the main act. The only question is where they choose to strike.'

Vine went silent for a moment, then he turned back to Amory, his tone sharper, more urgent.

'In Newton's correspondence with you, he talked about "the insurance" that you would safeguard in the event of his death,' he said. 'I've now told you everything I know. I believe Newton wanted me to pick up his trail, following the evidence to the same conclusion he reached before he died. I need to see whatever he left you to safeguard. Whatever it contains is the only information that will make sense of everything. Do you have it?'

Amory looked reluctant, staying seated for a moment. Then he got up and walked over to the painting behind his desk, lifting it up carefully to reveal a grey safe. He tapped in a passcode, reached inside the safe and drew out a single box. He placed it down on the centre of the desk.

'Don't ask me how Newton got this, or why,' said Amory. 'I suspect not by legal means. But I am just the courier. Newton had some romantic notion that Cecil would think twice before ordering a raid on the home of a parliamentarian. That's why he picked me as his fallback. Hence the Gmail account. From what you suggest about his visit to Buckland, he must have been trying to work up the case from legitimate sources before he died.'

Amory brushed a layer of dust off the top of the box, then opened it and reached inside, carefully lifting out a thin USB stick, balancing it in his hands like a prized object. 'You really think this can help you stop Gabriel Wilde?'

'Yes,' said Vine, more sure of the answer than of anything else. 'I think it's the only way to stop Gabriel Wilde.'

'Very well.' Amory clung on for another moment, before slowly passing the USB stick over to Vine along with a piece of notepaper containing two passcodes. 'Whatever is on there . . .' he began.

Vine didn't let him finish. 'Delete the Gmail account,' he said, as he pocketed the USB stick and started heading for the door. 'Cover your tracks. And, don't worry, your secret's safe with me.'

## 55

He barely noticed the hit of cold outside. Anticipation coursed through his body, a tingling rush. He hailed a cab, asked for Westminster, then checked behind and around for any sign of a tail. Minutes later, as the cab pulled into the Derby Gate entrance to Parliament, Vine paid and walked to the other side of Parliament Street. Then he quickened his pace, on to King Charles Street and down past the side of the Treasury on his left and the Foreign Office on his right. He ducked left at the end, crossed, then turned right into Old Queen Street. He hailed another cab and asked for Hugh Street. He checked for a final time, sure he'd lost any tail.

Once back in his room, Vine allowed himself a moment to order his thoughts. He took out the USB stick Amory had given him and considered it for a moment. The information it contained could be the final clue that proved Gabriel Wilde's treachery, showing how the MIDAS operation linked to the Nobody mole. He felt his pulse rise, a nervous sweat bristle all over his body. This would be enough to explain away Yousef's death, allow him back to his rightful place at Vauxhall Cross. The exile could finally end; he could come in from the cold.

He waited for his MacBook Air to jolt to life. Then he inserted the USB stick into the laptop and watched nervously as it loaded.

The first screen asked for an identification number.

He typed in the first number from the notepaper. Correct.

The second screen asked for an authorization code. He typed the second number in. Correct.

Then he waited as the screen whirred. He listened closely for any further sound nearby. Would a Special Branch team already be inside the hotel? Had they managed to creep up to his door without him noticing? He glanced towards it, knowing any second now it could splinter to nothingness.

The dial spun for the last time, opening up an ordinary-looking file named with a long series of digits. Inside the file was a single PDF document. He double-clicked and then peered closer. It looked like a scan, the lettering which had been redacted in the paper version at Buckland now clear. Vine read the top of the page.

TOP SECRET

STRAP 4

MIDAS OPERATION

The first thing that was unusual was the classification level. The header indicated that only those with STRAP 4 clearance could read the file. That excluded the bulk of the intelligence services and any Cabinet minister apart from the Prime Minister, Foreign Secretary, Defence Secretary and Home Secretary, alongside specially cleared aides in Whitehall.

The file was set out as a series of memos. Vine started reading through each one, pausing at certain passages, his confusion beginning to build.

MEMO: 2 September 2011
FROM: CSIS

TO: NSAWH, DNI, DCIA
CC: DGSS, AGOHMG

. . . I am writing to you following our recent Washington visit to confirm Downing Street's commitment to extending US–UK cooperation. As you know, the new operation has been designed to allow the UK to continue our special relationship beyond Five Eyes and be a full partner in your ongoing RPA programme. While political sensitivities domestically have thus far precluded action beyond a traditional military context, we are now convinced Special Forces can effectively partner the CIA in this exciting new frontier. The new US–UK operation will be codenamed MIDAS . . .

MEMO: 12 September 2011
FROM: CSIS
TO: NSAWH, DNI, DCIA
CC: DGSS, AGOHMG

. . . Since our previous exchange, I can now confirm that sign-off has been received for the MIDAS operational base at RAF Waddington. The select team there will be liaising closely with the 17th Reconnaissance Squadron at Creech and the wider 732nd Operations Group, under the management of a Joint Special Operations team reporting directly to Vauxhall Cross . . .

MEMO: 3 October 2011
FROM: CSIS
TO: NSAWH, DNI, DCIA
CC: DGSS, AGOHMG

. . . I am delighted to say that legal approval for the MIDAS operation has been received from the Attorney General's

Office, addressing all previous concerns about ROEs. Downing Street has therefore signalled that the MIDAS operation can now begin in earnest. Our two nations have a long history of intelligence sharing, from our role at Bletchley to defeating the threat of Soviet communism. Through the MIDAS operation, HMG very much looks forward to standing shoulder to shoulder with you once again in this vital work for the national security of the United Kingdom, the United States and, indeed, the world . . .

Vine looked down at the next document and read on.

ATTORNEY GENERAL'S OFFICE
OPINION: 3 October 2011
FROM: AGOHMG
TO: CSIS
. . . it is therefore our view that the MIDAS operation meets the necessary standards required by international law to protect HMG and CSIS from potential future legal difficulties . . .

As soon as he'd finished, Vine read through the memos again, then a third time, a savage sense of disappointment starting to crash through him. There had to be some terrible mistake. He had been convinced – more certain than anything in his life – that the truth about the MIDAS operation would finally confirm Gabriel Wilde's treachery. Newton had been clear, the file in the safe deposit box hinting at nothing less: the two pages had been deliberately placed together to suggest a connection, a causal thread that linked them both. Why else write MIDAS on the first sheet and then include a transcript about the Nobody mole on the second? Why would Newton risk everything, illegally stealing this file from Vauxhall Cross's own air-gapped system – or, perhaps, even infiltrating Langley's records – and asking Amory to safeguard it in the event of his death, unless it was the key to everything?

For the first time, Vine felt his confidence in Newton slip its moorings. He had always been so sure, nourished by an unblinking faith ever since that sunny afternoon in Cambridge sixteen years earlier. But what if that faith had been tragically misplaced? Newton had been old, frail, pensioned off from MI6 and given the role at the JIC as a last hurrah. But, even so, surely this couldn't be what Newton had meant? For a start, there was no mention of Gabriel Wilde at all. Vine began hurriedly combing through the acronyms and the dehydrated Whitehall jargon: RPA stood for remotely piloted aircraft, drones in other words, the lethal unmanned machines raining fire halfway across the world. ROEs, meanwhile, referenced military Rules of Engagement.

He turned to the distribution list and the bunched letters at the top of the memos: NSAWH meant the White House's National Security Adviser, the President's closest aide on security matters; DNI was the Director of National Intelligence, the person in charge of coordinating intelligence across the US government; DCIA referenced the Director of the Central Intelligence Agency. These were the high priests of the US intelligence world, for sure. But, no matter how hard he tried, Vine couldn't spot any link with Gabriel Wilde.

Struggling to maintain his composure, he moved his attention to the final part of the file. Frustration began to bite at him as he read the location names, the meaning once again drifting tantalizingly out of reach.

OPERATION LOG:
MISSION 1: 08.10.11. Location: Pakistan. Read out: sixty-one casualties. Summary: one confirmed target, sixty non-combatants.
MISSION 2: 24.10.11. Location: Pakistan. Read out: forty-two casualties. Summary: one confirmed target, forty-one non-combatants.
MISSION 3: 05.11.11. Location: Yemen. Read out: twenty casualties. Summary: two confirmed targets, eighteen non-combatants.
MISSION 4: 10.11.11. Location: Yemen. Read out: thirty-two casualties. Summary: no confirmed target, thirty-two non-combatants.

None of this made sense. The MIDAS file, the document Newton had risked everything to find and confirm, seemed unrelated to anything Vine had been pursuing, shedding no light on the investigation whatsoever. Almost despite himself, he began adding up the numbers, the ghastly bureaucracy of death. He looked again at the words – *sixty non-combatants, forty-one non-combatants, eighteen non-combatants, thirty-two non-combatants*. He considered the distribution list again. It was evidence of many things – mass extra-judicial killing, even a potential war crime, a black op at the very top of the British state – but he still couldn't see how it related to the case against Wilde, the truth about Nobody, the reason for Newton's death.

He closed his eyes and tried desperately to refocus. He rubbed them awake and turned to the bottom of the screen and the sender, the architect of the MIDAS operation. Was this what Newton had meant to direct him to? He checked it against the acronym at the top of all the other memos. It seemed the only possible linking thread, the sole echo of the words from Newton's file, a final hope that Vine felt himself cling firmly to now.

MIDAS operation terminated – ref CSIS.

*CSIS.* Chief, Secret Intelligence Service. MI6.
None other than Sir Alexander Cecil himself.

## 56

Vine closed the laptop lid and got up from his chair, feeling the walls of the hotel room lean in on him now, the crushing smallness of the place almost suffocating. A blast of different emotions whirled through his body: disappointment, anger, confusion. He had been so sure the truth about the MIDAS operation would be the key to everything, his ticket back to sanity, out of this room, wiping away the madness of the last few months. And yet he was left with nothing, just information about an obscure black op that resulted in mass casualties in the more dangerous corners of the world.

He took a deep lungful of breath, letting his arms rest by his side, closing his eyes to cut out all distractions. He drew up the information again in his mind, ordering it more neatly and then tracking through every detail to see what he could be missing. The first key point of interest was obvious: the scale of the civilian casualties. The MIDAS operation had undertaken four joint UK–US drone missions, with a horrendous loss of life. The numbers played in front of him again.

*. . . one confirmed target, sixty non-combatants . . .*
*. . . one confirmed target, forty-one non-combatants . . .*
*. . . two confirmed targets, eighteen non-combatants . . .*
*. . . no confirmed target, thirty-two non-combatants . . .*

The figures alone, if ever made public, would be enough to bring down careers and ruin reputations beyond repair. Inquiries would be launched, questions asked in Parliament, newspaper columns filled with calls to prosecute those who had signed off on what amounted to a war crime. Though it was well known that the CIA had carried out lethal strikes outside a traditional military context, the British government had always fiercely denied that MI6 had ever done so. If the MIDAS file was correct, Parliament and the public had been deliberately lied to.

Vine flicked back up to the text of the memos in his mind, sieving it for any further information that could prove useful, be teased out into a possible connection with Gabriel Wilde, the Nobody mole, a retaliatory attack on London.

*. . . the MIDAS operational base at RAF Waddington . . . will be liaising closely with the 17th Reconnaissance Squadron . . . under the management of a Joint Special Operations team reporting directly to Vauxhall Cross . . .*

The MIDAS operation had bypassed all the usual military command structures, placing an elite Joint Special Operations team and the power to order lethal strikes under the command of the Chief of MI6. To do that, Downing Street had signed off on a secret base at RAF Waddington.

*. . . I am delighted to say that legal approval for the MIDAS operation has been received from the Attorney General's Office, addressing all previous concerns about ROEs.*

The final memo confirmed that legal authorization had been provided by the Attorney General's Office, sanctioning the drone missions and ensuring that a way had been found to circumvent the normal Rules of Engagement that governed the conduct of British troops in battle.

Vine kept his eyes closed for a moment longer, scrolling back through all those details, parsing them for any more clues. He could feel his muscles tense further as he exerted every last ounce of concentration, willing himself to spot whatever speck or fragment he was missing, the same particle of information that Newton had glimpsed the night he died which brought everything into focus. But somehow all he could see were the facts, the gruesome procession of numbers and words.

Frustration began to well up inside him again, massing like an explosive force. Vine tried to let his muscles relax, his concentration sag, allowing his eyes to flicker open and take in the flaking paleness of the room.

But still nothing. The file seemed to be just another false start, offering no promise of redemption. For a moment now, he wondered how it would all end, hearing the sound of boots and weapons, any last chance exhausted in a final, hopeless hunt for the truth.

He was just about to shrug off such morbid premonitions, when a bark of noise snapped him back to full consciousness. He stopped, listening more closely. But there could be no mistake. The sound had been too loud to have come from anywhere else in the hotel.

Someone was knocking on the door.

## 57

He didn't move at first, trying to slow the tempo of his own breathing, suddenly conscious of the slightest creak of his feet. He looked towards the door, then turned to the window on his right. The curtains were threadbare, easily thin enough to spot the whirl of police sirens. Perhaps they had turned off the lights, decided on a stealth approach, knowing that the vaguest noise could send him heading for an escape route.

He tried to recall the exact frequency of the first two knocks. They had been firm and reasonably close together, loud enough to snap someone awake but not the usual battering-ram of sound. He waited for another second, then heard the rap of a further three knocks. They were quieter this time, as if nervous about making too much noise and attracting attention. Vine felt a bead of sweat slide down the side of his face, heavy on his skin.

He waited to see if he could catch the sound of footsteps retreating. But there was silence. Broken only moments later by another sound. A voice.

'Solomon . . . it's me.'

He moved over to the door and reached for the handle, gently teasing it open. Rose cast a quick glance behind her, before making her way in. Vine closed the door, relief allowing him to breathe again.

'How did you find me?' he said, checking the door was properly locked.

'I always remembered you telling me this was your back-up plan,' she said. 'Top room, top floor, Hugh Street.'

'A major operational mistake.'

'I'm not sure you were in fully operational mode at the time . . . I'm sorry. I checked my tail all the way here. I didn't know who else to turn to.'

He wondered how many times during the last few years he had imagined her saying something like that. Standing there, she looked more real than ever somehow, the glossy swish of hair tangled with rain, the curves of her face depressed by recent events. There was no distance between them now, the public face replaced by the private one.

His mind had been so full of disappointment at the MIDAS file and the lack of connection to the Nobody mole that it took him a moment to think of Wilde's hostage video. He dismissed all other concerns, hauling himself back to the present.

'When did you see the video?' he said. He walked over to the small plastic tray with a rickety hotel kettle on it at the end of the desk and began trying to find some mugs.

She looked exhausted even at the task of remembering. 'I was with Cecil,' she said. 'A final debrief on the Yousef surveillance.'

Vine tried to staunch a pang of unease. Was it Cecil who had sent her here? Were watchers taking up position around the hotel? 'They may have exaggerated it for the cameras,' he said, unable to summon any other comforting words. He wanted to tell her everything, pool his suspicions. But he stopped himself, feigning control. 'Have a seat,' he said, nodding towards the one chair opposite the chipped wooden desk. 'Coffee?'

Her lips creased into a near echo of a smile. Her voice was croaky. 'Coffee would be great.'

Neither of them spoke for a couple of minutes as the kettle boiled. Vine handed her a mug and then perched uneasily on the side of the desk, no other chair in sight. Bunched in here like this, he couldn't help but wonder what their marriage could have been like, to spend forty, fifty years discovering their unique routines. Sometimes he had imagined that future could still be exhumed and dusted down as new. Yet here – now – he realized that had always been nothing more than fantasy.

He tried to gather his thoughts, debating whether to ask her more about the hostage video, find out what Cecil had told her. But as he looked at her more closely, rain-soaked and huddled on the chair in front of him, he knew that she hadn't come here for an interrogation. She had yet to ask him about Yousef and could expect the same favour in return.

After an appropriate pause, he said: 'Now that the operation is over, what next?'

Rose took another sip. 'Back to Thames House in the long term. But there's a big UK–US commemoration service in Westminster this morning that Cecil roped me into a while back, lots of security grandees attending. The Speaker's Office was getting pressure from the US embassy, wanted someone as intelligence liaison. The usual drill. Nothing too exciting.'

Vine could already feel his attention being dragged elsewhere, unease beginning to crawl through his body. He thought of the fake hostage video again, unconsciously clutching the handle of the coffee mug tighter, fingers digging into the chipped enamel. The chaos of the last few days, the last few hours, pressed in on him again, clammy and distinct.

He forced himself to continue breathing, slowly – a gentle iambic rhythm – and not rush to react. And yet, strangely, all he could feel was the terrifying idea of absence, of aloneness so acute it was almost like a physical force.

She looked up now, the mug paused at her lips. Rain was still sliding down from her hair across her face, eyes splashed with make-up, limbs rocking softly with the cold. She knew him as well as anyone ever had, he realized, learning to distinguish the truths from the half-truths. There was no way he could bluff her. She peered at him just as she had when he first visited her flat what seemed like a lifetime ago, exposing all his calculated evasions.

He had promised himself he wouldn't say anything; but now, cornered by the look in her eyes, he knew he had to tell her.

He cleared his throat, turning away from her. The words felt clumsy and raw. 'Before he died, Cosmo Newton discovered something,' he said. 'Something about Gabriel's disappearance.' He heard the words leave his mouth, hover in the space between them. Ahead, he could see her interest begin to stir, body tensing slightly on the chair, disturbed and watchful.

'Newton left me some papers. Papers about the Nobody mole and a black op masterminded by Cecil called MIDAS,' he continued. 'Somehow he believed the truth about the identity of the Nobody mole was connected with the MIDAS operation.'

She didn't respond, silent except for the muffled rhythms of her breathing. She had stopped drinking, merely cradling both palms against the side of the mug, leeching off the warmth.

Vine paused, feeling the next thought catch. Every instinct told him not to do this, to find a way to persuade her without polluting whatever remained between them. But no answers came to him. Instead, there was just that sensation of absence again, of impending loss, stronger even than before.

She surfaced now, eyes pinched with confusion. 'What are you talking about?'

He heard his voice rise a fraction, self-control starting to loosen. 'What if nothing in this case is what it appears to be?' he said. 'The kidnap, the hostage video . . . what if something else is really going on?'

There was an almost imperceptible shake of her head, before her expression jammed for a moment, body locked rigidly forwards. She stayed like that for another second. Then it happened. Slowly her face seemed to weaken slightly, the tension caving in on itself, eyes darting warily back to his.

'You told me yourself that you sometimes had doubts about what Gabriel was doing. That you thought you might spend your life on the run,' he said. 'I looked back at everything. The evidence is all there . . . We just didn't want to see it.'

There was no reply. In its place the silence lingered, stretching out unendurably. His breathing was ragged and loud, and he tried to calm himself. But his heart continued to beat violently in his chest, a bone-rattling sensation that disorientated him for a moment. Now that he had said it, all he could think of was the sight of Gabriel Wilde in the soiled orange prison uniform, the knife cleaned and sharpened, etching its route around his neck. Of Rose seeing the footage for the first time.

Just when he couldn't bear the silence any longer, he heard a rustle of movement and glanced over to see her placing the mug down on the carpet, standing up awkwardly from the chair. She seemed unable to look at him, eyes carefully tracking the paces between her and the door.

'Please, don't . . .'

'This was a mistake,' she said, fastening the last of the buttons on her coat, addressing him almost like a stranger. 'I should never have come.'

Vine felt a different sensation grip him now, tracking slowly through his body, a heat clawing at his neck and up into his mouth. It tasted a lot like shame.

She was soon at the door, fingers grazing the handle. The words spilled out before he had a chance to stop them, a garbled rush: 'But Newton was convinced . . .'

She stopped him in mid-sentence, turning her gaze towards him for a final time. Looking closer now, he saw a thin line spreading itself down her cheek. For a second, he couldn't tell whether it was residue from the rain or something else entirely.

When she spoke, her voice was hoarse, broken, washed out with tiredness. 'Newton was an old man, Solomon. An old man with a crazy theory about my husband and a black op from half a decade ago. He might not have known better. But you should have.'

Without another word, she opened the door and slipped through, letting the crunch of the lock swing closed behind her, vanishing into the atmosphere as if she had never arrived at all.

## 58

Vine didn't move for a long time, body and mind numb from what had just happened. For once, his brain didn't whirr with thoughts. Instead, he just stood there, like a container emptied of its cargo, waiting to rust over and decay. Only as he saw the alarm clock blink towards 7.45 did he push himself forwards to the poky bathroom. He jabbed on the light and began peeling off his clothes, stepping into a lukewarm trickle. He stayed there as it went completely cold, unmoved by the icy hit on his face, still unable to wash away the hot, clinging feeling of shame. Finally, when his skin began to get scratchy with too much water, he reluctantly turned it off. He couldn't face crawling back into the clothes he had with him and wrapped himself in the brittle excuse of a robe that hung from the bathroom door, slopping moisture out on to the carpet with his feet.

From the corner of his eye, he caught a flicker of paper poking through from under the door. No longer caring about the consequences, Vine opened the door and stooped down to retrieve the edition of *The Times* that had been left outside.

He took a seat and glanced blankly at the front page. A screenshot of Gabriel Wilde from the hostage video stared back at him. He turned the page and then caught a photo of Ahmed Yousef, another of himself and several frenzied paragraphs concerning the ongoing police inquiry. He ignored both; his eyes fell on a story further down the page. EXTRA

SECURITY FOR WWII COMMEMORATION SERVICE.
He scanned down to read the main text:

> Security has been tightened around the Palace of Westminster in anticipation of a service today in the Crypt Chapel to celebrate the seventieth anniversary of Presidential Proclamation 2714, signed by President Truman in 1946 to formally declare the cessation of hostilities in the Second World War. Though the final guest list is not publicly known, sources suggest attendees will include key members of the Diplomatic Service, representatives from the White House, State Department and CIA as well as Britain's senior spymasters, including the Chief of the Secret Intelligence Service (MI6) and the Director-General of the Security Service (MI5). Following a short parade down Whitehall at 8.30 a.m. involving British and American troops, the service is scheduled to start at 9 a.m.

It was the service Rose had mentioned, a jamboree for the security establishment. Vine felt ill even at the memory of their conversation. He endured the story for as long as he could before folding the paper and chucking it in the direction of the bin. He tipped his head back and let his eyes fall shut again. Was Rose right? Had Cosmo Newton been just an old man with too much time, unanchored since his wife died, happy to lose himself in half-remembered spy games? Was Vine allowing his grief at Newton's death and unacknowledged feelings for Rose to affect his judgement, ultimately blaming Gabriel Wilde for his own failings? He looked around at the dull furnishings of the room and the threadbare carpeting. He could still taste the aftermath of Rose's perfume. For a moment, he saw all the paths he wished he had taken stretch out before him. There were so many decisions he wanted to undo. If he had been more malleable, more of a company man, willing to shelve his conscience and simply comply, perhaps then life would have been different. Instead, he was locked in a zero-sum game he was sure to lose. Every port would be alerted, as would all airports. It was only a matter of time now before they found him.

He was about to get up when he felt his left foot hit against a solid object beneath the desk. Vine bent down and pulled out his bag, still heavy with Wilde's edition of *The Odyssey*. He eased it out of the bag and leaned back in the chair, idly teasing the cover open and admiring the feel of the pages on his fingertips. There was still an unfathomable and unsettling quality to it. If he wasn't holding it in his palms, it seemed like something he might have invented at his most fevered and paranoid, an inexplicable oddity that defied all reason and explanation. Still the question beat at him: why had Gabriel Wilde sent this just a matter of days, hours even, before he disappeared?

Vine could feel the claws of his old obsessions begin to dig in, connotations starting to build. He stopped. That way madness lay. He had wasted enough time indulging in such fantasies, anything to avoid the fact that Cosmo Newton was dead, that he was now alone for good, trapped in a terminal solitude entirely of his own making. He looked over at the discarded copy of *The Times*, debating whether the bin was large enough to house the book as well, content with the thought that it would be gathered up by a cleaner and spirited out of his life for good.

He was just about to try, when he caught himself glancing down at the inscription, hovering instinctively over each word.

*Dear Solomon,*

*In case we don't meet again, I want you to have this. All wisdom lies
in this book. Take care of Rose for me.*

*Yours,*
*Gabriel*

He couldn't help but weigh the words again, one final time.
*In case we don't meet again.* It seemed like a taunt, daring Vine
to catch him. *All wisdom lies in this book.* The meaning appeared simple, ditching any need for cipher and plaintext.
And yet it meant nothing, simply a shapely line without
substance.

Vine found his eyes lingering over the rest of the page.
There was the title of the book, Wilde's name and then the
library codes carefully outlined in pencil near the bottom.

He was about to obey the voice in his head telling him to
shut the book and stop himself, when he paused for a
moment on the library codes. He had checked for any mathematical pattern before and dismissed them as numerical
nonsense. And yet now they seemed to itch at him, a detail
he had paid little attention to before. He had been so caught
up in chasing other explanations, propelled by the weight of
emotional history, that he had never given his mind the
chance to disentangle them.

He peered more closely and noticed the handwriting
looked different, the swirls of the inscription contrasting
with the prim neatness of the pencil markings. The codes
looked so forgettable, barely legible against the firm cursive
of the inscription. If Wilde had meant to obscure them from
view, it had been expertly done.

Everything told him to walk away, to stop before he drove himself further into the ground. But Vine found his body disobeying his brain, hands scrabbling around in his jacket pocket for Newton's first sheet of paper from the file. He uncapped a pen and began noting down the numbers on the piece of paper.

034

697

15024

On the surface, they looked meaningless. He was sure they were a numerical jumble, with no logic behind them. That narrowed down the potential solutions. He could feel his heartbeat racing as he then turned to the book again and began trying to flesh out any possible pattern. He took the first three numbers, ascribing each number to the most logical progression he could think of.

034. Page 0. Line 3. Word 4.

Page 0 seemed to make no sense at first. The opening line of the translation began on page 1. The most likely candidate before that was the title page with the inscription.

Vine looked at it once again. Line 3. *In case we don't meet again, I want you to have this. All wisdom lies in this book. Take care of Rose for me.* Wilde had always been something of a grammatical purist, given his classical education. The dependent clause in the first sentence wouldn't have counted as a line in itself, despite the fact that it took up a line's worth of page space. Vine concentrated, instead, on the third sentence.

Word 4. He carefully counted along to the fourth word to make sure there was no possible chance of a mistake. If this was a proper old-fashioned book cipher – the sort that had been used ever since the codex was first invented – exact accuracy in tracking from the cipher to the plaintext was essential. One careless misattribution and the entire message could be rendered useless.

*Take (1) care (2) of (3)* Rose *(4) for (5) me (6).*

Curiosity piqued, Vine slowly noted down the word, double-checking for errors. Then he turned to the second trio of numbers.

697. Page 6. Line 9. Word 7.

He methodically turned the pages until he reached the sixth page. With the pen in hand, he counted down to the ninth line. But he felt his resolve lessen as he read the half-sentence. It appeared to be meaningless. Even so, he tapped along to the seventh word with the tip of the pen and noted it down.

*. . . not (1) even (2) from (3) rumours (4) that (5) he (6) is (7) returning (8) home (9).*

He checked again that he hadn't missed anything. Once he was sure he hadn't, he turned to the final set of numbers. 15024. Page 150, Line 2, Word 4. His fingers tensed harder as he made his way to the right page. Already, he could feel his chest beginning to constrict further. The mild curiosity began to morph into something else. His breathing became heavier, more rapid. As he slowly flicked through to the right page, another thought struck. A line echoing back at him, the voice clear and distinct: *An old man with a crazy theory about my husband and a black op from half a decade ago.* The room seemed to grow smaller by the second, the silence pressing in on him until he was almost struggling to stay still. He tracked back through everything he had said, words rushed out in fear and confusion. Yet, deep down, he was almost positive – no, certain, in fact – that he had never mentioned the date of the

MIDAS operation. *A black op from half a decade ago.* How could she possibly have known?

He reached the page and counted down to the second line. Then he moved along until the pen rested on the fourth word. He looked at it for several seconds, but he had no need to check this time. The line was already ingrained in his memory, like a bullet ready to fire at the right moment. It was the line that had damned Gabriel Wilde and seemed now to be his vindication.

*My (1) name (2) is (3)* Nobody (4) . . .

Suddenly, the rest of the world began to dissolve, losing all coherence. Vine saw a lifetime of memories start to crumble as he read the line on the piece of paper beside him, wondering whether insanity had temporarily overwhelmed him, obliterating the last of his reason. Three words, he realized now, that Gabriel Wilde was speaking from beyond the grave.

ROSE IS NOBODY.

## 59

He did nothing more for the first minute than stare down at the letters in front of him. He considered the chance of human error, one incorrect number leading to a wildly mistaken conclusion. But none of the possible excuses survived for long. Somehow, deep inside himself, the truth of it overwhelmed him.

Without warning, Vine felt vomit start to fill his throat, surging up uncontrollably. He staggered towards the bathroom sink just in time, heaving up the little food he had left in his stomach. Once it was done, he rested his head on the cracked surface of the mirror, splashing cool water against his face. He grabbed at a hand towel and dabbed his face dry, staying there as the torrent of memories began to assault him.

Cosmo Newton had been right after all. The answer to everything rested in the connection between the MIDAS file and the Nobody mole, the one explaining the other. Two details came to him now, both taking on a new, terrible clarity. The first was the line from the memos, the meaning deliberately silenced by the ponderous prose, bled of consequence: *I am delighted to say that legal approval for the MIDAS operation has been received from the Attorney General's Office.* The second image was far more human, busy with life and hope. It was the photo he had found hidden in the drawer at Rose's flat the day he proposed to her; the memento in her coat pocket at the safe house. The photo of the family she had lived with for a year after Harvard, adopting her as one of their own – 'Pakistan 2005' scrawled carelessly on the back. He saw the exuberance of her smile, remembered the dissonance of it, the gap between the past and the present. He couldn't be sure – perhaps he would never be sure – but everything told him that somewhere among the rubble of the MIDAS missions would be the faces from that photograph, that family, one of the many caught in the wrong place at the wrong time, paying for such cosmic bad luck with their lives.

The MIDAS operation – the operation responsible for the death of over 150 people, most of them innocent civilians – had only gone ahead thanks to a legal opinion drafted by the Attorney General's Office. Each piece of the puzzle began to slot slowly, hideously, into place. Rose had been with the Attorney General's Office in September 2011, their lead counsel on intelligence matters; she had been the one to draft that deadly vindication, using every ounce of her intellect and academic ingenuity to approve a massacre. It would only be later that she would make the connection, truly realize what she had done. In another age, another era, perhaps, she could have remained mercifully ignorant of her actions, continued with her life. But she had made the mistake of living in an era of Facebook, Twitter, Instagram, of tweets and blogs and posts. A memo could be drafted in Whitehall, a trigger pressed in the depths of RAF Waddington, a wedding ceremony turned to ashes in Pakistan and a Facebook page fall fatally silent all within the space of days. If he was right, then Rose's words had killed that family as sure as if she'd pulled out a gun.

The smiling faces in the photograph refused to leave him now, the grandmother, parents, the eight sons and daughters, the sight of Rose in the middle wearing a smile unlike any he had seen before. He wondered how much pressure Cecil had put on her to sanction his plan. She would be bound in from all sides, discarded as soon as her job was done. Locked alone with her grief. The operation was classified as STRAP 4: one word and she would be put away for life under the Official Secrets Act. She couldn't run to a paper, couldn't confess the cause of her guilt to a priest or counsellor. Boxed in, she had been left with only one means of rationalizing what had happened, of continuing to function as a human being. Denied justice, she had instead, over time, settled on something far more deadly – revenge.

He saw her slot in beside him now on the pew at St Martin's. Every action, each phrase, had been tailored specifically for him. His only sin had been to work in counter-espionage, tasked with rooting out the moles, the doubles, the breaches. Once she had blinded him, she moved on to Gabriel Wilde, Cecil's protégé, the confidant. To destroy Cecil, she had to destroy his greatest creation, silently subverting Wilde's every move. Vine had been so sure that Gabriel Wilde was guilty, allowing theory to disfigure the facts. Yet he saw now how they had all been played – Wilde, Yousef, Cecil; all merely symptoms of an establishment that punished the innocent and protected the guilty.

So much began to take on a sharper focus, the chaos of recent events revealing their own impossible logic. The set-up that day in Istanbul, Wilde's sudden disappearance, the watchers at Oxford and Guy's, the deaths of Newton and Yousef – she had gone so far that each further step must have felt like a necessary evil, prelude to a final act of absolution.

And that final act? He heard her words again, spoken right in front of him: *there's a big UK–US commemoration service in Westminster this morning that Cecil roped me into a while back, lots of security grandees attending.* Several loose thoughts started to coalesce near the front of his mind: the barriers being put up down Whitehall as he had made his way towards Portcullis House to meet Amory; the signs in Westminster Hall during his second interview with Olivia Cartier; and the words from the story in the paper this morning: *sources suggest attendees will include key members of the Diplomatic Service, representatives from the White House, State Department and CIA as well as Britain's senior spymasters, including the Chief of the Secret Intelligence Service (MI6) and the Director-General of the Security Service (MI5).* Everyone involved in the MIDAS operation would be sitting in that chapel. As Vine saw the past rewrite itself, the numbness began to fade. He looked at his face in the mirror again, surfacing from the shock, snapping back to himself. He turned towards the room and glimpsed the alarm clock near the bed: 08.32 a.m.

Hurriedly, he began searching for his clothes. As he finished dressing, he heard the sound of vehicles parking outside, the oddly muffled shutting of car doors. He inched closer to the window and lifted the curtain, peering down to the top of Hugh Street below.

There were two vehicles dancing with lights. She must have alerted them soon after she left, calling in his location.

The police had arrived.

## 60

He looked round the scene again. Enough of his posses-
sions were scattered throughout to establish beyond
doubt that he had spent the night here. The receipt for a
train ticket to Edinburgh was carelessly dropped underneath the bed: not showy enough to scream of tradecraft,
but obvious enough that a team could locate it with a
bit of hunting. It wouldn't buy him long, but enough for
what he needed to do. He closed the door and made his
way down the hall.

When conducting an initial assessment of the building, he
had spent time memorizing the sole escape route. There was
a fire exit near the kitchens that led straight out on to Belgrave
Road. He reached the door to the back stairs now and went
through it without pausing. The stairs down to the fire escape were thin and crumbling, starved of any functional
lighting and existing in a permanent greyness. Vine could
imagine the progression of the team behind him, a crab-like
scuttle up the floors; nearing the top now, soon to swoop on
his room.

He reached the final flight of stairs, cars thrumming past
on the road outside. The only question was whether the team
would have people stationed around the immediate vicinity.
Given resource pressures and in order not to alarm the public near a major transport terminal, Vine guessed it was a
small team, not more than four. They would only be carrying
standard-issue Glocks, rather than clearly visible weaponry.
With two taking the immediate task of scouring the room

and one patrolling the downstairs, that left just one other to guard the area outside the front door.

He readied himself, swallowing down the emotions that were rising through him. He had to clear his mind and stay focused now. No matter how practised he was in the art of remaining hidden, he had always known that sheer numerical force would eventually overwhelm him. It was only a matter of time – each second diluting his chances.

He rehearsed his route one final time and then inched open the rusty fire escape door and slipped on to Belgrave Road.

As soon as he felt his feet touch the concrete, he told himself not to look round. He proceeded at a calculated speed in smooth, unhurried movements. From the initial glance, he had seen the back of a police officer talking into a radio by the passport office. He calculated that he had no more than ten seconds to escape her sightline before she turned and saw him. He quickened his pace now, using the jam of traffic to snake his way through to the pavement opposite and up on to Eccleston Bridge.

As he reached the back entrance to Victoria station, he risked one split-second look backwards. The police officer was walking in the direction of the hotel, past the fire escape door. Her Airwave radio was holstered on her ballistic body armour. There was no other sign of significant police activity that side of the building.

Vine followed the crowd in the direction of Buckingham Palace Road. He silently clocked the cameras around the station and made sure to duck his way free of a direct shot, crossing to the other side.

He increased his pace forwards, trying to silence the tangle of thoughts. He wished more than anything that time could be reversed, that knowledge could be unlearned. But he knew there would be no retreat into ignorance.

He stopped for a moment, his mind still swimming, body raw and hurting. As he tried to collect himself, he saw a taxi heading his way, the light mercifully lit. He began searching for his wallet, pulling out the last remaining cash he had as he raised his arm and saw the cab slow up ahead.

Vine sprinted towards it, yanked open the door and handed over a twenty-pound note.

'Where to?' asked the driver, scooping up the money and casting a cautious eye over his new passenger.

'Westminster,' he said. 'Take me to the Palace of Westminster.'

## 61

Vine looked at his watch: 8.49.

There were eleven minutes before the commemoration service in the Crypt Chapel began. The taxi was still at the back of Parliament Square, jammed in a haze of exhaust fumes and parping horns, barely nudging forwards.

As another car sounded its horn, Vine broke out of his numbness. He pressed his phone into life and called Valentine Amory, getting an answer on the fourth ring.

'Valentine, it's Solomon Vine.'

Amory's voice sounded wary. 'Do you have the answers you were looking for?'

'Yes,' he said. 'Everything finally makes sense.' Vine rubbed a hand across his forehead. He tried to think what to do. One hundred guests. One hundred possible casualties. 'There is going to be an attack on the Crypt Chapel. We only have a matter of minutes to act. The commemoration service. That's the target.'

'Why?' said Amory. 'What does the file mean?'

'It means we've all been duped,' snapped Vine, the last of his composure beginning to melt away. 'Ahmed Yousef, Gabriel Wilde, the Prophets group at Oxford. It was none of them. Rose Spencer has been behind everything that has happened. She was used by Cecil when she was intelligence counsel at the Attorney General's Office to sanction UK involvement in a top-secret drone operation codenamed MIDAS. The operation was eventually shut down. But not before scores of innocent civilians were killed.'

'And the commemoration service?'

'It's the only option,' said Vine. 'The biggest UK–US event of its kind for years. Rose Spencer is planning to blow up every former spook and mandarin who participated in the mass slaughter of civilian populations . . . And we've just given her the chance to do it.'

He thought back to Newton dead on the railway tracks and Yousef slumped over his desk; the words on Yousef's phone planted to frame him. Then he thought of the meeting in the Pugin Room, Olivia Cartier pushing him towards believing Yousef was behind the attack, further disinformation culled from a nameless source within the intelligence world. All of it had been Rose.

'She's using her position to infiltrate the security team,' he said. 'She has a pass to any building on the Estate.' He looked out of the taxi window and at his watch again: there were now exactly ten minutes until the service started. He peered at the golden-brown sweep of the Palace of Westminster up ahead and imagined it deformed by bomb blasts.

'Alert the Palace authorities,' he said. 'Try to stop Rose Spencer getting anywhere near the chapel . . .'

## 62

Eight fifty-two.

Vine looked at his watch again, willing the numbers to self-correct. But they remained stubbornly in place. He felt adrenaline seize him, plugging the gap where fear should have lurked, opening the taxi door and throwing himself out into the road.

He narrowly avoided the rush of cars, navigating his way across to the grass of Parliament Square. His breathing was jagged, muscle movements edged with purpose. The crowds of tourists were already thick, slowing him down as he slalomed through them, contorting his body, eyes locked on the hands of Big Ben.

*In case we don't meet again, I want you to have this. All wisdom lies in this book. Take care of Rose for me . . .*

It had all been there, staring at him. He cursed himself again for missing it. Wilde had been forced to disguise it, knowing the scale of the opposition he faced. Anything too obvious and it would have been intercepted long before it reached Wellington Square. Vine forced himself onwards, ignoring the stab of uncertainty in his midriff, all the time checking to make sure the Palace was still intact.

He was nearing the end of Parliament Square now. Four lanes of traffic separated him from the Palace entrance. He saw the other pedestrians stop and jab for the green man, ignoring them all and wading out into the sludge of traffic. He swerved to avoid a passing grey Mercedes, then darted on, brakes screeching all around him. There was the sound of another horn and the narrow miss of a Land Rover. He had no time to dissect the experience. He just kept on until he felt the sure ground of St Margaret Street underneath his feet.

He shouted at tourists to move and let him pass. But still they bunched up, forcing him to detour round them. A chilly blast of anger worked through him. A shout of frustration caught itself in his chest.

Sweat soaked through his shirtfront and stung his eyes. His view was obscured by the spark of a camera flash, smartphones held aloft like trophies, a collection of toothy smiles.

For a moment he hovered, the honking chaos of Whitehall and Parliament Square jumbling his senses. He felt his breath drain out of him. What was he doing? He was a wanted man. If he made a scene he would be signing his own arrest warrant. Or – this close to flanks of armed DPG officers – much worse. He should let the security services, the police, the paraphernalia of the state deal with it, and with the consequences. Damn the lot of them. They had most surely damned him.

He cast one more look at the side of the Palace and began to hear chatter rising from within the Parliamentary Estate. Then, from somewhere, he felt instinct grab him again, a primal energy that overrode all logic. It was channelled through his chest, the same feeling as before, pushing him forwards, this time careless of the wounds he inflicted as he jousted with his arms and used his brute strength to get to the turning.

Finally, he swerved left towards the queues for St Stephen's Entrance, the best route to the Crypt Chapel. He cast a glance back towards Big Ben and saw the oversized clock hand creep towards 8.55.

Five minutes . . .

Further ahead, he could see the Peers' Entrance surrounded by cars, passengers hidden behind tinted windows. He froze for a moment, wondering what he could do now.

It was then that he saw him, walking peacock proud in his long black coat, hair ruffled slightly by the breeze. Alexander Cecil was making his way up to St Stephen's Entrance.

Vine broke into a new run, dodging through the queues. There was not enough time to persuade the police guards to let him into the Parliamentary Estate or get the authorities to understand.

There was only one option now.

He reached the barriers as he saw Cecil nod to the police officer and begin walking up the steps to Westminster Hall.

He stopped for a moment and tried to recover his breath.

Then he shouted: 'It's Rose.'

## 63

The coated figure turned slowly. Vine caught the weary dip of the head, pausing on the steps as if debating whether to go back or press onwards. Vine walked up to the officer guarding the entrance and saw Cecil reluctantly descend the steps and make his way over.

'What the hell are you doing here?' he asked.

Vine shook his head, trying to control his breathing. 'We have to get everyone out of the Crypt Chapel.'

Cecil sighed. 'None of this is any longer your business, Vine. One word and I could make sure you never see daylight again. The service is just about to start.' He began to move away. 'I'm sorry, but I really can't . . .'

'I know about the MIDAS operation,' Vine shouted, at last. 'About what happened. It was your creation. You covered it all up, of course, made sure there was no investigation. And you used Rose to absolve you.'

Up ahead, Cecil came to a halt, suddenly rigid. He turned and looked back, his face drained of colour. He didn't say anything, just retraced his steps as if in a daze.

'Yousef's testimony about the Nobody mole wasn't about Wilde. There was a real mole all along. It was about Rose.' Vine stopped. 'Everyone involved in the MIDAS operation is sitting in that chapel. That is the real target. *You* are the real target. You always have been . . .'

Cecil looked directly at Vine, struggling for air. 'And the video?' he said.

'Gabriel Wilde signed his own death warrant the minute he began pretending to be a double and helping Langley with their drone programme.' Vine tried to keep his voice clear. 'We have to get everyone out. You have to damn well let me in.'

'Not possible . . .' Cecil shook his head. 'The bomb squad has sniffer dogs through Westminster Hall every day. They'd have picked something up.'

Vine was newly conscious of the tourists and spectators beginning to stop at the sound of raised voices. 'She's played us all. She was the one behind the death of Newton. She was the one behind the death of Yousef. She had all the freelance contacts she ever needed from her time at Thames House, used them against Newton and Yousef and to frame me in Istanbul. She's been planning this for years. She has access to every part of the Estate, even got you to assign her to the event. Rose is Nobody. It's been her all along . . .'

## 64

Slowly, Cecil began snapping out of shock. He nodded, then stared at his watch and resumed control. His face began reclaiming some colour.

'Let him in,' he said to the police officer. His voice was terse and commanding. 'We need to lock down the Palace immediately. Code Red to all security stations. Get every Cabinet minister out of the Estate as soon as possible. Evacuate Portcullis House, Norman Shaw as well. Alert Downing Street, tell them the Chief of the Secret Intelligence Service has just ordered full lockdown protocol.'

The police officer seemed to hesitate, fussing with his radio.

'Do it!' bellowed Cecil.

Vine was already pushing past, through the entrance directly into Westminster Hall and the purer quiet inside. He clambered up two flights of stairs and then ran straight across to the entrance for the Crypt Chapel.

There was one police officer on the gate, checking passes and invitations. Vine approached, calculating the quickest way in.

'Need to see your invitation, sir,' said the officer. His weapon bobbed uneasily around his upper chest, cutting off easy use of his left hand.

Vine seized on the weakness. He didn't bother to apologize for what he was about to do. He calculated the exact force necessary to successfully incapacitate his opponent and then delivered a brutally efficient volley of movement – a punch to the head, simultaneous knee to his ribs, then the elbow crushing down on the neck. The combined effort sent the officer sprawling. Almost immediately, mutters were starting to accumulate around him. He could pay for it later, if there ever was a later.

Vine ignored the sound and ran through the wooden door, moving quickly down the stone steps. A rustle of chatter and a heavy burst from the organ rose up to greet him.

He was through the Western Entrance now, confronted by the massed reality of the crowd. He began scanning the rows of people. Despite recent tightening, the security around the event was lighter than might have been expected, with most resources deployed elsewhere in Whitehall. The people here weren't politicians, but senior civil servants, spies and military chiefs. The protection surrounded politicians who would be in office today and out of it tomorrow. These names were only known to those on the inside, like a secret currency. They were largely free from the trappings of the security state – a sitting target, the puppet masters behind the strings.

He noticed one former Permanent Under Secretary from the Foreign Office. The current Cabinet Secretary and the Principal Private Secretary from Number 10 were sitting in the third row. There were two former Director-Generals of MI5, as well as the serving Director of Special Forces alongside a procession of retired MI6 officers.

He moved further into the chapel. 'We need to evacuate the building,' he shouted. He felt his voice die off amid the noise of the organ. 'This is an emergency. Evacuate the building. This is not a drill. Evacuate the chapel. *Now.*'

No one moved. Vine bellowed at the organist to stop, spotting a fire alarm near the end of the front row. He moved down the aisle and broke the glass with his bare hands.

'There is a bomb somewhere in this building,' he shouted, a wail of noise covering the space around him. 'You need to evacuate now.'

As he looked across, Vine clocked Cecil emerging from the doorway with two DPG officers from Central Lobby. Both officers began barking out the order, hurrying people away from the chairs. Vine stared round at the smallness of the chapel. It was the perfect place, insulated underground. There was nowhere else for the blast to go.

They would all be killed.

With the fire alarm now sounding, the panic levels had risen, the surge threatening to turn into a fatal crush of activity. As people began stampeding for the exit, he turned and saw a familiar figure emerge from the baptistery. He felt an irrational surge of hope. There was still a chance he could be wrong. Everything could be explained somehow, the inferences and logical connections disproved. He would rather face a lifetime of chaos, of formless anarchy, than live with the pattern he had discovered. But even as he entertained the idea, he felt the other half of his brain absorb a detail, computing its implications.

Rose Spencer was reaching for something in her jacket.

## 65

For a man approaching retirement age, Sir Alexander Cecil still moved with speed, apparent as he used the split-second to lunge forwards and knock the mobile from her hands, sending it skittering over the hard surface of the chapel floor, the screen smashing.

Rose retaliated with forensic efficiency, a blow to the head that sent Cecil stumbling towards the organ, holding his palm against the wound. He slumped to the ground, blood seeping out across the floor.

Vine felt his breathing become heavy as he approached her, moving back down the aisle. She would have used her position to get through the security barriers unchecked, planting the explosives just before the service started, set on an automatic timer; the phone that had been in her hand was just for insurance, a back-up should anything unexpected happen.

He looked at her again now, desperately searching for some way out. He held her gaze, willing her to look away. But, as he stared at her, he found himself taking in a different person. She had been true to her calling: targeting, recruiting and turning him. He had been nothing more than a means to an end, an operational detail. The eyes he saw glaring back at him were ones he didn't recognize – tougher, unforgiving, propelled only by the purity of the cause. Guilt had hollowed her out, reshaped her into something else entirely.

He allowed himself to look away, scanning the rest of the chapel to try and figure out where the explosives could be located. The Crypt Chapel lay directly underneath St Stephen's Hall. If the chapel went, the rest of the flooring above would collapse too, potentially initiating a domino effect on the whole of the Palace. The Estate was crumbling and had been in need of urgent repair for decades. An explosion could bring the entire structure down, and thousands of people along with it.

Sweat began to slide down his palms, his mouth consumed with dryness, as if he had never tasted water. One of the police officers had gone back to the top of the steps, trying to shepherd the guests safely out into the daylight.

Vine turned to the second police officer. 'We need bomb disposal down here now. This could go off at any minute. Go.'

There was the sound of final footsteps leaving the Crypt Chapel. The space was now empty. Apart from Cecil's unconscious form, it was just the two of them.

He waited for a moment, watching what she did next. Then he inched closer, slowly, methodically, showing her that he posed no danger. There was only one question he had left, one final answer he needed.

'The photograph,' he said. 'The family in the photograph.'

She didn't say anything, punishing him with her silence. When eventually she spoke, the words seemed to pain her, wounds that had no hope of healing. 'The first strike,' she said, letting her eyes fix on him again. 'The intelligence was wrong. The drone hit a wedding instead. Their eldest daughter was getting married . . .'

The rest of the sentence remained unspoken, the terrible consequences filling the void around them.

He stayed there, looking down at Cecil still lying on the floor, knowing there might only be seconds left to act.

On instinct alone, he reached down and grabbed for Cecil's arms and started dragging his weight with him towards the door. As he did, he saw Rose watch them silently, blankly; the masks gone, the screams beginning to dim, the weight of her own actions and inactions slowly lessening. Finally tired of all she had done, at peace with what she was about to do. Soon, very soon, it would be over.

Vine was nearly at the entrance to the stairwell. He began lifting Cecil's body up behind him, straining under the weight, seeing the first glimmer of light from the doorway above them. But it was too late. It had always been too late. As he reached the steps, everything began to slow. His final memory was a haze of colour, more like a dream than reality: the lone figure of Rose in front of him, the golden echo of the chapel carrying her into its fold.

There was a brief pause, a blinding flash. A snowstorm of pieces signalling the start of oblivion. Then darkness fell.

# Epilogue

'Just here's fine,' he said.

The taxi pulled to a stop. Vine paid the driver and then looked up at the first of the spring sun as he walked down the rest of the way towards the main entrance of Trinity College.

He reached the porter's lodge now and stated his position as a former student.

'I'm here to see the Master,' he said. 'The name's Vine. He's expecting me at twelve.'

He sat in the waiting room for ten minutes until he was collected and led through Great Court to the Master's office. He heard the voice before he saw the figure, the slimmer version of Lord Cecil of Burford squeezed into his wheelchair, dishing out instructions to a group of administrative assistants in the outer office. When he saw Vine, Cecil nodded, finished off his instructions and added in a croakier version of his old newsreader's baritone: 'Do you mind doing the honours?'

Vine took the handles of the wheelchair, pushing through into the Master's study, a vast room with views straight out to Great Court. A bulky oak desk sat at the back of the room, covered with a large desktop and piles of paper either side. The room was lined with bookcases, older books kept in glass cabinets under lock and key, others paraded along the walls on either side.

'Just over here will do nicely, I think,' said Cecil, indicating the two armchairs slightly apart from the cream sofas in the middle of the room. 'Do you fancy a tipple of some sort,

Vine? One advantage of my new role is a free hand at the college cellar. The embarrassment of riches is quite extraordinary. Some very good Scotch. Margaret, one of the better bottles would help us along, I think.'

Vine helped ease Cecil over from the wheelchair to the armchair, feeling the bonier underside to the arms and body, the effect of months on nothing more than hospital food. Once seated, Cecil seemed to readily adopt his more recognizable shape, almost fattening back to his full plumage.

'Damn nuisance that thing,' he said. 'But, I suppose I should be grateful. A few inches either way, and the wheelchair would have been the least of my problems.'

Vine took a seat in the armchair opposite. He couldn't help but remember their conversation five months earlier, stuck in the equally decorous surroundings of Cecil's country estate. Since then, the news had focused on little else but the blowing up of Parliament and the mysterious figures found in the stairwell of the Crypt Chapel, the famous stone all that saved them from certain death.

A few minutes later, Cecil's PA returned with a silver tray, a bottle and two glasses. Vine poured and handed a glass to Cecil, who raised it.

'Cheers,' he said, taking a long sip. 'So . . . consultant for the National Security Adviser, or so the rumour goes. Hefty day rates, I hope, all at the expense of the public purse. To what do I owe the pleasure?'

Vine put down his Scotch and crossed his legs. He gazed around the study. During his three years at Trinity, he had only ever been admitted here twice, all to sip lukewarm sherry and make polite chitchat with other scholars in the college. The prospect of entering the secret world had been little more than a hazy possibility in an unknown future. Often he wished himself back to those days, treasuring an ignorance he had once been so desperate to lose.

'I've been sent with a message,' said Vine, turning his gaze to Cecil now. 'About the MIDAS operation and the details that came to light.'

Cecil bowed his head. 'Ah. Some sort of plea deal, I suppose. I write down my confession, and you give me someone to make sure my door is locked at night? That's why you came?'

'No,' said Vine. 'I came because Cosmo Newton was the best person I've ever known. I came because, without you, Gabriel Wilde might still be alive. I came because justice has yet to be done . . .'

At this, Cecil's face creased with what looked like a frown before flowering into a gale of laughter. 'Very noble,' he said. 'Perhaps I imagined it, but I thought I heard you weren't going to be charged with handling stolen classified information. But justice is for other people. Bad people like me, I suppose.'

'That's different,' said Vine.

Cecil laughed again. 'One day you'll get it,' he said. 'Newton never did, that's what killed him. You're not a hero, Vine. You're a spy. We don't deal in right and wrong. We deal in advantage and disadvantage. We don't live in an age of armies and total war, or nukes and mutually assured destruction. We live in an age where death roams our streets. You fell for Rose because you were seeking an absolute – love, justice, truth. Leave truth and justice to the judges, the politicians, the media. We live in the shadows, the grey areas, the no man's land. No matter how you like to get yourself to sleep at night, you have always been part of it. We exist because we have to. By fair means or foul.'

Vine sat there and traced his finger around the top of his glass. He had said what he wanted to say and could at least visit the graveside with a clear mind. He put down his Scotch, lifted his briefcase and pulled out a folder. 'I spoke to Number 10 this morning. They will be supporting Valentine Amory's call for a full inquiry into black ops under previous administrations. All witnesses will be under oath.' He pushed the folder across the table. 'As you can see, you will be summoned first.' He closed his briefcase and got up from the armchair. 'Good luck, Alex. Enjoy your Scotch. While you can . . .'

He nodded to the PA outside, then followed the stairs down to Great Court. He looked up and took in a last sweep of it all, the sense of cloistered quiet, suddenly tired of Cambridge, of the stately buildings masking their weight of secrets.

He walked back to the train station, letting the conversation replay itself in his mind. He tried to shake off the shiver of disgust he had felt as he sat in that room and absorbed the cold reality of the words. He could already see the excuses being prepared, all guilt obscured by official rank and title.

Back in London, he reached the cemetery just after seven o' clock. The sun was withdrawing and the plots were deserted. He walked down to the gravestone, standing there for hours and letting the lukewarm breeze massage his skin, brushing off the traces of his visit.

As he looked down at Newton's gravestone, he longed for some answers, to once again distinguish between black and white. Instead, he was merely consumed by a rush of feeling. As a trickle of rain began to beat on the tip of his nose,

Solomon Vine closed his eyes and allowed himself one final memory. Then he turned and started back, still able to hear the haunting echo of her voice, growing fainter now until it merged with the wind and the crackle of the trees, somewhere fading into silence.

# Acknowledgements

This book wouldn't exist without the work of Euan Thorneycroft and Pippa McCarthy at A. M. Heath. I owe an incalculable debt to both for turning me into a published author. Thanks, too, to Robert Dinsdale for vital editorial advice early on.

My next huge debt of gratitude is to Rowland White at Penguin for believing in the book and taking it on, honing it even further and providing an invaluable masterclass in the art of suspense writing. Thanks also to Emad Akhtar for his editorial insights, Victoria Bottomley for managing the publishing process and everyone else at Penguin for getting it into the hands of readers. Particular thanks to Chantal Noel and her rights team and to Nick Lowndes and David Watson.

Going through the life cycle of a book has been a fascinating insight into new worlds. Huge thanks to Conrad Williams at the Blake Friedmann Literary Agency for guiding me through the universe of TV production with such style and graciousness. Thanks also to Daniel Nixon.

In Westminster, my ongoing thanks to George and the team. It is a great privilege to work with you all.

To Clare, for her extraordinary generosity over the last few years, both in terms of phenomenal career advice and speechwriting opportunities.

To Professor John Carey at Merton for taking the time to answer the queries of a graduate student and for one of the most fascinating lunches I've ever had.

Thanks, too, to Eddie Bell for encouraging my early writing, and to Laurence Paul, Rosanna Boscawen, Vincent McAviney and Kevin Macnish for conversations that have been indispensable along the way.

Finally, my greatest debt of gratitude is to my family. To my parents, John and Ruth, my siblings, Peter and Sarah, and to Mary, aunt extraordinaire. Whether putting up with me writing on Christmas Day or listening patiently to yet another redraft idea – you've always gone far beyond the call of duty. I couldn't have done any of it without your unstinting love and support.

# He just wanted a decent book to read ...

Not too much to ask, is it? It was in 1935 when Allen Lane, Managing Director of Bodley Head Publishers, stood on a platform at Exeter railway station looking for something good to read on his journey back to London. His choice was limited to popular magazines and poor-quality paperbacks – the same choice faced every day by the vast majority of readers, few of whom could afford hardbacks. Lane's disappointment and subsequent anger at the range of books generally available led him to found a company – and change the world.

*'We believed in the existence in this country of a vast reading public for intelligent books at a low price, and staked everything on it'*
**Sir Allen Lane, 1902–1970, founder of Penguin Books**

The quality paperback had arrived – and not just in bookshops. Lane was adamant that his Penguins should appear in chain stores and tobacconists, and should cost no more than a packet of cigarettes.

Reading habits (and cigarette prices) have changed since 1935, but Penguin still believes in publishing the best books for everybody to enjoy. We still believe that good design costs no more than bad design, and we still believe that quality books published passionately and responsibly make the world a better place.

So wherever you see the little bird – whether it's on a piece of prize-winning literary fiction or a celebrity autobiography, political tour de force or historical masterpiece, a serial-killer thriller, reference book, world classic or a piece of pure escapism – you can bet that it represents the very best that the genre has to offer.

## Whatever you like to read – trust Penguin.